MASTER
of DESIRE

Lacey Alexander

ELLORA'S CAVE
ROMANTICA PUBLISHING

What the critics are saying...

∞

SEDUCTRESS OF CARALON

5 Angels "Lacey Alexander cleverly portrays the sexual tension between Jalal and Enrick during there battle of wits. [...] *Seductress of Caralon* is a sizzling, arousing tale of honor, duty, and bravery during war. *Seduction of Caralon* is an engrossing, steamy tale of a future without technology. Lacey Alexander deftly depicts the fear and yearning Jalal experiences upon spotting Enrick. I eagerly anticipate the next book in the Brides of Caralon series." ~ *Fallen Angels Reviews*

MASTER OF DESIRE

5 Angels "Passionate, outrageous, intense, and very erotic are just a few of the words that can be used to describe Lacey Alexander's latest futuristic story. With a mixture of Dominant/submissive, sexual slavery, and plenty of other erotic escapades, Ralen and Teesia come to rely on each other for their very existence. [...] It is nonetheless a powerful and truly evocative look at the dramatic and tension-filled emotion of love. [...] Kudos to Ms. Alexander for creating a tantalizing and fairly sinful story of love, lust and everything in between in an interesting futuristic setting." ~ *Fallen Angels Reviews*

An Ellora's Cave Romantica Publication

www.ellorascave.com

Master of Desire

Trade paperback Publication June 2008

MASTER OF DESIRE

ജ

SEDUCTRESS OF CARALON
~11~

MASTER OF DESIRE
~51~

SEDUCTRESS OF CARALON

ঔ

Dedication

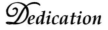

*The Brides of Caralon series is dedicated
to Leonie Daniels,
who first encouraged me to try my hand at erotica,
and to Anya Bast,
who gave me a helpful tip or two along the way.*

Chapter One
3565 A.D.

৯০

Jalal concentrated on the wooden tiles arranged in a pyramid before her. She would turn nineteen tomorrow, so word of her bridegroom might come at any time—she must be in practice with the Maran tiles that would determine her wedding night rituals.

She looked up as her maid entered the room, the woman's tunic of thin fur brushing her plump thighs. "Won't you please tell me now, Relah? Just a hint." Some said it was actually better not to do well at the game, that skill with the Maran tiles was overrated, but that hardly made sense to Jalal.

The stern maid planted her hands at her hips. "You know very well you'll not find out until after your vows."

"Did they use the Maran tiles back in the Before Times?"

Relah rolled her eyes. "How would I know?" Then she turned more thoughtful. "But I suspect not. They were very different times, likely very different people."

Indeed, Jalal couldn't imagine the lives of the people who had inhabited the colossal crumbled cities to the north like Yorkland, Delphia, and Washton, where new, smaller cities now grew from ancient debris. "But surely the people of those times had the same thoughts, feelings, desires we have. So perhaps they did have their own version of—"

Relah's tired but venomous look stopped Jalal cold. Relah often claimed she talked too much. "Don't vex me, girl."

Jalal sighed, wishing she'd been born a man. If she were a man, she would know the secret of the tiles. If she were a man, she'd have some choice in her future. By Ares, if she were a man, she'd build a great army and overthrow her father—she'd march into all the domains rising throughout Caralon and soon rule each and every one.

"Your father summons you," Relah said.

Jalal dropped the tile she'd just lifted from the second tier, her eyes going wide as she looked up. Her stomach churned, her breasts turned heavy beneath her silken chemise, and the slit between her thighs tingled with anticipation. This was it—he'd called her before him to announce her bridegroom!

Ten minutes later, Jalal entered the grand hall, which looked more run-down than ever before. And to her surprise, no crowd of people had gathered, as she'd expected. Still, her limbs went weak with anxiety as she pulled her best fur wrap about her shoulders and walked up the uneven floor toward her father's small throne, which he nonetheless had elevated so high that it was necessary to lean her head back to meet his eyes. "You summoned me, Father?"

Osren's hair was the warm gray of an alpha wolf's winter coat, falling about his shoulders, but the crags in his face revealed his years. She was the last of his daughters to reach bride's age. "Scouts tell me Enrick treks this way, that even now his forces are weaving through the western mountains."

Jalal drew in her breath, tensing. "Enrick the Attacker?" What was he saying? That Enrick the Attacker was to be her bridegroom? Please, Ares, no! The region between her legs seemed to shiver with fear.

"Yes, Enrick the Attacker. It is predicted he will reach the borders of Myrtell in only two to three days' time. As you know, most of my armies are not here, daughter. They are split, guarding my borders to the north and south. We never expected an attack from the mountains. I'm calling on you to detain Enrick while my armies are assembled."

Jalal blinked. What? This had nothing to do with her nuptials? Her birthday? "Me? How?"

"You must seduce him."

The words hit her like a physical blow, leaving her breathless for a long, painful moment. She'd known her father was a vulnerable and often desperate ruler, but... "What of my virginity, Father? You're willing to give up my bride value?" While most women of Caralon were free to indulge their sexual urges at will, daughters of the upper classes were kept virgins until they were traded in marriage to whomever their fathers chose. It was a practice Jalal despised, but it at least held the likelihood of a life of comfort, a marriage to someone of means.

Her father's stalwart expression never wavered. "What good is your bride value if Myrtell is toppled by Enrick?"

Jalal swallowed nervously. Her father truly expected her to seduce Enrick the Attacker? "What could I possibly know about seduction, Father?"

"You need know very little given the ripeness of your breasts, the lushness of your curves, the satin of your skin."

She sighed. She'd been told of her rare beauty her whole life. Her father had always been fond of saying she'd fetch quite a price. She'd always imagined going to a wealthy young ruler, someone strong and handsome who might even pamper her if she were lucky. But this changed everything.

"I still haven't the first idea how to pleasure a man. What of my Orientation?" The stirrings in her body these last years had actually made her look forward to the week prior to marriage, which she would spend with a handpicked Orienter — a woman who would teach her the ways of sex.

"We haven't time for a proper Orientation. But Gilda will come to you tonight and try to prepare you for your task. You'll be taken into the mountains at sunup." He leaned slightly forward, the lines in his face deepening as he added, "Do not fail me, Jalal. Distract Enrick with your body long enough for my forces to gather — or you shall answer to me when this is over."

Maybe you'll be dead when this is over, she thought, her eyes narrowing on him. She'd always doubted the man held any love for her in his heart, and this proved it. She wanted to spit on him. She wanted to trample his bravado under her feet.

But a woman's place in Caralon was not such that she could ever rule over any man. She had no choice but to do what her father demanded. She had to attempt to learn the ways of seduction, then give herself to the feared Enrick, a beast of a man who inhabited children's nightmares—had even once inhabited *her* nightmares. Like it or not, it seemed, he would soon enter her bed in a whole new manner.

* * * * *

Osren's fifth wife, Gilda, swept into Jalal's room, her voluptuous body swathed in the sheer fabric created by the silkworms her father had gathered from near and far. Waterfalls of sea green fell over Gilda's ample breasts, then spilled again from her hips toward the floor, the more intimate curves of her body visible beneath.

She dropped a puddle of blue silk on the bed next to Jalal. "Ah yes, just as I thought. The blue looks enchanting with your dark hair. You shall have to let it down, you know."

Jalal reached protectively to the silken twine that currently wrapped her long locks in a single row down her back. To let one's hair down was to announce to all that she was no longer innocent. Jalal's hair had stayed bound her whole life, and of course it would make sense to release it now, if she were to perform a seduction, but she somehow felt almost violated by the suggestion. This was not how she'd intended to lose her well-guarded virginity.

Picking up the scant garments made of the same translucent silk as Gilda's, she gasped. "They are as see-through as…" She glanced at her stepmother, older than her by only a few years, then lowered her eyes. "Well, as yours."

Gilda's nipples shone like dark flowers through the transparent green fabric.

Rich laughter rang through the room. "Of course. We want Enrick to see all you have to offer—your lush breasts, your lovely pink cunt."

"Cunt?"

Gilda smiled tauntingly. "You don't even know what your cunt is?" She rolled her eyes. "By Ares, they do protect the rich ones. Too much, in my opinion. I can't believe I'm expected to ready you for fucking in one short night."

With that, Gilda drew back her sea-colored skirt to reveal the slit between her legs—the place on Jalal's body that had caused her such frustration for years. All the hair had been removed from Gilda's mound, leaving it shockingly bare. "This is the cunt. Sometimes called the pussy. It's what a man treasures most on a woman's body, what Enrick will penetrate when you've done your job."

Jalal couldn't hold in her gasp. "Penetrate?"

Gilda drew in a tired breath, reaching into a small leather sack and drawing out a cylindrical object of clay, like a mushroom with a swollen, overgrown stem and a very small top. "This is a cock, what a man has between his legs. He uses it to fuck you."

Yet another new word that left Jalal feeling ignorant and helpless. Why couldn't Gilda explain better? "Fuck?"

"Yes, fuck. Means when he puts it in your pussy and moves it in and out."

Jalal was certain she looked lost. All she could think was that the cock appeared enormous—it must have been seven or eight inches in length—and it was to go inside her body?

"Here, let me show you," Gilda said, climbing up onto the bed next to her.

Kneeling with her legs spread, she placed the clay cock between her thighs and—oh, Ares!—pushed it up into the pink slit parting there. "Mmm," Gilda moaned softly, driving the clay up into her until it nearly disappeared. Then she began to slide it in and out, in and out.

Jalal was aghast, her eyes locked on the intrusion of the clay cock. "Is it painful?"

Gilda's laugh this time was deeper, like a warm purr. "Oh no, dear. A cock is a tool of pure pleasure."

Jalal could scarcely believe it.

Clearly reading the doubt on her face, Gilda said, "All right, yes, there might be a bit of pain at the start, but once you've had it, you shall crave it, Jalal. Your body shall yearn for it. Your cunt will ache for it."

Jalal swallowed nervously. Perhaps that was why her cunt had tingled and tickled so badly these last few years. When she'd reported it to Relah, fearing the physician need be summoned, Relah had only chuckled and told her it was normal for a girl to have such sensations there, in preparation for her bridegroom. Now it was a dull throbbing that tortured her daily. "So then, you're saying it won't be horrible—seducing Enrick."

Gilda tilted her head. "Well, Enrick the Attacker—who can say? I've never seen him, but from the stories…" Gilda ceased working the clay cock and her voice trailed off, a look of dread gathering in her features, until she finally forced a smile and refocused on Jalal's eyes. "Sex is not horrible, no. I can't imagine living without it."

With that, Gilda cast a coy look toward her cunt and began moving the clay cylinder again. "And a big cock filling you up, Jalal," she said, her voice going husky, "will help drive you toward climax."

Jalal bit her lip, watching as Gilda used her free hand to reach down and spread the very upper part of her slit, revealing a small pink nub of flesh. "This is the clit. Stimulating it, especially while you're being fucked, will bring you the greatest pleasure of all."

Still moving the cock up and down in her cunt, Gilda began to rub two fingers over the glistening protrusion. "Oooh," she moaned. "Yes. Oh, yes."

"It feels good?" Jalal asked.

"Mmm."

It seemed to Jalal that Gilda was lost to her then, her eyes falling shut as she continued using both hands to pleasure herself. Jalal watched in utter astonishment as Gilda thrust the false cock harder and harder up into her cunt, releasing low sounds of delight with each rough plunge, her fingers moving at lightning speed over her clit. Jalal's own cunt went hot, wishing she had the courage to mimic Gilda's demonstration, but it seemed like a thing she'd rather experiment with alone.

Jalal's nipples hardened, jutting against her silk gown as Gilda's breath came raspy, labored. Jalal's gaze was drawn from her stepmother's impassioned face to her cunt, still taking a pummeling from the clay tool, until finally Gilda cried out, shocking Jalal. "Oh! Oh! Oh, Ares, yes!" she sobbed, thrusting her pussy roughly against her hands and the play cock.

When Gilda's squeals finally ceased, she calmly withdrew the clay cylinder, rose from the bed, and walked to Jalal's cleansing bowl, where she proceeded to immerse the cock and wash it. "You see what pleasure a man's shaft can bring you now," she said, still sounding a bit breathless. "And fucking you will bring him great pleasure, too. But another way you'll please him is by taking his cock in your mouth."

Again, Jalal gasped. She'd wondered long and hard about sex, but she'd never imagined her *mouth* would be involved.

Gilda laughed. "I would demonstrate that for you, as well, but the clay tastes foul. Nonetheless, you should always be eager when you suck a cock, licking it in every way you can, then taking it as deep into your throat as possible, sliding your lips up and down."

Jalal swallowed. This was all beginning to sound impossible. Maybe it was a blessing her father had no current plans for her to marry. And as for Enrick, well… At least that was only temporary.

"After some time of fucking your cunt, or your mouth, your man will spurt his seed inside you, so be ready for that — especially if he's in your mouth. You'll want to suck and swallow at the same time. I won't mislead you — it's a skill one has to work at to do well — but the better you do it, the more pleased he will be."

Dropping the freshly cleaned cock on the bed, Gilda reached into her bag once more and this time extracted a small jar — clearly expensive, one of the glass artifacts so hoarded by the traders. "Now lift your gown over your pussy and spread your legs."

Hesitantly, Jalal followed the command, raising her silk skirting to her waist and parting her thighs across the bed. Glancing down, she could see her cunt had parted with desire. "What are you going to do to me?"

Gilda unscrewed the jar's lid, dipping her fingers inside. Jalal tensed when her stepmother smeared a thick, yellow paste down one side of her slit, then the other. "This will remove the hair." She reached for another dollop, spreading it across the top of Jalal's mound. "Only the wealthy can afford the luxury, so be thankful. It's even possible your pussy will be the first hairless one Enrick has seen — it should drive him mad with lust."

A few minutes later, Gilda began to wipe the paste off with a cloth. Indeed, Jalal's dark pubic hair came away, leaving the sensitive skin beneath as soft and smooth as a baby's bottom. Gilda crossed the room to retrieve Jalal's greatest treasure from the Before Times — a rare viewing glass that had been pieced together from ancient fragments. Gilda held the viewing glass down between Jalal's thighs. "Look how pretty you are there now."

18

Jalal's stomach quivered at the sight of her bared cunt, still open to reveal the pink flesh inside. "There you see your own clit," Gilda said, pointing. "Rubbing it against anything will bring you pleasure." Then she pointed lower, to a small opening guarded by miniscule flaps of pink skin. "And that's where his cock will go."

In that tiny hole? "How will it possibly fit?"

As usual, Gilda's laughter reverberated through the room. "Trust me, dear. He'll make it fit."

Laying the viewing glass aside, Gilda smiled. "Now, put on the outfit I brought. I want to see how you look in it."

Rising from the bed and turning her back to the other woman, Jalal let her silk gown fall to her feet and slipped on the barely-there swathes of blue.

Gilda propped the rectangular viewing glass on a table, then stood back with Jalal as they both studied her crackled reflection. The thin skirt reached the floor in back, but tapered and overlapped in front, barely covering her pussy. Not that it mattered — the naked flesh could be seen clearly through the fabric. The top Gilda had brought puckered across Jalal's full breasts, a tie just beneath them pulling the hem snug to her body.

Reaching up, Gilda pulled the blue material resting upon Jalal's shoulders down onto her upper arms, making the outfit even more alluring. Then she moved behind Jalal, reaching around to softly cup Jalal's breasts in her hands. "He will lust for these. He will caress them and suck on them."

"Does it hurt?"

Again, Gilda chuckled, releasing Jalal's breasts. "Well, if it does, it's in the best possible way."

What did *that* mean? Jalal resisted asking, tired of Gilda's amusement with her naïveté.

Walking back to the bed, Gilda lifted the gray, clay cock. "You can practice with this tonight," she said. "If you practice, it will be less painful when Enrick fucks you for the first time."

Soon after, Gilda departed, leaving Jalal to stare once more, with a combination of shock and arousal, at her body in the viewing glass. Tomorrow she would shed all innocence. She would seduce Enrick the Attacker for the good of Myrtell. Maybe if she did well, her father would begin to love her. Maybe he'd still try to find her a good marriage, and perhaps they could even devise a way to disguise her lack of virginity — she'd heard of such tricks succeeding.

All she knew was that she had to be brave — she had to use her body to make Enrick want her badly enough to delay his march into battle.

Shedding her seduction costume, she lay down in bed, reaching to take up the clay cock Gilda had left her. With the Maran tiles no longer of importance, this was the game she should practice now — she should try inserting it into her pussy and fucking herself as Gilda had shown her.

Yet before she even placed it between her thighs, worry and exhaustion coupled to immerse her in a deep sleep.

Chapter Two

ହ

As Enrick bent toward the stream and lifted a handful of water to his mouth, a flash of blue borne not of nature caught his eye. He lifted his gaze to the most comely creature he'd ever seen. She reclined on the opposite bank, her head propped on one elbow, her raven locks falling wild and tantalizing about her shoulders. Her luscious breasts pointed full and erect through the alluring scrap of fabric that covered them—her nipples dark and large and begging at first sight to have his tongue laving them. As their eyes met, she lifted her leg, bending it at the knee to reveal a smooth, bare pussy of nobility. Reaching down, she stroked her middle finger teasingly through the slit.

His cock had risen to its full length in the few short heartbeats it had taken to study her. Enrick knew two things. She was trouble, sent by a ruler who meant him harm. And he was going to have her.

He strode boldly through the shallow water, splashing his way across, his gaze never wavering. As he neared her, his muscles went taut and his cock grew still more rigid.

Her eyes went feral, her breath heavy, even before he kneeled in front of her, firmly parted her legs, and bent to rake his tongue up the center of her glistening cunt. A quivering moan left her as the taste and scent of her salty-sweet juices filled his senses.

"Who sent you?" he asked, narrowing his gaze on her sapphire eyes.

The vixen still trembled, looking fraught with pleasure from just that one lick. "Sent me? No one sent me."

He arched one brow. "Am I to believe you simply dropped out of heaven, a gift from Ares for a hungry warrior?"

She shook her head. "I've come from a village to the south, through the mountains." She pointed. "When I heard Enrick the Attacker was marching past, I could not resist traveling to see such a legend."

Amused, he dropped his gaze to her pussy, still spread pink and lovely below. "Came to see me, did you?"

"To seduce you," she clarified.

He could not hold in a slight grin. "Why?"

The raven-haired beauty bit her lip and let her eyes rake over him. "Look at you. You're as muscular and handsome as any combatant has ever been. How could I know such a man was passing through without wanting him, wanting his cock?"

Enrick could not hold in his smile. She was the most alluring female he'd ever met. She was clearly too ignorant to realize, however, that her silken clothing and denuded cunt gave away her background. The only question that remained was which of his enemies had commissioned her seduction.

Reaching down, he thrust aside his thin fur vest and pulled the tie that laced his pants—revealing his erection. His seductress gasped. "Dear Ares—it's even bigger than I expected."

"What's your name, vixen?"

"Jalal." She looked utterly dazed as she stared at his cock.

"Well, Jalal, do you like what you see?"

Appearing breathless, the girl nodded with enthusiasm.

He edged closer to her, until his cock stood but a few inches from her lovely face. "Do you want it? Do you want it in your pussy? In your delicate little heart-shaped mouth?" He reached out to run his thumb over her full lower lip.

Finally drawing her gaze from his shaft, she looked up at him. "More than I've ever wanted anything before."

Again, he allowed himself a small smile. She might be bait, but he liked an eager woman. So did his cock.

Reaching down, he ran his hands briskly over her breasts, her sides, her hips, then parted her legs and took a close look at her pussy. She released a trembling sigh. He'd been fairly certain there was no place on her scant ensemble to hide a weapon or poison, but he'd had to make sure. Finally, he glanced over his shoulder and called out in the direction from which he'd come. He'd left his two most trusted men just beyond the copse of trees that lined the stream. "Wansel! Morl!"

A few seconds later, the two men appeared. Wansel grinned. "What have you there, Enrick?"

He gazed down into the beautiful wanton's eyes and smiled. "A captive."

* * * * *

Jalal sat in Enrick's tent, reliving the past hour. Her senses were on overload.

Upon reaching the area near Enrick's encampment, her father's guides had searched him out, and only when they'd seen him heading toward the stream had they left her. She'd felt so uncertain she could complete the task given her that she'd almost been tempted to run—anywhere—but escaping alone into the mountains would probably be fatal, so she'd stayed to face her fate.

The moment she'd seen Enrick, her cunt had spasmed. He was...amazing. His light hair had fallen about his face like a sun-kissed mane, his shoulders were broader than any she'd ever seen, and his chest rippled with muscles. When he'd crossed the creek toward her, she'd been certain he would hold her down and fuck her—and she found herself hoping, waiting, for that grand intrusion she'd learned about last night.

She'd nearly fainted when he'd licked her pussy. Ares above, Gilda had not warned her he might use *his* mouth on *her*. Her entire being had prickled with a pleasure so intense it was almost agonizing.

And then he'd unleashed his cock—a tool much longer and thicker than Gilda's clay one. Fear had lurched inside her, even as a hunger and want unlike any she'd ever known raced through her, leaving her utterly confused and excited.

Oh, how she'd wanted him to end her suspense and plunge himself between her legs on the creek bank. She could not have been more shocked when he'd announced he was taking her captive.

He'd chuckled in the face of her obvious fear as his men drew her hands behind her back, tying them with twine. As she'd stood glowering up at him, he'd gently lifted her chin. "I shall see you soon, Jalal." Then he'd brushed a tantalizingly soft kiss across her lips, sending a rush of sensation skittering through her body.

As the two men had led her through the enormous valley encampment, Enrick's soldiers had all gaped and ogled, yelling out obscenities as she passed. She'd sensed their eyes on her breasts and cunt, but rather than feeling appalled or ashamed, their stares had only added to the intense arousal that left her legs streaming with her own juices.

Upon reaching the largest tent in the camp, Enrick's men had untied her hands, although one of them had leered at her, saying, "I'd advise you not to leave this tent, pretty. If you do, all the men will get to enjoy you, not just Enrick."

Now she sat looking around, surprised at the luxuries a man like Enrick possessed. Rather than the dull, cold warrior's residence she expected, the tent teemed with the expensive silks of the wealthy, and he slept on a feather bed—on which she currently rested. Across the tent, she noticed he even owned a viewing glass, much like her own, remnants and shards of the ancient glass pieced together to form a whole.

How long would it be before he came to her? Night would fall soon—surely then, if not before. Drat it all, she should have done as Gilda had advised and practiced with the clay cock so she'd have some idea of what it would feel like, what to expect. For even as her whole body burned with a desire like none she'd ever felt, her cunt quivered in fear, as well. Gilda had said it might hurt at first, and upon seeing Enrick's massive cock, Jalal now worried what his penetration would do to her.

She peered frantically around the tent. She'd not brought the toy cock with her, but perhaps she could find something just as good. Of course, despite the lavishness of Enrick's tent, items to choose from were few, but her eyes did fall on a plump candle wedged in yet another antique—a brass holder whose dents and tarnish made it no less exquisite.

Biting her lip, Jalal rose from the bed and snatched up the half-burned candle. It was not as wide or as long as Enrick, but it would be better than nothing.

After positioning the viewing glass across from the bed, she lounged back on the silk coverings, parted her legs, and looked at her pussy's reflection. Reaching down, she used both hands to part her cunt and locate the entrance Gilda had pointed out to her. Then she freed one hand and picked up the candle, positioning its end just so.

When she first began to attempt insertion, she met resistance—it felt strange to be putting something in her body that way. But when she thought of Enrick, her arousal bloomed fresh and her pussy seemed to open, allowing the end of the candle inside.

Oooh, how strange and erotic for her cunt to be swallowing something so sizable. Peering at the viewing glass, she experimented, beginning to move the candle in and out, pushing it slightly deeper with each slide. The sight of the candle slipping in and out of her pussy was as exciting as the sensation itself. Oh, Ares, she wanted to be ready for Enrick.

Captive or not, despite her fear and uncertain fate, she wanted all the pleasure the hulking warrior had to give.

* * * * *

Enrick stood at the entrance to his tent, thoroughly tantalized by watching his tempting little captive fuck herself with his candle. It had taken but a few inquiries among his men to learn Jalal was the name of the youngest daughter of Osren of Myrtell—Myrtell, a domain so small and poorly guarded that Enrick had, up to now, possessed no particular interest in taking it just yet. He'd been weaving through the interior mountains, planning to turn north soon and attack the growing domain of New Bern. But if this Osren was so afraid of him that he'd sent his daughter to—what? detain him?— well, then, to Myrtell his troops would go.

It was easy to see why she'd been sent—a woman so lovely and sensual could easily lure most men's thoughts away from war and onto heat. Fortunately, he wasn't most men—he knew well how to enjoy a woman without surrendering completely.

Her cunt looked ripe and ready, the candle slipping easily in and out of her inviting passage, reminding him of the long lick he'd given it earlier—the tart-sweet taste of her still lingered lightly in his mouth. A shame she was an enemy, but that didn't mean they couldn't enjoy each other.

In and out, in and out, she smoothly moved the candle. Letting a lecherous smile creep over his face, he drew back the tent flap and stepped inside.

She gasped, her blue eyes going wide as she extracted the candle, letting it drop between her legs.

"No," he said, moving closer and bending down to pick it up. He smoothly re-inserted it into her pussy, then physically wrapped her hand around it. "Don't stop. I wish to watch."

He took a seat in a wooden chair a few feet away, focusing intently on her. He'd never seen bigger, bluer eyes, her lashes long and lush—she stayed focused on him as she slowly began working the candle again.

"Good girl," he said softly. "That's right. Fuck your pretty little pussy for me."

"Don't you want to fuck it yourself?" she asked, lowering her chin provocatively.

He let another grin steal over him. "All in good time, Jalal. Now, fuck your cunt and tell me who sent you." He knew the answer already, but he wanted to make her admit the truth.

"No one sent me." In and out, in and out. "I told you, I came from—"

"Who sent you?" he snapped. When she ceased moving the candle, he spoke more gently. "Don't stop. Keep going and tell me."

The candle resumed its slippery fuck as she said, once more, "No one sent me. I'm here of my own accord."

Enrick rose from the chair and closed the distance between them, kneeling before the low bed. "Keep working your candle," he instructed, then closed his hands around her full, rose-tipped breasts through the transparent fabric. She moaned. He kneaded the firm mounds and his cock throbbed with wanting her.

Finally, he lowered the blue material over her plump breasts, securing it underneath. "These are beautiful," he whispered, dipping to rake his tongue across one taut pink nipple.

Another soft moan left her. "Oh Ares," she purred.

He cast a devilish grin up at her as he lightly closed his teeth around her nipple, pulling, gently biting. Then he whispered to her, "Even Ares can't help you now, Jalal."

Reaching down, Enrick took possession of the candle—she released it easily into his grip. As he suckled one puckered nipple, he thrust the candle into her pussy, harder and deeper than her own strokes.

She cried out at each drive of the tool, and he sucked at her furiously. She held his head to her chest, crushing him against her, and he buried his face in her lush softness, the valley between her breasts seeming to swallow him. It would be easy to forget his task, so easy, but Enrick hadn't gotten where he was by being vulnerable—even when faced with the most entrancing body he'd ever had the privilege of touching. He'd never let himself be bested; he never let anyone even *think* they'd bested him. She would admit to him why she'd come.

With one deft move, he released the candle, gripped both her wrists tight, and pushed her back onto the bed until his face hovered only inches above hers. "Tell me who sent you, Jalal. Tell me who was stupid enough to give me your body in a useless attempt to save their little domain. Tell me exactly what you came here to do."

"I came here to be fucked by you. But no one sent me."

She was utterly enticing, yet her lies were beginning to wear thin. "No one sent you, eh? That's all you have to say? All you're going to give me?" Shifting to secure both her wrists with one hand, he reached down between them, untying the waist of his pants until his cock burst free.

He'd had enough of her lies and wanted to scare her now—scare the truth from her. Squeezing tight on her slender wrists with his roughened hand, he planted his knees on her thighs, spreading her wide. "Tell me now, vixen, or suffer my wrath."

The girl stayed silent, her big eyes wide with...what? Fear? Or anticipation? She was clearly ripe for sex, but she was also young—how experienced could she be? In fact, given that she was the daughter of a ruler—dear Ares, had Osren sent a virgin to seduce him? Would the man actually sacrifice his daughter's bride value?

Every nerve in his body ached to know the answers, even as he burned to wring honesty from her. If he took her virginity, the one thing that gave her value among Caralon's upper classes, he should be cursed to hell, but Ares...he was weak. His rigid cock throbbed where it lay against her slit. Every limb, every pore, drove him onward, needing to know the sweet depths of her cunt. "Last chance to save yourself," he bit off.

When she remained silent, those warm blue eyes seeming to dare him, he couldn't hold back. With a mighty thrust, he rammed his cock inside her, making her cry out. Ares above— she *was* a virgin. The telltale wall of defense inside her hadn't held, of course, but he'd felt himself break through.

Now her lips trembled, her breath came ragged, but her eyes... Given the size of his cock, he might have expected to read in them pain, anguish, fear—but instead, he saw only fire raging in Jalal's gaze. She was still daring him, daring him to do more.

"You *will* tell me," he ground out as he drove his cock deep into her wetness. "By Ares, you will." He rammed against her once more.

Again and again, he thrust into her warm, tight passage, trying to drive the truth from her lips, but her cries were those of delight and nothing else. *Harder*, he willed himself. *Again — harder*. Her sobs grew more feral, yet those sparkling eyes of hers remained defiant, wild with pleasure.

As Enrick fucked her, harder, faster, he kept telling himself the power of his large cock in her tiny hole would wrench an admission from her eventually, that a virgin could not take what he was doling out, but for long, intense moments, the heat and bliss that assailed his body banished all other thoughts. Her lush breasts jiggled below him with each thrust until he used his free hand to seize one, squeezing it firmly, bending to draw on her beaded nipple once more. He sucked it deep, deeper, feeling it elongate between his lips, her fevered moans fueling him. *Harder, fuck her harder.* Each deep thrust into her pussy made him groan, the sound mixing with her high-pitched squeals. "Tell me!" he yelled. "*Tell me!*"

The devirginized vixen ignored him completely.

And finally, a sense of calm anger washed over him. She was enjoying being held down far too much, enjoying the hot drive of his cock too deeply.

Suddenly he understood how to lure the truth from her.

Releasing her wrists from his tight grip, he sat up and eased his cock out of her cunt until only its tip teased her pink flesh.

Her labored breath was the only sound.

He wanted more of her, wanted it like he wanted to breathe, but there was also immense satisfaction to be had in other ways.

Her lips trembled when she spoke, her voice soft, needy. "Please."

"Please what, vixen?"

"Please...don't stop. Please fuck me."

He felt the slow smile creep over him. "You want more of this big cock, Jalal?"

She nodded against the bedcovers. "Yes. Oh yes!"

"Then tell me who sent you."

Even now, she remained quiet other than her ragged breathing.

Glancing down, he could almost see her pussy pulsing with need. She rubbed it against the head of his cock. Temptingly wet, but he didn't move, only stared down at her. "If you want it, tell me what I ask of you."

Without answering, she reached down for his cock with one hand, beginning to finger her clit with the other. Hungry little vixen.

"No!" he snapped, closing his hands around her wrists once more, pinning them to the bedcovers at her side.

"But I—I'm so—"

Desperate for cock? He hoped she was desperate *enough.* "You'll only get more when you've answered me." Letting go of her wrists, he reached behind him to the table at the end of the bed. He lit a candle—dusk had grown deeper and he wanted to see every second of his encounter with Jalal. Then he reached for a long string of twine, left over from erecting his tent earlier.

Turning back to his captive, he rolled her onto her side, pulled her hands behind her back, and tied her wrists snugly together. "There," he said. "Now you get only what I give you."

When she raised her gaze to him, though, her expression was wilder than ever. Subduing her hands had done nothing to squelch her raging heat. As her raven mane fell about her face, he thought she looked like a hungry animal, caged but still fighting. *Ares,* he wanted her.

"Tell me who sent you, Jalal, and I'll loose your hands. I'll loose your hands and I'll fuck you all night long." A promise he wanted to keep.

Her deep-set eyes were just as beautiful and untamed as ever, and when she opened her mouth, the noise that came out sounded more animal than human. Even without the use of her hands, she jerked to a sitting position, her eyes darting down between her own spread legs and then between his, to the cock jutting from the soft leather of his pants.

Without warning, she propelled herself forward, bending over, grabbing onto the head of his cock with her tender mouth. "Oh Ares!" he groaned. She was the hottest, hungriest little beast of a female he'd ever encountered. And now that his cock was in her mouth, it depleted some of his strength— this was a pleasure he couldn't resist.

She shifted to her knees, dipping to slide her wet mouth up and down as much of his length as she could take between her delicate lips. Even without her hands to help her, she worked vigorously, her mouth latching onto him like a tiny vise. He had no choice but to lean back and watch the beautifully erotic sight of her lips wrapping around him, her mouth being filled with his width and length. He couldn't help thrusting lightly, thinking, *Deeper, vixen, take me deeper.* Wondrously, she did, allowing him to fuck her sweet mouth as they both moaned their pleasure.

Enrick's weakness was killing him. He didn't like his inability to stop. Domains had been lost over lesser failings. But his cock was immersed in the sweetest, wettest mouth he'd ever felt, and her wild enthusiasm was too great for him to fight.

Just when he feared he might climax, she raised her head, lips swollen, eyes wild and untamed. "Fuck me," she pleaded. "Fuck me!"

Enrick drew in a deep, trembling breath. *Don't give her what she wants. Tie her up better. Tie her to the chair. Make her beg until she delivers what you want.*

"Fuck me, Enrick! I need your cock. I have to have it! Put it in me."

The last time Enrick had responded to a woman's demands was…never. He'd always been the one in control, had never come across a woman brave enough to question his authority in bed. But Jalal was different. She was fire. She was lightning in a bottle.

He couldn't help himself. Her sweet pussy was too tight, her tigress's role too enticing. Gritting his teeth, he pulled her to her feet, then pushed her to her knees on the floor. "Bend over the bed," he commanded.

She obeyed, suddenly eager to please now that she knew she was getting what she craved. She was a vision of pure allure, blue clouds of fabric hanging in lovely disarray around her body, her hands tied behind her back as she awaited the fucking she'd begged for.

He thought about issuing threats, warnings, but at the moment, all he wanted to do was sink his cock where it belonged—deep in her pretty, wet cunt. He still couldn't believe her newly deflowered pussy could take him so well, a thought that added to his need. He couldn't wait another second, dropping to his knees behind her, lifting her ass, and plunging his cock to the hilt.

Her cry of pleasure took him to heaven and he fell into the same hot, hard rhythm as before, pounding her pussy over and over again as her sobs filled the candlelit tent.

Hard, hard, hard, he fucked her. Wet and tight, in and out, his cock grew stiffer with each thrust. How long would she take it before she begged him to stop? Amid his fucking, he issued a wry chuckle. This girl? She'd probably take it all night, drain him of his seed over and over and still plead for more. Born to fuck, he thought. Born to fuck *him*.

That was when she began moving her bound hands behind her, reaching, clawing—for anything, it seemed— another wild reaction to be being fucked. Her cries intensified as her slender, willowy fingers flailed about in desperation.

Peering down, watching his cock slam into her, he saw one of her stretching fingers collide with her anus. "Oh," she moaned at her own touch, and he had the distinct feeling she'd just discovered that part of herself.

Indeed, after that one stroke, her fingers returned there, her hands struggling against the bindings as she rubbed the puckered fissure and let out another groan of pleasure.

His own heat increased, watching her caress her tiny asshole with more and more fervor. She sobbed with frustration, though, when the twine at her wrists prevented her from stimulating it exactly in the manner she pleased, and Enrick was so enraptured by the sight of her touching herself there that he was sorely tempted to reach for the blade at his hip and slice the twine away.

But then a better idea occurred to him, and without ever easing up on his strokes, he reached around her and closed his fist around the abandoned candle. The moment he placed its rounded end at her ass, she released a moan of gratitude and relaxed her hands. Her hunger astounded him, propelling him to twist the still-moist candle back and forth against the fissure until it slowly began to ease its way inside. As her cries filled the tent, as his cock continued to plunge deep into her warm pussy, he applied just enough pressure on the candle to drive it gently deeper, deeper.

"Oh!" she cried. "Oh Ares!"

She was soon taking five, then six inches of the candle into the expanded opening of her ass. He matched the thrusts of his cock with those of the candle, filling both holes again and again, each stroke making her cry out. Her sobs, growing still more wild and laced with abandon, slashed through him with a deep satisfaction that reached his very core.

Jalal could barely understand what was happening to her. She'd never imagined such insertions into her body could spill so much pleasure over her every limb. It raced through her veins, it ran to her fingers and toes, it made her unable to think or reason. In one sense, she felt beyond replete with pleasure, as if her body might reach a point where it was so full, so well-fucked, that she might simply disintegrate. Her arms ached, stretched behind her, her knees were sore from being planted on the hard ground—yet the other sensations in her body were so overwhelming that everything else became minor, barely registering in her brain. Yet in another way, there was something more she wanted—needed. It had to do with what Gilda had told her about her clit. It tingled madly, longing for attention. Each drive into her from behind seemed to make the spot in front scream out in frustration.

She didn't want to give up the wild pleasure of his cock, or the candle—suddenly in a place Gilda hadn't even mentioned—and yet, after so much of his powerful fucking, she couldn't help begging for what else she needed. "Lick me!" she pleaded. "Like you did earlier, at the stream. Please lick me, Enrick!"

Behind her, his fierce strokes softened slightly, and she gathered the strength to peek over her shoulder at him. She found her handsome captor wearing an utterly wicked grin as he continued sliding his cock deep into her cunt. "You want me to lick your clit, vixen? You know what you have to do. Tell me what I ask."

He still wanted to know who sent her. Couldn't the insufferable man just forget about that and concentrate on pleasure? It was certainly all Jalal could think of, and her clit begged her to just tell him. After all, why did she think she owed her father so much loyalty? Why was she protecting him at all? Up to now, she'd thought saving Myrtell might save *herself*, ensuring a decent life of the luxuries she was used to, but in reality, it didn't. If her father would forsake her by sending her to surrender her bride value, what made her think he'd protect her in any other ways, especially now that her bride value was gone? So maybe she had nothing to lose— nothing but the pleasure that was begging for release.

"I…" she began. "I came…"

He slid his cock into her pussy, the candle into the opening above. "Yes, Jalal? You came from where?"

But what if she were wrong? What if telling Enrick the truth would send him marching on Myrtell with even more fury? What if her father's domain was toppled, leaving her with nothing—no place to go?

"Clearly you need a little help remembering," he said, then drew both his cock and the candle from her nether regions.

"Oh," she moaned on a shudder, his departure leaving her body strangely empty.

"Lie down on the bed."

Jalal could barely move, he'd weakened her so, but gathering her strength, she slowly climbed onto the soft mattress. Reclining on her back, she looked up past his massive, jutting cock into eyes filled with dark determination. "Spread your legs," he commanded.

She obeyed. Would he do it now, would he lick her clit once more? Had he finally quit harassing her for information? Would he end her sweet, hungry agony?

As he eased onto the bed between her parted thighs, she thought, *Yes, yes, he's going to lick me again!* But instead, he reached behind him, digging beneath the bedclothes to the mattress, finally drawing out a downy white feather.

Leaning over her, he blew slightly on the swollen pink nub that protruded from her folds and yearned for his attention. "Unh…" she moaned, the exquisite sensation at once a joy and a torture because her poor clit needed so much more. As Gilda had promised, it seemed the key to her pleasure.

Next, Enrick brushed the feather teasingly across the little mass of nerves. The touch was even lighter than his breath a few seconds before, sending her ache into a soaring spiral of desire.

When she spoke, her voice trembled. "Please, more. Your mouth."

"Please me with *your* mouth first, vixen. Use it to tell me what I want to hear." He concluded by dragging the fluffy feather lightly across her mound, leaving it to tingle with a combination of delight and torment that nearly buried her. She jerked involuntarily at the twine holding her arms beneath her. Dear Ares, she had to get free, had to rub her agonized clit on something, anything to end her hot misery. But, of course, the bindings held tight, only frustrating her more. Meanwhile, Enrick reached up to rake the excruciatingly ticklish feather across one of her hard, sensitive nipples, then into the valley between her breasts before grazing it up onto the other. A light, high sound of pure anguish left her as she watched the tantalizing cruelty.

As he trailed the feather down over her stomach, it left a ripple of pleasure in its wake. She tensed herself against the sensation as the feather once more brushed over her cunt, but there was no help for her desperate desires. All that mattered in that moment was gaining what she sought—his mouth between her thighs. "My father," she blurted. "My father, Osren, ruler of Myrtell, sent me."

An expression of satisfaction reshaped Enrick's face as he abandoned the feather and stroked his thumb over her clit—*oh yes!* That was so much closer to what she needed. "And the reason he sent you is...?"

"To detain you while he gathers his forces from the far borders."

He raked his thumb over the sensitive nub once more, sending a hot frisson of heat through her veins. "Myrtell is not big enough to have far borders," he said with an amused smile.

Her breath came labored. "Well, they are far to us. When he heard you were marching in our direction, he sent me to slow you down, to seduce you, so he could be ready for battle when you arrive."

Enrick's dark eyes narrowed as he gazed at her, sensuality taking over his expression completely. "Good girl, Jalal. And now you get your reward."

Chapter Three

❧

Jalal bit her lip, raising her head slightly to watch as he bent to lick her — his tongue leaving a trail of fire from the bottom of her cunt to the very top, where her sensitive clit resided. She made no attempt to hold back her moan as the harsh pleasure swept through her.

His eyes locked again on hers, his tongue still lingering on the engorged nub. "Is that what you want, vixen?" he asked, his expression alight with passion. "Or would you like this better?" Never taking his gaze from hers, he lowered his mouth fully around her clit, then sucked.

"Oh Ares!" she cried as heat flashed through the distended little knob of flesh, making it feel as if it were the biggest part of her. "They're both...too good for words. Do them both to me."

"Greedy," he said with a lecherous grin, then dropped back to work his tongue over her clit once more.

At first, he merely flicked the tip of it over the swollen tissue, and Jalal released a series of high-pitched gasps in response. Sensation buffeted her like the waves on Myrtell's sandy shores. His licks grew longer then, more languid and lingering, as if her cunt were the finest delicacy and he was savoring each taste, licking deep and thorough, in an effort that spanned her whole pussy. "Mmm, Ares, yes," she purred.

As he continued to pleasure her, Jalal experienced the strangest sense of climbing, higher and higher, or working to reach a summit — it was as if each hot lick from Enrick's tongue elevated her that much more, taking her up, up, closer to the prize. "Oh, more, please. More." Her words were breathy, difficult to get out in the midst of such passion.

At her request, he latched onto her clit with his mouth, again closing his lips firm around the aching nub. "Yes, suck it," she whispered. "Suck it for me."

She sobbed with delight as Enrick drew that tiny part of her deep into his mouth, sucking it so hard her pleasure bordered on pain. Still she suffered the sense that she was ascending—higher and higher—somehow nearing an entirely new plane of existence, perhaps the climax Gilda had told her about. She could not resist the urge to lift her hips toward Enrick's mouth, an attempt to somehow increase the already incredible pressure on her pussy. As she lifted, he slid his large hands under her ass, squeezing her cheeks as he suckled her clit. "Mmm, yes," she breathed, her body humming with near-bliss. Just a little further, she somehow knew—a little more and she would reach that zenith of tremendous pleasure.

"Oh!" she cried when one of his fingers sank into the tight opening where he'd placed the candle earlier. "Oh Ares!" she screamed.

The slight penetration seemed to scream through her, forcing her hips to buck against his mouth, forcing her to cry out with desperation as her pleasure grew, grew—until finally she was crashing down, the heat and sensation exploding inside her, racing through her pussy and outward in pulsing waves of release and pure ecstasy. She lost herself to it, writhing in his arms, against his mouth, sobbing as it rushed through her with a power she'd never dreamed possible.

As the throbs in her cunt began to fade, as she ceased jolting against him, she seemed to sink deeper into the soft feather mattress as a wicked sense of satisfaction stole over her. Her bride value was gone, but she couldn't have felt more fulfilled.

When Enrick rose up from her pussy, his mouth, his face, were wet with her. "Did you like that, Jalal?"

She nodded, beginning to feel sleepy, her limbs exhausted. "Will you untie my hands now?"

He responded by helping her roll to her side, drawing a small blade from the sheath at his hip and handily slicing her free. Her arms felt heavy as she drew them around and turned onto her back once more.

"Was it worth giving up your secret?"

Again, she didn't hesitate to nod. "There's nothing I wouldn't trade for such pleasure, Enrick."

"Now," he said, a small smile creeping over his handsome face, "you get to pleasure *me* some more."

The very concept shook her exhaustion away, made her hungry for more of this man and his sex. "What shall I do?"

"Just lie still for now," he whispered, moving up to straddle her hips, then moving higher, until his cock—still beautifully strong and rigid—lay between her breasts. Peering down at it, she bit her lip, then watched as his hands closed around her breasts and drew them up around his shaft. Leaning his head back, he let out a small groan and then returned his eyes to her chest as he began to gently slide his cock into the deep valley of her breasts.

On impulse, she reached out her tongue, letting it flick across the tip of his cock, licking away the dot of fluid there. Another groan left him and his cock began to slide easier between her breasts as his moisture and hers combined to wet the path.

She let out a light moan, surprised the sensation of his hard shaft between her soft mounds filled her with such pleasure.

"Ah, you like me to fuck your lovely breasts, vixen?"

"Mmm, yes," she sighed.

Lifting her own hands, she closed them over his, pressing her breasts tighter around his hard column. Then she opened her mouth into a wide "o", yearning to have his cock inside it again.

"Ares above, you're amazing," he said, his voice low with lust as he slid the hot shaft between her welcoming lips. She closed them around him, relishing the sensation of having that powerful cock nestled there once more, slowly fucking her mouth even as he fucked her breasts.

"Sweet, hot Jalal," he whispered, his eyes like dark diamonds, twinkling with heat. "You push me to the edge."

The edge of what? she wondered, sucking deeply on his enormous cock, wishing she could take even more of him into her mouth, her throat.

"Ah, Ares, you push me too far," he breathed hotly, and then he pulled out of her mouth, holding his shaft down, and she didn't know why, what was happening, until he released a mighty groan and shot hot white fluid onto her breasts, her stomach. She gasped, remembering Gilda had told her about this part, yet mere words could not have prepared her for the satisfaction of watching his seed spurt forth, of knowing she'd made it happen.

But Gilda had said it would happen inside her or in her mouth, so Jalal grabbed onto the shaft and pulled it roughly between her lips, wanting to taste him before his climax ended, wanting to drink him, swallow him. She sucked voraciously at the sweet fluid still oozing from his cock as his groans grew more and more ferocious. And when finally he seemed spent, going quiet, she raised her gaze to his, releasing his cock and licking her lips.

He looked like she felt...overwhelmed.

"You are...a true seductress, Jalal."

* * * * *

Jalal woke in Enrick's arms to sunlight glancing through the tent fabric. She could scarcely believe the night they'd shared—it hadn't been a dream. Waking with her curves molded to his hard, sinewy flesh reminded her just how hard one particular part of him could get and how much pleasure it could deliver.

Before last night, she'd known so little about being with a man—and maybe she still knew nothing, for she had no idea if she should follow the instinct that urged her to lower her lips to his. Her heart beat faster as she pressed a kiss to his mouth—it was warm and moist, a salty taste lingering there.

When he met the pressure, returning the kiss, her body flooded with heat. And when he slipped his tongue between her lips, she instinctively met it with her own. Just the power of his kiss turned her pussy wet again.

"Good morning, Jalal," he said with a soft smile.

"Good morning."

"Daylight's upon us, so we'd best rise. We'll be traveling today, and you'll ride with me."

Ride—that meant he had a horse, a rare and treasured animal. "Toward Myrtell?"

He nodded. "Sorry, vixen. It has to be done."

Jalal bit her lip, suffering mixed feelings. In one sense she was worried for her homeland and its people, feeling as if she were a traitor. But her father had never been a particularly good or giving leader, and perhaps Myrtell's citizens would fare better under Enrick's rule. The only thing she knew with certainty was that her heart ached and her stomach churned when she thought of Enrick going into battle. "Have you ever been injured in an attack?" she asked softly.

"Of course."

Everything roiling inside her tightened into a hard knot of dread. "I...don't want you to be hurt. You must be careful."

He offered a good-natured chuckle, lifting one hand to push the hair from her face. "Don't worry, Jalal. It might not be much of a battle. I'll give your father a good reason to avoid it."

"What reason?"

"You. I'll be offering you in exchange for a peaceful surrender. You're his daughter—he'll have no other choice."

Jalal's heart seized—she only wished she were as sure as Enrick of her father's actions. As it was, he might well be willing to sacrifice her and go to war, and what would happen then? Would Enrick die in battle? Would Myrtell fall or stand? And would anyone care about her in the end—or would Enrick be just as willing to toss her away when this was done?

* * * * *

"Sorry, vixen," Enrick said as he tied the last knot, binding her once more, this time to the wooden triangle topping the pikes upon which it was mounted. "I don't like using you for this, but war is never pretty."

His hot, delicious captive looked stalwart, strong. "Don't worry—it isn't the first time I've been used to avert a battle."

The words made his heart pinch a bit. She didn't deserve to be a spoil of war. Even so, it might bring his meeting with Osren to a peaceful conclusion and add another domain to the region he now controlled. As for sending Jalal back to her father, well…his heart constricted a little at that thought, as well. But war was not a matter of the heart.

"Commence marching!" he commanded his troops, and they moved as one massive entity toward the hilltop over which Osren's fort lay.

An hour later, his army stood face to face with that of Myrtell—or at least whatever forces Osren had managed to gather, given that Jalal's mission of distraction had worked, but her mission of delay had failed. As he'd known, he could take Osren easily, so hopefully the man would surrender without bloodshed. The man who sat on an elevated throne being supported by a number of his men looked old, spent—and even from a distance, he disliked Osren's eyes. Unlike Jalal's, they were filled with venom. It was hard to reconcile his vixen having come from this man's loins.

"Raise the captive!" Enrick demanded, peering over his left shoulder to watch his men lift the triangle to which Jalal was bound. Her swathes of blue had been adjusted to cover her lush breasts and bare cunt, but the transparent fabric left little to the imagination.

"Surrender peacefully, Osren of Myrtell, and we will return your daughter to your safekeeping. If you do not surrender, however, Jalal will be passed around among me and my men, a sex slave." It was a lie, but would no doubt produce the quickest surrender.

"If Jalal is no longer a virgin, she's of no use to me," Osren replied. "Unfortunately for you, Enrick the Attacker, I do not care what becomes of the girl, so it will take more than a threat against her to win Myrtell — you'll have to fight for my domain if you care to take it."

Enrick's heart shriveled in his chest. He knew from his travels and battles in Caralon that men of this region often saw women as objects, possessions — especially among the wealthy ruling class. Yet he'd also witnessed much love for women, and the very concept that Osren would cast his daughter so carelessly away stung him deep. Perhaps it shouldn't have surprised him, given that the same man had sent her into an army camp with instructions to surrender her virginity, yet this seemed even more unfathomable. What father wouldn't save his daughter from a life — or even death — of sexual slavery? This one, apparently.

"Very well, Osren. Prepare to fall."

* * * * *

Jalal waited in Enrick's tent in the new camp that had been erected before the march to her home. Her heart swam with uncertainty, worry, pain. She'd not been surprised to hear her father reject her so bluntly, yet it had still hurt. Now, she worried for her fate, and for the fate of Enrick, as well. Her captor. How could she care so much? And would he truly pass

44

her among his men? Her heart ached with a need she feared only he could fill, and her cunt hungered for his strong cock.

When the tent flap was flung back, she flinched.

Enrick stepped inside, his body covered with dirt and thin stripes of blood — shallow cuts made by daggers.

Her first thought was to leap up and run to his arms, so thrilled was she to see him safe. But instead she only swallowed nervously. She had no idea what would happen now — to her, to her home. She had no idea if Enrick cared for her as she cared for him.

"Myrtell is now mine," he said, settling into the chair near the bed where she rested.

"And my father?"

"He's being put out on one of the border islands. There will be food and water enough for him to survive. The few of his men who would not agree to join my army will be placed there with him."

"And the rest of those in my household?" She could not help fearing for Relah, Gilda and others.

"They were given a choice. Pledge loyalty to me or be cast out to the island."

Well, that was fair. Whichever option they'd chosen, she would not have to worry for their fate.

"Your father was lucky," he said. "I was sorely tempted to drive my blade through his heart."

She drew in her breath. "Why?"

He tilted his head, no longer the wicked, tempting captor of last night — his expression now held nothing but raw, honest sincerity. "Because he was willing to sacrifice you, to place a mere domain over your safety."

Jalal's heart seemed to swell in her chest, even as her clit tingled beneath the thin blue sheath of her skirt.

"I don't wish for you to be my captive anymore," he said.

Oh Ares—was he turning her out? Where would she go? And how would she live without him now that she knew the pleasures of love and passion, as well as the joys of his cock? "But I...I would willingly be your sex slave."

"I'd prefer you to be my wife, vixen. Given my other victories and more to come, I'm the ruler of a vast domain—all of Caralon before I'm through. When I'm done, I'll need a wife. Children. I want you to rule Caralon with me, Jalal."

"Me?" she asked, splaying her fingers across her chest. What he offered was the sort of existence she could only dream of, yet...she could only imagine how many women Enrick had been with. Why her?

"Your passion and enthusiasm last night went beyond anything I've ever experienced with a woman. Your strength this morning was equally remarkable. I want you, Jalal. Always."

She bit her lip, nearly overcome with emotion. "Oh Enrick—I'd love nothing more than to be your wife...and your sex slave, too."

He grinned, reaching out for her. She left the bed and let herself be pulled into his lap for a searing kiss that set her cunt on fire. "Although," she added, "I guess I won't need my bridal Orientation now."

His rich laugh rang through the tent. "No, vixen, I'd say not."

Jalal tilted her head, remembering one last mystery of sex. "But what about the game of Maran tiles a virgin bride plays? Tell me what they indicate."

He leaned his head back slightly. "On the wedding night, before the new husband takes his wife, other men stimulate her with their hands and mouths, driving her arousal to a fever pitch so she'll be ready for her man. The number of tiles the bride cannot successfully remove from the game board determines how many other men will pleasure her."

As shocking as she found the explanation, her pussy seemed to bloom with fresh desire. "I suppose we will dispense with that tradition, as well."

He cast a soft smile, one hand rising to cup her breast. He stroked her distended nipple with his thumb. "Unless you would like it."

Jalal tried to imagine that much stirring pleasure, that many hands and mouths all there to please her. "Tempting," she concluded, "but I think you're all the man I can handle. And why would I want others to get me ready for you when I'm already constantly hungry for the big shaft between your thighs? In fact, I'm hungry for it right now."

They both peered down at his bulging crotch. Licking her lips, Jalal rose from his lap and together they unlaced his leather pants until his cock sprung free, just as tremendous and arousing as she recalled.

As she kneeled between his legs, he once again flashed that deliciously wicked smile she'd seen last night. "Consider me your feast, vixen."

MASTER OF DESIRE

Dedication

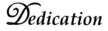

The Brides of Caralon series is dedicated to Leonie Daniels, who first encouraged me to try my hand at erotica, and to Anya Bast, who gave me a helpful tip or two along the way.

Prologue

3587 AD

એ

Teesia's skin prickled with awareness as she shifted her attention to the dark man across the room. As she'd suspected, his gray gaze burned into her, forcing her to look away quickly. Her heart pounded in her chest and the juncture of her thighs tingled.

Despite the quick glance, she'd gotten a good enough look. Smooth raven hair, as dark as her own, fell past his shoulders, and a shadowy stubble dusted the bottom half of his olive-hued face. Black leather encased his body from his broad shoulders all the way to his boots. He was a study in darkness, a creature of the night—simply leaning against the wall, arms crossed, staring.

Beneath the long feasting table where she sat, she grabbed onto her older sister's wrist. "Maven, who *is* that?"

Maven turned from where she'd been speaking with her husband, Dane. "Who is who?"

Teesia could hardly point the man out, of course, and now she didn't even want Maven to look, lest he know they were talking about him. His gaze continued to brand her. "Don't turn your head," she warned, "but he's clad in black, with dark hair, and…" *Something about him makes me feel like I'm melting from the inside out.*

"And what?" her sister asked impatiently.

Teesia swallowed past the lump in her throat. Ares above, she'd never had such an instant and visceral reaction to a man. It was at once frightening and scintillating. "And he keeps looking at me." She took a long sip from her wine goblet to distract herself.

Teesia watched as her sister cast a subtle sideways glance across the room. Fortunately, he was easy to spot — not the sort of man who blended with the crowd. "Ah," Maven said. "That's Ralen of Charelton."

"Charelton?" The region lay only a few days journey south of Teesia's own home in the Myrtell area of Caralon, and like Myrtell, bordered the sea. "Why have I not heard of him before?"

"He came into power there only within the last year, I believe, on the death of his father, Granick."

Teesia pulled in her breath and took another sip of wine. No wonder the man looked so fierce. Granick had been known throughout all Caralon as a ferocious and terrifying warrior, not to be angered — and the reputation had persisted even into his old age. As a daughter of Enrick, Ruler of Caralon, Teesia knew Granick had guarded the domain's southern border her entire life. "Does this Ralen now guard Caralon to the south, as his father did?"

Maven nodded. "Dane tells me this is the first time he's met Ralen, but he considers him a formidable man of power and thought it wise to make his acquaintance." The autumn feast in Dane's northern region of Rawley was a celebration of Maven's pregnancy, but as royal daughters, both girls knew that any meeting of such wealth and authority in one place became political, as well. And if Dane, of all men, considered Ralen formidable, then it was a description surely well-earned.

Teesia was sorely tempted to gaze back at him, bold and brazen. But she couldn't quite make herself do it. Perhaps more wine would help. She reached for the wineskin on the table before her, refilling her goblet.

Maven glared. "Mother said *one* cup for you."

But Teesia only smirked. Now that Maven was married and pregnant, she thought she could treat Teesia like a child?

Just then, their younger sister, Laela, approached behind them, bending to whisper loudly in Teesia's ear. "That man is watching you!" And then she pointed!

Horrified, Teesia spun to push Laela's arm to her side. "Must you be so obvious?"

Laela's eyes sparkled with her usual immature excitement. "*He* is obvious. So what difference does it make if we are, too?"

Teesia swallowed nervously, deciding Laela might actually have a good argument. "But even so..." she reprimanded, then let out a sigh.

"Perhaps it's your gown. I told you it was cut too low."

Teesia glanced down at the sea green silk draping her breasts, which now tingled beneath the soft fabric. It was the most revealing thing her mother had ever permitted her to wear, and Laela was simply jealous.

"In fact, if not for your braid, a man might think you were not a virgin," Laela accused.

Teesia pulled in her breath in mock outrage, yet secretly, she was pleased. The long plait which she and Laela were forced to wear to indicate their royal virginity hung as heavy as a chain from the back of her head, and the idea that she might be thought of in some other way, especially by the mysterious man across the room, was infinitely titillating.

How she longed to reach bride's age as Maven had some months back, so that she, too, could finally know the pleasures to be found with a man. Other girls her age knew, now even Maven knew—*everyone* knew, it seemed, except for her and Laela. Such was the price of being a royal daughter, her virginity her greatest asset. Or *her father's* greatest asset, she amended.

Maven had been traded in marriage for protection of the northern border—it was only lucky for her that she seemed to have found happiness with Dane. Teesia and Laela, too, would be bartered into arranged unions. But Teesia wasn't afraid. Her status in life meant she would marry a man of power. And surely a man of power would be a man of great sexual prowess, as well.

Sex. A word her parents, even her sisters, had no idea she knew. But her friend Bella, from the village, had been persuaded to tell her much over the last few months. Bella, the young widow of a prosperous businessman in Myrtell, was very fond of Teesia and seemed to find it hard to deny her anything—even secrets forbidden to be shared with a royal daughter. So instead of being kept totally in the dark about sex as tradition demanded, Teesia had already learned something about it. And she already *craved* it. Bella had made it sound like the most wondrous part of life and Teesia couldn't wait to learn more, firsthand.

Rising to her feet, Teesia thrust her breasts slightly forward for the benefit of Ralen of Charelton. A glance down revealed that her nipples puckered the fabric prettily. The warmth that climbed her face resulted from both nervousness and anticipation, the inner heat of desire. "I'm going to take a walk," she announced, pushing past Laela.

"All right. I shall go, too."

"No," Teesia said quickly.

Laela looked wounded. "Are you mad at me? Just because I said your dress was cut too low?"

Teesia gave her head a quick shake. "No, Laela. I just...wish to be alone, that's all."

"Is something wrong?"

No, something's right. Or it might be anyway, if I can ever get away from this crowded room. "Not at all. I just...want to give you some time with Maven." She motioned to the chair she'd just vacated. "Here, take my seat. We've not seen our sister in many months. You should be given some time to speak with her, as I have."

Laela smiled, believing the explanation. "You're right, Teesia. Thank you."

As Laela slid into the seat, Teesia's body began to hum with heightened anticipation. She had no idea if the man in black would seek her out, but maybe, if she were lucky, she'd get a taste of the mysteries of sex that so haunted her these days. She simply didn't think she could wait until bride's age to experience it, and even as much as his stare intimidated her, she realized this was an opportunity that would never return to her if she passed it up.

Of course, her father would kill her if he had any notion what she hoped for, and she knew wanting to be with this feral-looking man was wrong, but she couldn't help her feelings, her body's urges. Ralen of Charelton had brought them to boiling level with just a glance, and she couldn't help wondering what *else* he could make her feel.

She slipped from the fortress's great hall into a corridor that led to the garden—which she thought would be a delightful place for a seduction. But she stopped when she caught sight of herself in an enormous viewing glass, its rare and jagged pieces from the Before Times pasted together on the wall. Her father owned many of the valuable antique viewing glasses, but she'd never seen one so large, and it reminded her what power and wealth lay *outside* the royal fortress, as well. Maven had married well and Teesia could only hope to be as lucky.

A sconced candle lit the space only dimly, yet highlighted the shadows and coves of her body. The manner in which the green silk clung to her curves reinforced the notion that she was becoming a woman.

Then she noticed her hair, pulled back from her face. No man would touch a girl with braided hair—it was unthinkable, an offense punishable by death if her father found out.

Dare she? Dare she take away the one aspect of her appearance tonight that identified her as a virgin, a girl with a valuable bride's price between her legs?

If her parents or sisters saw her hair flowing free, she'd be in immeasurable trouble...yet somehow, just now, the risk seemed worthwhile. Maybe it was the wine driving her to such lengths, or maybe it was the stark lust she was experiencing for the mysterious Ralen—but whatever the reason, she wanted to be beautiful. A real woman, not just a girl on the way to becoming one. She wanted to be a desirable, attainable woman that the forbidding dark-haired warrior in the great hall could want—and have!

Biting her lip as she peered into the jagged-edged viewing glass, she reached up and began untwining her hair. She could re-plait it later easily enough. And even if the dark man did not seek her out, she could at least look on herself at her most exquisite—with her hair falling loose around her shoulders, framing the pale green silk that highlighted her feminine curves.

Soon enough her hair was free, somehow setting *her* free, too. She smiled boldly into the viewing glass and thought, *Come and get me, dark warrior from the south. Come and make me a woman.*

"Lovely," said a deep voice from behind her in the darkness.

She flinched and turned, but could only make out the shadowy shape of a man.

"It was designed by my friend, Bella," she said nervously, glancing down at her gown, "and the fabric came from the silkworms on our estate."

The man chuckled. "The frock is very fine, too, but I was referring to what's underneath."

She drew in her breath, but tried to hide her reaction as her pussy—that's what Bella had called the feminine parts between her thighs—spasmed softly. "Come out where I can see you," she demanded.

Ralen of Charelton stepped into the light.

His dark eyes glimmered with flirtatious intent even as something within them signaled danger. He stood even taller, his shoulders stretching even broader, than she'd realized from across the room. His smooth, straight, onyx-colored hair seemed almost too soft for such a hard man, but it added to his masculine beauty. Her heart beat so violently that she feared he could see it pulsing within her chest.

"What's your name?"

Still holding her breath, Teesia thought fast. She couldn't identify herself as Enrick's daughter or Ralen would likely flee the corridor in a heartbeat, fearing Enrick's wrath. Even if it was difficult to fathom *this* man fearing *anything*, better safe than sorry. "Tee...Teenya," she said.

He tilted his head, his expression possessing a hint of mischief. "You unbraided your hair."

She gasped gently, reaching up to touch it. Then she remembered what she'd so quickly forgotten in the flurry of wanting to hide her virginity. Dratted wine! "You saw me in the great hall."

He gave a short nod, and she thought of a lie.

"My family is not from this region. Where I hail from, the braid signifies nothing. It was only as I spoke to the mistress of the estate, Maven, that I learned what it indicates here."

He cast a wicked grin. "So you quickly rid yourself of it, for it would be terrible if anyone thought you a virgin."

A wave of fresh heat echoed through her. "Yes. For I...well, I am not. And I would not want to give a false impression."

She couldn't read his smile—it seemed laced with secrets. "Perhaps that's my good fortune."

Another burst of flames ignited inside her, filling her breasts and pussy with a startling warmth, a warmth she wanted to invite him into. "Perhaps," she said, the word coming out huskier than she'd intended.

"You must know how creamy and ripe your breasts look within that dress," he said deep and low, taking a step toward her.

She swallowed nervously, unable to reply.

He moved ever closer. "And you must know that your every curve is accentuated, on display for men to see."

She found her voice, wanting to be bold. What she yearned for felt as if it were almost within her grasp, and she couldn't risk losing it now. "I wish for men to see what I have to offer. I have nothing to hide and much to give." If other women in Caralon could give freely of their bodies to anyone they chose, she could, too. At least for tonight.

His voice went lower still, his eyes darker. "Do you wish to give it to me, sweet vixen?"

She felt deliciously captured by him already. "If you wish to take it."

Sex tinged his smile as he moved even nearer and whispered, "Turn around. Look back into the viewing glass."

She tried to breathe evenly, stay calm, even as her pussy hummed with longing. As he stepped up close behind her, he reached around, splaying one large hand across the green silk that fell down her stomach; the other he poised softly on her shoulder, bare but for the dress's thin strap. His touch was like a strike of lightning, but nothing compared to the shock he delivered when he leaned forward into her! Bella had told her about cocks and erections, but Teesia couldn't have imagined *how* big, *how* hard, one could be. Now Ralen of Charelton's nestled tenderly against her rear and she thought she would explode from the desire churning inside her.

"Tell me you're certain, little vixen," he whispered in her ear. His fingers splayed wider, his thumb brushing the underside of her breast. Her tense heartbeat now pulsed through her pussy, as well.

"Oh yes, I'm certain," she breathed. She wanted this big, fearsome man to teach her the mysteries of sex more than she'd ever wanted anything in her lifetime.

As he lowered a light, scintillating kiss just below her ear, her head fell back, her eyes shutting in passion.

"Open your eyes," he said.

When she did, their gazes met in the veined shards and pieces of reflecting glass.

"Look at us together," he instructed, "and tell me once again, vixen. Tell me you're sure you desire this."

She let out a breath of frustration, even within his heavenly grasp. "Why do you doubt me? Yes, I desire this, desire *you*. *Please*."

His unbelievable erection hugged closer against her bottom, making her sigh with heated pleasure, as he gently cooed, "All right, little vixen, all right. I'm convinced. I'll give you what you want."

She sighed with relief—and anticipation—then bit her lip as she watched his hand in the viewing glass, drifting down over her belly, his fingers slowly edging over the green silk to ease into the crux of her thighs. Unimaginable pleasure shot through her, forcing a broken, thready moan from her lips.

More kisses rained across her neck, then her shoulder, as his fingers sank deeper into the thin silk barely separating pussy and hand, and she parted her legs to let him touch her more easily. Her breath was the only sound as he slowly began to stroke...stroke...stroke with those big, magical fingertips. "How do you like that, little vixen? Does it feel good to your sweet cunt?"

Cunt. She didn't know that word, but she didn't have to—the meaning was easy to decipher. "Mmm, yes," she purred. "Yes."

"Watch in the viewing glass," he reminded her again, his voice warmly demanding at her ear. "Watch me touch you."

She focused on the reflection before her, but it was hard to believe the girl she saw was *her*, Teesia of Myrtell, royal virgin, writhing in the grasp of a dangerous man in black who she'd never met before. Hard to believe—and delicious. A most decadent indulgence that would've made her throw her head back with wicked laughter had she not been so deeply caught up in passion.

The large hand between her thighs began to bunch and gather the fabric of her dress, closing it into a strong fist. Gathering, gathering, slowly pulling her formal skirting higher and higher, revealing first calf, then knee, then thigh.

Her desire rose higher, too, with each inch the silk climbed, with each bit of her body his hands revealed to both their eyes.

He'd stopped kissing her neck now, both of their gazes locked on the viewing glass. His other hand twined around her waist, making her feel all the more captive within his well-muscled arms, and he used his hand to pull back what remained of the sea green skirting until her pussy was on display.

"Oh," she murmured. She'd looked at that part of herself in the viewing glass in her chamber at home, but the vision before her now was the most erotic she'd ever witnessed. And she was at the very center of it. "Touch me," she pleaded.

Ralen let out a small growl as his fingers sank into her wetness, making her cry out.

"Shhh, quiet," he cautioned, reminding her for the first time that they were still in the fortress and that someone could come upon them at any time. Dear Ares, talk about risk!

But his fingers stroking so deep into her pussy produced the most wonderful sensation she'd ever felt, so rather than think about risk, she chose to concentrate on pleasure.

She watched in the glass as he fondled her with fingers clearly experienced at the task, and soon she found herself moving, gently thrusting to meet his hot touches. "Yes," she whispered. "So good."

His eyes, next to hers, glazed with pleasure as he witnessed her response. "That's right, little vixen, fuck my fingers."

Fuck. Another word from Bella. It meant the sex act, but she thought it must mean more than just the cock and pussy coming together given his usage just now. It spurred her to move more energetically against his hand, to soak up the delights he delivered more enthusiastically.

"Mmm, yes, good," he said. "Just like that. Just like that."

Teesia began to feel lost in his incredible caresses, her limbs going weak, every part of her feeling heavy, hot—her whole body tingling with a maddening intensity.

"Keep going," he urged, and she realized her instinctive thrusts heightened the joy not only from his fingers, moving in rhythmic circles over her wet flesh, but also brought her into firmer contact with the powerful erection at her back. She found herself grinding her bottom against it just as feverishly as she ground her pussy against his hand.

His breath had gone heavy, too, by the time she realized something was happening, growing inside her, the heat getting hotter and hotter, like the flames that turned from orange to blue in the ovens at home.

"Oh Ares," she moaned, reaching up to brace herself, flattening her palms against the viewing glass. She didn't plan it, simply did it, understanding instinctively that she needed the leverage to lunge more powerfully against his fingers. "Yes. Oh yes."

And then— Oh, oh, oh! It thundered through her like a hundred horses racing over the land. Sweet, hot echoes vibrating like enormous heartbeats through her entire body. Total pleasure. An amazing transport to someplace entirely new. Nothing else existed.

Nothing else...until it faded and she opened her eyes to find her dark man of mystery studying her in the glass. "Lovely," he murmured, clearly pleased by her reaction to the startling sensations—but he didn't seem nearly as surprised by it as she did.

"Fuck me." The words shot out of her without forethought, a request Bella had told her filled a man with great desire. *Fuck me, because whatever just happened to me, it wasn't sex, and I still don't know how it feels, and I want that wonderful hardness in your pants, I want to know it better.*

They were up close to the viewing glass now, since she'd leaned forward against it, and his eyes felt ominously near. She drank in his musky scent as his heated gaze devoured hers.

"Goodnight, my little vixen," he whispered, a hint of a smile playing about his lips.

And quick as that, he kissed her on the cheek and disappeared into the darkness from which he'd come.

Chapter One
3589 AD

ဆ

Teesia stood before her father's throne, peering up at him and her mother, who sat at his side. She couldn't help beaming. She had finally reached royal bride's age and had been summoned to the great hall of her father's fortress to learn the identity of her husband-to-be.

Everyone who lived and worked in the fortress at Myrtell had gathered to hear the news, as well, but Teesia thought only of her parents—her strong father, whom she knew instinctively had chosen for her an equally strong and powerful man, and her raven-haired mother, still a beauty and much beloved by her husband many years into their marriage. Jalal was the wisest, most influential woman in all of Caralon and Teesia not only admired her mother greatly, but she also admired her mother's *sway* over her father. All Teesia's life, people had said she favored Jalal, both in looks and temperament, and she'd never been prouder to be her mother's daughter than she was today.

"Daughter Teesia," her father Enrick began in his deep, authoritative voice, "you have reached the age to be given in marriage, and the man I have chosen for you is Ralen of Charelton."

Pure joy flooded Teesia's body from head to toe. She'd *known* it would be Ralen—she'd just *known* it! And whereas Maven had at first resented being awarded in trade for border protection, Teesia had no such concerns. It was the way of their world, and she was only thankful that her fervent prayers to Ares these past two years had been answered—she was to be wed to her dark warrior from the corridor, a man whom she knew, both from experience and intuition, would pleasure her infinitely.

"Very well, Father," she said, still smiling wide, certain her happiness must be evident in her eyes. "When shall I be given?"

Enrick delivered a soft grin, clearly pleased that she liked his choice. Much talk had been made about the looks exchanged between Teesia and Ralen at the feast two years past—but only *she* knew about the delights he'd delivered in the hallway. "You shall be given tomorrow, daughter."

She drew in her breath. Tomorrow! That was highly unusual. "So soon?" She was anxious to begin her new life, certainly, but there was so much to be done first!

Enrick nodded. "Ralen and his entourage camp outside Myrtell even now, awaiting the Giving Ceremony. He and I met only yesterday and he seemed eager to take you as his wife, so we agreed to dispense with the customary waiting period."

Teesia nodded, but said, "What about my Orientation?"

Her father only laughed—probably at the enthusiasm in her voice, or the fact that she was broaching the subject before everyone in the great hall without a care for their presence.

It was Jalal who answered with her motherly yet regal smile. "Not to worry, dear. You and I shall discuss everything shortly. Perhaps, though," she said with a glance to her husband, "we should adjourn, as there *is* much to be accomplished before tomorrow morning."

"Agreed," he said, then looked down on Teesia. "Tomorrow at dawn," he announced in a loud, ceremonial voice, "you shall be given to Ralen of Charelton, daughter!"

The crowd filling the hall cheered their approval, and Teesia's heart felt near to overflowing. All her dreams were about to come true! She couldn't wait to take Ralen as her husband, and she couldn't wait to discover the joys to be had in his bed.

* * * * *

"What about my Orientation?" Teesia asked again, kneeling at the center of her fur-covered bed as her mother entered the room.

"Well, obviously, you will not have the usual three nights, so your Orienter will have to work fast."

"Who is it and when will she be here?" The Orienter was always another female, someone close to the bride-to-be, and her job was to teach the royal bride what she needed to know about sex before she entered into marriage. For most royal and wealthy girls who were kept so ignorant of sex until Orientation, it was a large task—but given what Teesia already knew, she'd hopefully not miss out on too much. Thank goodness Bella had broken the rules for her!

"Soon, soon," Jalal answered with a light laugh. "And you shall see who your Orienter is when she arrives. For now, daughter, might I suggest you practice your Maran tiles?"

Teesia let out a heavy breath, trying to absorb how quickly everything was happening. And yes, that was a good suggestion. Maven had had three whole days to keep practicing the sacred game in between her nights of Orientation. Ares above, maybe being given over to Ralen tomorrow wasn't so wonderful, after all—a girl needed time to prepare! Then yet another thought struck her. "But if I practice the Maran tiles, who shall pack my things?" There was simply no time!

"Relax, my dear," Jalal said in a calm, soothing tone. "Willa has already emptied your chamber of most of your belongings and set about putting them in trunks. You didn't even notice?"

Teesia looked around her. Indeed, other than the fur bedcover, leather wall hangings, and a thin silk nightslip, her maid had emptied the room of everything personal. It was startling in a way—to think she'd never again see the bedchamber of her girlhood as it had always been, filled with her clothing and hair ribbons and everything else that was distinctly her own. "I've a lot on my mind suddenly, I suppose," she said, feeling sheepish.

Her mother sat down beside her and took her hand. "You must be calm now, daughter, and trust that all is as it should be. Tomorrow you go with the man with whom you'll make your life. Use today to prepare for that life, and to anticipate it. Everything important has already been taken care of—your only task for today and tonight is to ready yourself to be a wife." With that, Jalal leaned in to deliver a kiss to Teesia's forehead, then rose from the bed.

Opening the heavy wooden door, she looked over her shoulder with the reminder, "Practice the tiles, Teesia," and was gone.

Teesia was determined to heed her mother's advice. Like all royal girls, she still didn't know how the ancient Maran tiles fit in with the marriage rituals, but was always told she would learn soon enough. She settled before the same set of tiles Maven had used to learn the game before *her* betrothal, and tried to focus—both on playing and relaxing.

Her whole world was changing, but that didn't mean she couldn't be civilized and adult about it. She wanted more than anything for her new husband to think of her as the woman she'd wanted to be for him that night two years ago. To this day, she didn't know why he'd left her in the corridor without taking their encounter further, but soon she would learn all there was to know about him. And she didn't want him to mistake her for any sort of young miss or little girl. She wished to be all woman for him in every way, and that included behaving in a mature and confident manner.

She had just finished the first practice game—successfully clearing the board of nearly all the tiles!—when a prim knock came on the door.

She almost thought she recognized the knock, but couldn't be sure. She blinked and looked toward the door, hopeful. "You may enter," she called.

Her beautiful friend Bella swept into the room, a charming smile gracing her face. Voluminous red hair spilled over her shoulders and eyes as green as the rare and ancient marbles from the Before Times glimmered in the pale light admitted through the high, thin windows. Her silken frock was green, as well, the shade of summer leaves, draping her womanly curves in such a way that no one could miss them.

Teesia pushed to her feet. "Bella! Is it you? Have you been chosen to orient me?"

Bella's smile widened. "I have, my sweet little Teesia."

Teesia padded quickly across the smooth stone floor and gave her friend a long, heartfelt hug. Bella's arms folded warmly about her as their bodies pressed together, and she'd never felt more content. It was fitting and perfect that her dear older friend be her Orienter, especially given how much Bella had already taught her about the ways of sex. "I'm so glad it's you."

Bella held her at arm's length and gave a conspiratorial grin. "Fortunate, given our shortness of time, that I've already oriented you quite a bit on my own, yes?"

Teesia nodded. "Indeed. Otherwise, I'd be left completely unprepared for Ralen."

At the mention of his name, Bella's smile took on a wicked slant. "He is a strong, virile man, my Teesia. Everything you could hope for in a husband."

Teesia let out a dreamy sigh as she plopped backward on the bed, the juncture of her thighs swirling with fresh desire for the man who would soon be her husband. "Mmm, I know." She'd told Bella about Ralen stroking her pussy at Rawley two years ago. That's when she'd learned the word *orgasm* from Bella—which had explained the heights of pleasure his fingers had lifted her to.

"But never fear, my girl—we will have you good and ready for Ralen's cock, I promise you that. Good and ready for him in every way he could want."

Teesia lay back on the bed, turning on her side and propping her head on one fist. "What else can you tell me to make me ready, Bella? Is there more I don't yet know?"

Bella joined her, lounging lengthwise next to her, the green silk clinging to her ample breasts and curving hips like dramatic ocean waves. "Do you have any questions I haven't answered? Anything you're not clear about?"

Teesia tried to think through it all. She knew from Bella how their bodies would come together, and she knew about the fleshy little knob at the top of her pussy called the clit, which was the source of orgasm. She knew about the cock, how it grew—and mmm, she remembered with pure delight and longing the way *Ralen*'s had grown against her bottom in the hallway! She also knew how it would spurt seed, into her or onto her, depending upon her husband's whims. She knew about sucking his cock, too, and that he, in turn, would lick her pussy, and that all of it would culminate in insurmountable pleasure for them both. "There's only one thing," she said, wondering if Bella would dare break one last rule.

"What's that, sweet Teesia?"

"What significance do the Maran tiles have? What will happen when I play the game on my wedding night?"

Bella's eyes sparkled with a hint of wildness at the mention of the Maran game—but then she disappointed Teesia, as she always did when Teesia asked this particular question. "You know good and well that you are not meant to find out until the game is played. If you knew, it would…" She let out a lascivious little laugh. "Well, it would wreck your concentration, to say the least, and affect the outcome of the game."

Teesia gave her head the persuasive tilt that so often prodded information from her friend. "Not even a hint? *Please.*"

Bella let her head drop back to the fur bedcover with a sigh. "All right—I'll say only this. The Maran tiles will bring you more hot and decadent pleasure than I have ever known."

This surprised Teesia, so she leaned over to look into Bella's eyes. "*You* have never known these pleasures? The ones *I* shall soon know?" Bella was a widow with many lovers, so it seemed impossible.

The woman's curls fanned out about her like a wild mane. "You forget, my girl, only the royal experience *this.*"

Bella had been married to a well-to-do clothier before his untimely death—she was a very well-respected and financially comfortable woman, even now, having taken up the business herself. But she wasn't royalty or even part of the truly wealthy. Bella was so elegant and beautiful that Teesia sometimes forgot certain boundaries separated them.

"So then, it's something truly unique—something the average woman cannot do?" Teesia pried.

Bella let out another rich trill of laughter. "Oh, the average woman *could*, my sweet—and someday I may just indulge in such wantonness myself—but not many have *this* treat, no. And, I daresay…" She stared up at the ceiling, looking thoughtful. "I suspect it will be better for you than it would for me, for there comes a certain added pleasure in having such delights thrust upon you unexpectedly, without thought or decision." Finally, she rolled to her side, graceful as a cat, and peered into Teesia's eyes. "Trust me when I tell you, Teesia, to enjoy every minute of this pleasure when it comes. Savor it."

Bella let out another long, languid sigh, as if imagining the joys to be had after the Maran game, and Teesia couldn't hold back a shiver. Her pussy wept with curiosity and anticipation.

"Now, though," Bella said, sitting up, "we must make you clean and tidy for your husband."

Teesia sat up, as well, going a bit rigid. "Clean? I am quite clean already, thank you."

But Bella only laughed, then walked to the large wooden door, opening it wide. "Bring it in," she said to someone outside, and Teesia watched as four strapping young men who worked about the fortress carried in one of the rare and valuable bathing tubs from the Before Times. She noticed it was the grandest of those in the fort—a crisp white with shiny, curling brass legs.

"There is more to this tidying than you know," Bella said with a conspiratorial wink in her direction as the boys began filling the tub with ewers of hot water. Bella sprinkled in red rose petals to scent it as the surface slowly began to rise.

"What do you mean?"

Just then, Donnell, a particularly attractive young man who, it was rumored, had once fancied Maven, entered carrying a smaller round tub, which was soon filled with water as well.

Finally, when the boys departed, Bella instructed her to stand up and shed her dress of soft, thin leather. She'd never had occasion to disrobe in front of Bella before, and as the dress dropped to her feet, her nipples tightened, her pussy tingling softly. Perhaps it was the warm gleam in Bella's gaze as she boldly perused Teesia's curves that caused the unexpected response.

Teesia swallowed around the sudden lump of nervousness in her throat and said, "Well, what do you think? Will Ralen like my body?"

Bella's smile, like her movements, reminded Teesia of a sensuous cat. "Oh yes, my sweet girl, he shall be very happy when he sets his eyes on those lovely round breasts with their pretty pink points." Bella moved closer to her then, kneeling beside her and reaching to smooth a gentle palm down over Teesia's bare stomach. "And such soft, flawless skin and ripe curves."

When Bella tenderly cupped her pussy, Teesia flinched.

"And this," Bella said, "this he shall love wildly, but he will love it even better after we have put it on display for him."

Teesia blinked, taken aback, her cunt grown warm in Bella's hand as she looked down on her. "On display? What do you mean?" She wondered if she would leave Bella's palm wet.

Pulling her hand away, Bella reached for a woven sack next to the bed. Dyed the same green as her gown, Teesia had not even seen her friend carry it in. From inside, she extracted a valuable antique jar of clear glass filled with a bluish paste.

When Bella uncapped it and began to use her fingers to smear the blue cream on Teesia's thigh, she asked, "What are you doing? What is that?"

Bella's cat's smile returned. "You shall see, sweet girl, you shall see."

Given the discussion they'd just had, she shouldn't have been startled when Bella spread the paste not only up and down her legs, but also between them, covering the mound of her cunt. She hissed in her breath slightly as Bella rubbed it there, covering the area thoroughly. Again, she wondered if the wetness from her slit would moisten her friend's hand with something other than the blue ointment.

Some minutes later, Bella instructed her to step into the wooden tub Donnell had delivered, after which she used a sea sponge and water to begin rinsing the paste from Teesia's legs. It was only when she removed the blue from between Teesia's thighs that she realized what was happening—all the hair was gone! Teesia gasped at the sight of her bared pussy.

"Fear not, sweet girl," Bella said, smiling up at her briefly before refocusing on her work below. "Ralen will be madly aroused by your hairless cunt."

"But...why?"

Bella shrugged. "Who can say why certain things arouse us? But count yourself lucky. Only the wealthy can afford this, for it's very expensive. And the naked flesh between your legs, my dear, is…mmm…very pleasing, indeed."

Teesia thought Bella was overly thorough—rinsing and re-rinsing the area with sponge and water long after all traces of blue were gone and making the sensitive area feel swollen and tingly all over again. When her friend finally ceased, rising back to her feet, Teesia asked, "Do *you* use the cream, too?"

Smiling, her friend reached down and pulled up the flowing green billows of her gown to reveal smooth legs and a bare cunt of her own. "Yes, my dear. Very expensive, but a luxury I indulge in."

Teesia bit her lip, studying the other woman's pussy. She'd never seen any other besides her own. Bella's appeared fleshier, hints of pink peeking out from the center slit.

"Into the bath with you now," Bella said, letting her dress fall.

As Bella carefully bathed her with another sponge, which she lathered with a thick square of soap made by the washer women, she spoke in soothing tones about relaxation being the key to sexual pleasure. "No boundaries, Teesia," Bella said softly. "Relax and your boundaries will fall away. Relax and you will discover desires yet unknown to you. Open yourself to passion, to whatever feels good. Let your husband please you however he wishes—take joy not only in the acts themselves, but in the giving of them. Give back just as freely. Follow your instincts and urges, never push them down." Teesia had let her eyes fall shut, and it made her all the more aware of the sensations as Bella's sponge ran slowly over her breasts, curving down her stomach and between her thighs. She parted her legs, following the inclination, and let Bella thoroughly wash her there. "Hands, mouth, even skin—they are your tools of pleasure. And more than that, you will discover other tools—not of the flesh—which bring joy."

This confused her, but she kept her eyes closed, trying to remain in her lulled state of relaxation. "Tools not of the flesh?"

She sensed more than heard Bella's soft titter of sensual laughter as she abandoned the sponge and began unbraiding Teesia's waist-length hair. "It is not for me to tell you more, really. It's for your husband to teach you, if he chooses. But from what I've heard of Ralen, you may expect some…yes, some *tools* to come into your relationship. Yet trust me, sweet Teesia, when I say you need not fear them at all. It's only a way to vary the pleasure, to take it deeper, with your husband's help."

Bella began pouring small pitchers of warm water over the length of Teesia's hair, and somehow even that became a sensual experience—she was unusually aware of how her hair became weighted, how the weight pulled slightly at her scalp, making it tingle.

Bella washed her hair with slow, firm fingertips, massaging so deeply that Teesia let out a small moan at one point. Opening her eyes, she looked up at Bella, hovering over her, and they shared a smile.

When her hair was clean and rinsed, she wordlessly stood and stepped out onto a fur rug placed next to the bathing tub, waiting patiently as Bella slowly, thoroughly ran a drying cloth over her. Her entire body prickled with awareness as Bella drew her thin white nightgown over her head, then took her hand and led her to stand before the viewing glass mounted on the wall in her chamber.

Her nipples shone through, dark and pink, and the fading light of day made a shadow at the juncture of her thighs, even though it no longer shone dark with curls.

Bella brushed Teesia's hair until it was nearly dry, then said, "Lie down on the bed."

"What now?" Teesia asked, lounging comfortably on her back.

Bella crawled up next to her on the fur bedcovering. "I've told you as much as I can about men and sex," she said. "The only way to teach you more, sweet Teesia, is to show you."

"Show me?" What did Bella mean?

A small smile played about her friend's red lips, which always looked to Teesia as if perhaps they'd been stung by a bee—large and prettily swollen. "First, you must learn how to kiss."

With that, Bella leaned over, lifting one slender hand to Teesia's cheek, then lowered a soft, short kiss to her lips. Teesia couldn't help being surprised at the skitter of sensation that shot down through her body at the gentle contact. Then she let out a small laugh. "That was easy, but surely that's not how a wife kisses her husband."

Bella smiled. "No, sweet girl, it's not. It's more like this." Her next kiss was slightly firmer, longer...it was more searching, Teesia thought, as if trying to pry something out of her. She returned the kiss, trying very hard to do it in just the same way, trying to learn how she should kiss Ralen of Charelton.

She'd thought they might stop and evaluate the kiss afterward, but instead, Bella kissed her again and again, the kisses growing deeper, more sensuous. Teesia soon forgot about *trying* to kiss well and simply found herself kissing Bella back, meeting her lips, moving her mouth against them, finding herself inspired to continue the pleasurable lesson without conversation.

When Bella's tongue swept past her lips, Teesia was at first surprised, but then understood—it was just another way of kissing, and she had to learn them all. She welcomed her friend's warm tongue and met it with her own, sensing from Bella's response that she was learning quickly and doing well.

When Bella's hand glided from Teesia's cheek to her neck, then down to cover her breast, she moaned at the touch. Bella kneaded her through the thin, flowing silk, rubbing the fabric so gently against her skin that she thought she'd die from the tender pleasure. Could a fierce man like Ralen touch her this softly? She had to wonder.

But at the moment, there was too much pleasure in Bella's lesson for Teesia to broach the question. After all, Bella was the Orienter—Teesia decided she should simply accept the lesson as it was and ask questions later.

Soon, Bella's lips left hers, only to descend to her neck—and oh, what sweetness her dear friend's mouth delivered to the sensitive flesh there! She heard her own breath turning labored, coming in sighs. But all of that measured nothing when Bella pushed her sleeping gown from her shoulder, baring her breast, then lowered her mouth to the stiff pink peak.

Teesia moaned unabashedly as Bella's kisses echoed through her body like the sort of thunder that shook the ground. She watched as Bella ran the tip of her tongue around the hardened nipple, again and again, setting off spiraling waves of heat in Teesia's flesh.

"Oh Bella," she breathed, "that is exquisite! Will Ralen do that to me, too?"

Delivering another tender kiss to Teesia's breast, Bella looked up with amused surprise. "I never told you about that? I suppose it must have seemed so obvious to me that I simply forgot. But yes, Ralen will love your breasts and you will learn that they're wonderful play toys for you both."

"I'm already learning," Teesia purred.

Bella imparted another sensual smile, then freed Teesia's other breast, using her hands to lift them, push them together until they looked to Teesia like two twin mountain peaks. Bella began licking, suckling her, moving from one eager breast to the other.

She moaned her pleasure as she watched Bella work, wondering how her friend knew so well how to do the things that a man—her husband—would soon do. She was well aware of Bella's plump breasts pressing against the curve of her waist and she suffered the faint longing to feel them against her own, the stiff nipples brushing over hers, or even raking across her tongue.

Finally, Bella looked up from her task, still caressing Teesia's breasts as she spoke. "You already know what it feels like to have your pussy fondled by eager fingers, how wet and wild it grows with longing. But what you don't know is how it feels to take a cock—so that shall be the next part of our lesson."

With that, she left the bed, and Teesia wondered what on earth Bella had in store for her! How could Bella have a cock? Teesia raised her head from the fur to find her friend returning with her green bag, from which she produced a bizarre-looking cylindrical object made of clay. Teesia flinched, stunned at the sight.

And Bella grinned. "This, Teesia, is a cock."

Teesia blinked, still a little dumbfounded. She'd felt Ralen's behind her, but she'd never imagined it to look so…well, so long. So prominent. She'd imagined it as more of a mass of flesh that perhaps pushed up out of the body for sex—not as something that could be thought of as another limb!

"Not a real one, of course," Bella said on a laugh, "but a reasonable representation. And most suitable for acquainting you with a man's rod."

She'd heard Bella call the cock that before, but had never known why. Now she understood. A rod indeed.

"Some will be smaller than this, some larger," Bella explained, "and they are not stationary in size—they grow and harden when aroused, then later retreat, becoming a smaller, limper thing. I wish I could teach you how to suck it, sweet girl, but the truth is, the clay clock is rather foul-tasting, and I don't wish to leave you with any sort of unpleasant impression. But here," she said, beginning to run the cock gently across Teesia's breasts, "feel it against you. Become accustomed to its length and width against your flesh."

An oddly alluring thing, she thought, watching Bella rake the smooth clay cock back and forth, teasing one of her nipples with it.

"Is a real cock this hard?"

"Mmm, yes, thank Ares," Bella said on a throaty rasp.

At the moment, Teesia couldn't decide if that news were good or bad. She keenly recalled how hard Ralen's cock had felt against her rear, and how exciting that had been, yet at the same time, something this hard was a little frightening, forbidding.

Her green eyes glittering with delight, Bella began to drag the cock in wide, swirling motions down over Teesia's belly, still covered with a thin layer of silk. "Get used to how it feels on you, dear girl, and know that as foreign as it seems now, you will soon relish it."

When Teesia felt the light fabric drifting up her newly denuded legs, she knew her friend was raising her sleeping gown. She glanced down in quiet anticipation as Bella's cool fingers swept the gown to her waist and began to gently glide the head of the clay cock against her slit.

Without decision, she parted her legs to feel it better. Oh yes, hard *was* good. Feeling the cock stroke into her wetness reminded her of the pleasure brought by Ralen's big, strong fingers, yet somehow she knew the urge of wanting this *inside* her, of feeling empty even as it moved against her. She instinctively spread her legs wider, wider, aware that both she and Bella watched the clay tool move smoothly through her pink, open flesh.

A tool! Was this what Bella had meant when...? "Is this the kind of tool Ralen will use in our marriage?"

Bella's eyes met hers. "Perhaps. Perhaps not. There are many such pleasure tools."

"Truly?" How many could there be?

Another cat's smile graced her friend's face. "Not all use them, sweet girl. And many are known only to those who…well, those who enjoy finding ways to seek out more…*uncommon* sexual pleasure. But yes, this might be the sort of item you will encounter. Again, I cannot say with certainty, but I have heard that Ralen…well, that he seeks many sorts of carnal delights, so you should be open-minded."

"That's what you meant about having no boundaries?"

Her nod came with a certain heat, dripping from her eyes, and Teesia realized Bella had begun to drive the clay cock softly at her pussy now—a sweet thrust, then another, another—and to her surprise she was involuntarily pushing back against it, trying to take it inside her. Oh, dear Ares! A true Orientation this was! Only she had not known one could have sex with a cylinder of clay!

Teesia met the gentle thrusts, beginning to feel her pussy stretching, slowly opening further. Then a horrifying thought broke through her longing. "Will this make me no longer a virgin?"

Bella tilted her head, her red curls falling to drape Teesia's bare thigh with lustrous tresses. "Well, it depends upon how you define virginity. As a purely physical thing, a part of the body to be breached? Or as being had by a man, your husband."

Teesia swallowed nervously. "I would not wish him to think I've come to him without my virginity intact." She, of course, had lied to him that night in Rawley, and wine and arousal had had her ready and willing to surrender her bride price had he chosen to take it—but even after he realized he was marrying the girl he'd stroked to orgasm in Dane's corridor, she would still be Enrick's daughter, a *royal* daughter, and he would still expect her virginity. She'd better have it to give.

"It's quite possible, sweet dear, that what happens after the Maran game will…um, destroy that evidence, same as I'm about to do now." She continued her gentle thrusts, even rising to kneel between Teesia's parted thighs, working the cock with both fists, watching its point of entry with intensity.

"He'll have no way of knowing you weren't entered *then*, during the Maran rituals."

Ares above—the Maran game *did* hold amazing secrets!

"Trust me, Teesia. After the Maran tiles are played, you will understand that your bride price is more about your husband being the first *man* to take you. Dildos such as this do not count."

But Bella had said it was only *possible* the evidence of her virginity would be destroyed following the Maran game. "What if my physical virginity is *not* breached after the game? Won't he have reason to think I've been with another man?"

Slowly, Bella stopped driving the cock at Teesia's slowly parting pussy. She pulled in her breath, then let out frustrated sigh, looking uncharacteristically forlorn. "I suppose you're right, dear. I...I don't know what came over me. Selfishness, I presume."

"Selfishness?" Teesia asked, her legs still spread wide, her friend still situated between them.

Bella raised her gaze, looking shockingly...guilty. Up to now, the only expressions Teesia had ever seen on her friend's face were joy, confidence, sensuality—nothing like this. "I just...well, I so wanted to show you how it would feel, so wanted to push this cock up inside your lovely pussy."

Teesia bit her lip as her cunt tingled, even without the cock thrusting against it. "Is it? Lovely? He'll like it?"

Bella ran her fingers over it, seeming to pet it, her fingers stroking down into Teesia's wetness. "Mmm, yes, I promise you he shall."

But Bella's eyes remained sad, and Teesia couldn't abide that. Bella had been such a wonderful friend to her, making her beautiful dresses, spending countless hours with her and treating her like a real adult, telling her the secrets of sex—and now she was her Orienter, too. She couldn't bear to see Bella look so bereft. "What's wrong, Bella? What suddenly makes you so unhappy?"

Bella moved to lay next to Teesia once more. Teesia considered pushing her gown down over her cunt, lifting it to cover her breasts, but it seemed pointless given all they'd just shared.

"I suppose your Orientation simply has me, well, wishing for sex," Bella said confidingly.

"But don't you have it all the time? What about Oren, the baker? And just last week you told me of a romp with the servant boy who works in the orchard."

Bella smiled, as if to herself. "Yes, both have wonderful cocks, and both are generous lovers. But I suppose...I was curious to see how it might feel to be on the other end, if you will. I wondered what it would be like to...be the man. To push a hard cock into a soft, tight pussy."

Part of Teesia wished she hadn't felt the need to stop Bella from indulging her wish.

Looking up at her, Bella read her mind. "But you were right, sweet girl. I don't know what I was thinking, nearly risking your bride price that way. It could have been disastrous. Passion got the best of me, I suppose."

Then Teesia got an idea. Bella had always been so generous to her, in so many ways, perhaps this was the least she could do on the last night they would see each other. "Would you like for me to push the clay cock into *you*?" She leaned over her friend.

Bella smiled boldly. "Would you? Would you like to?"

"I will if you wish it."

Bella gave her head a speculative tilt against the fur. "It might be a good way for you to learn even more about the pussy."

Teesia drew in her breath and picked up the tool where it had been abandoned between them. Together, they pulled up the flowing green fabric of Bella's dress until her parted legs revealed moist pink folds and a dark little opening Teesia had never seen on explorations of her own cunt—so surely this was where the cock entered. Leaning down near her friend's cunt, she nudged the clay cock at the tiny passageway.

"Don't be gentle, Teesia," Bella said, her voice taking on a hard, lusty edge.

"Really?"

"I would have been with you—you're a virgin, after all. But for me—no, it's not necessary. Make me feel it."

Gathering her courage, Teesia thrust, and watched as—amazingly—the cock sank neatly into Bella's cunt. Teesia gasped and Bella moaned. "Now fuck me with it," Bella demanded.

Teesia began pushing the tool in and out of Bella's opening, her excitement growing as she watched it glide so easily in and out of the astounding little hole. "Oh Bella, it's incredible!"

"Oh, I know!" she moaned. "Don't stop! Do it harder!"

Teesia tensed, her entire being infused with the same passion emanating from Bella as she began ramming the clay cock more firmly into her friend's wet, accepting pussy. If this was what it was like to deliver pleasure to her husband, she would enjoy it.

"Harder!" Bella said again, so Teesia plunged the cock as forcefully as she could, realizing a woman's cunt must be a strong and resilient little cave to take such violent thrusts with pleasure.

Just as her arm began to grow weary from working the tool, Bella reached down and began frantically rubbing her fingers over her clit. Teesia drove the cock deeper and deeper, watching. Witnessing her friend's pleasure was almost like experiencing her own—her pussy had grown even wetter now than it had been before, when Bella had been nudging the cock at it.

Teesia had touched herself the same way Bella touched herself now, ever since learning from Ralen that a hand could excite so much, but she wasn't sure she'd ever moved her fingers with such wild ferocity as Bella did. Her beautiful friend moaned long and loud, thrusting herself against the clay cock in Teesia's grip as she stroked herself so fast that her fingers were a blur.

Finally, Bella's groans changed, growing shorter, her breath seeming to catch—and then she cried out with such abandon that Teesia knew her dear friend was climaxing. "Oh! Oh Ares! Yes! Yes!" she cried, and Teesia continued thrusting, thrilled to have helped Bella reach her ecstasy, until her friend's movements finally ceased, her head dropping back to the bed in exhaustion.

Teesia slowly drew out the toy, still watching Bella's open cunt, amazed at the female body. To think *her* body would soon take a cock like this! She clenched her teeth with anticipation, her pussy humming.

Just then, she caught Bella studying her, likely seeing the desire that surely shone on her face. "Lie down," Bella instructed, her voice taking on a whole new softness Teesia had never heard from her before.

When Teesia lay back on the fur, Bella rolled toward her, placing her hands on Teesia's shoulders. "I can't leave you like this." Then Bella began to kiss her again—long, passionate tongue kisses that Teesia eagerly returned, thinking of practice and also succumbing to pure pleasure. Her Orientation had taken her deep into an unexpected passion that she wanted simply to *feel*—she wanted to surrender to it all.

Bella's kisses soon strayed from Teesia's mouth, arcing down over one breast, then onto the other, suckling her nipple deeply. Teesia sighed and moaned, involuntarily arching against Bella's lush, pliant body. Her friend's mouth moved lower, delivering scintillating kisses across her stomach, through the silk, then lower, just above her mound.

Teesia was lost to Bella's generosity, amazed by her friend's sensual lessons and how much she'd learned, and was *still* learning—about giving, and succumbing. When Bella's hands pushed her thighs apart, she didn't resist, and when

Bella's lush mouth sank to Teesia's hungry pussy, she cried out. "Oh Bella!"

She'd never imagined such raw pleasure as that which Bella's tongue delivered in long, languid licks through her pink, wet flesh. She shuddered and bucked uncontrollably. She thrust her fingers through Bella's beautiful red tresses. She lifted her cunt, begging for more.

It didn't take long until Teesia knew orgasm was hovering, hovering—and then she toppled, seeming to fall, deep, deeper, until the fur bedcovering caught her, wrapping her in warmth and satiation. A satiation she'd certainly never expected to find in her Orientation.

Soon, Bella moved up next to her in bed and leaned close, her nipples jutting against Teesia's arm through the silk that covered them. She gently kissed Teesia's lips, then whispered, "There now. You'll be able to get a good night's sleep. Your all-too-brief Orientation is complete, my sweet Teesia, and my only regret is that I can't have more of you. For tomorrow you go with your husband-to-be. Tomorrow your new life begins."

Chapter Two

ဢ

Ralen of Charelton stepped into the great hall of Enrick's fortress, well ready to set eyes on his new bride. Enrick had assured him she was lovely, but what father wouldn't make such a claim about his daughter, especially during marriage negotiations?

As the Giving Ceremony was a private affair, the hall was empty but for Enrick, his comely wife—whom Ralen had met before, and the dark-haired girl who sat perched on a large silk pillow below the two thrones.

His footsteps echoed in the cavernous room as he crossed the floor, growing closer, closer, until finally he was near enough to see that—yes, indeed, Teesia was a beauty. As promised, she resembled her mother—shiny raven hair, blue eyes, creamy skin and pleasing curves that tempted his touch already. His cock stirred to life in his pants at the sight of her, and at the knowledge that she would soon be his.

Only—he'd seen this girl before.

With her now-braided hair cascading down her back and over her shoulders.

With her legs parted to him before a viewing glass in Rawley.

Ares above! The little vixen from the hallway was Enrick's daughter? His wife-to-be?

"Welcome to Myrtell, Ralen of Charelton," Enrick said as Ralen drew to a halt before the throne, masking his shock.

"Thank you, Enrick," he answered, eyes still pinned on the girl. She sat mooning up at him as if he'd hung the sun in the sky, an expression that might well have pleased him under other circumstances. But did the girl think he'd not remember her? What in Ares' name was she smiling about? Did she think it would please him to realize his bride had heretofore gone about offering herself to men she didn't know?

"You are acquainted with my wife, I believe," Enrick said, and Ralen shifted his gaze to the beautiful Jalal, a woman held in high regard throughout the land.

He gave a nod of respect, trying to reconcile the fact that the wanton who'd offered herself to him so freely at Rawley was this stately woman's offspring. "My pleasure to see you again, Jalal."

The ruler's wife offered him a small, regal smile. People professed that Teesia took after Jalal both in looks and personality, but they were clearly mistaken on the second count. Caralon was a place of freedom—sexual and otherwise, so he did not judge the girl on *moral* grounds. No, he judged her on *royal* ones! Royal and wealthy girls knew their duties to their families, and *most* obeyed the rules, as they should.

He'd not believed her for a second that night when she'd claimed her braid signified nothing, nor had he believed she was not a virgin. But he'd never suspected she was Enrick's daughter, sister of Dane's wife!

His own damnable fault, he supposed, for not seeing a family resemblance, but he'd never expected a young royal daughter to be giving herself to men in the back hall. At the time, he'd presumed she was a wealthy girl of other parentage, seeking excitement. He had burned to open his pants and explore her cunt deeper than his fingers had been able to, but had not wanted to ruin the girl, both for the sake of herself and her father.

As for wealthy girls with a bride price seeking sexual release—well, it had been fine when she was a stranger, someone he would never see again. But to discover that same girl was to be his bride… He could only wonder how many *other* male hands had dipped beneath her costly silk skirts.

"I have promised you my middle daughter, Teesia," Enrick continued the ceremony, a tradition suddenly tainted for Ralen.

Looking again to the ruler and trying to hide his ire — for it was not Enrick's fault he'd raised a misbehaving tramp — he gave a nod of recognition.

"Do you vow you can provide her with a comfortable life?"

Define comfort, he almost asked, yet held it in. He was suddenly inclined *not* to offer his new wife the ease of life she surely expected. But could he give her material possessions, keep her well-fed, a sturdy roof over her head? "You know that I can, Enrick," he replied. Enrick had visited his estate — he knew what Ralen possessed. He need not know any of the more punishing thoughts that swirled in Ralen's head just now.

Enrick nodded. "And do you vow you can fulfill her physical needs and get her with child, so that my line is guaranteed to continue?"

"Oh yes, Enrick, that I can do," he answered with bold confidence. He'd do more than fulfill them — he would make sure she knew who her sexual master was.

"Very well, then," the ruler of Caralon said. "I send her with you knowing she's in capable hands."

Capable? Indeed they were. And he'd intended, until a few moments ago, for them to be loving hands, too — but Enrick's wayward daughter had ruined that wish. For what he had on his capable hands, it seemed, was a girl who had been slinking around back hallways and Ares knew where else, giving herself over to any man who would have her. For all he knew, she *wasn't* a virgin.

But he wouldn't hold Enrick responsible for that. Enrick was honorable and Ralen respected him — always had. He certainly had no idea of his hungry little daughter's appetites and that she'd already been doing her best to get them filled.

And he, like Enrick, was a man of his word. He'd agreed to guard Caralon's southern border until the time of his death or Enrick's, whichever came first, in exchange for the girl and a place in the royal family.

All this meant was…well, that he would not have the marriage he'd expected.

And that his new bride would have to be punished. Severely.

His royal bride was supposed to be his and his alone. She was supposed to be totally ignorant of sex other than what she had learned in her Orientation. She was meant to be his to mold and teach and train and nurture.

Well, soon enough she'd understand unequivocally that she *was* his, body and soul, to do with what he pleased, to treat as he would, to use in bed in whatever manner he wished.

He was a man of unusual sexual desires. Some women had gone so far as to call his tastes frightening, chilling, bizarre. Up until this moment, he'd had every intention of initiating young Teesia into his decadent sexual world ever-so-slowly, exercising the utmost care and concern for her feelings and her pleasure. But to his surprise, he was marrying a woman who was not to be trusted, who might well think she could fuck every man she liked — and she'd have to be brought to heel, taught to know good and well to whom she belonged.

The good news was that he no longer had the slightest care if she enjoyed his sexual tastes or not. And he would no longer worry about going slow or being gentle. Punishment was not meant to be soft — it was meant to teach a lesson, and he'd be certain his wanton little vixen would learn it.

"Daughter, stand and take Ralen's hands," Enrick instructed.

The silly girl hopped to her feet at lightning speed, anxious to get in his pants, he presumed, if his last meeting with her was any indication. He closed her much smaller hands in strong fists, wondering if she could sense the anger in his grip, if she could see the cold determination in his eyes as he gazed down on his lovely, naughty little bride.

"I hereby give to you my daughter, Teesia of Myrtell, Teesia of the House of Enrick. She now belongs to you, Ralen of Charelton."

* * * * *

Teesia's entire body was atingle as Ralen led her away from her parents, out the door into the bright Myrtell sunlight. "Do we start for Charelton now?" she asked, peering up at his strong, handsome face, the lower half covered with rugged stubble just as when she'd first met him. He was just as dark, dangerous and arousing as she remembered, and the mere touch of his hand made her heart beat faster.

"Yes, my caravan is waiting," he said without looking at her.

That pinched a bit, making her lustiness die a little. She'd thought he'd be more…well, more like *she* was—excited and thrilled and ready to begin their new life together.

Perhaps she just needed to express herself better, let him know how pleased she was to become his wife. He still held her hand in his firm—truthfully, too tight—grasp, so she took the opportunity to stroke her thumb lightly over the back of his knuckles. Bella had taught her that little touches could be used to ignite flames in a man. "I am thrilled to be going to your home, Ralen, thrilled that we will soon be married."

Only then, as they walked, did he glance down at her with stern eyes. "That makes one of us, then."

Teesia flinched and instinctively tried to pull her hand away, but his grip was too constricting. She was aghast, trying to fight off the sting of his words. "You…you…do not wish this marriage?"

"I wish this union with the royal family," he stated plainly.

Teesia swallowed back the pain that threatened to make her collapse. Ralen's entourage had just become visible in the distance, but she kept her eyes on her husband-to-be. "I thought that...well, I thought we would fit well together," she said, sorry for the depth of emotion that leaked from her voice. "I thought you would wish a happy marriage, as I do."

He stopped walking, pulling her to a rough halt, and stared down into her eyes. "Do you think I'm so thick that I don't recognize you, vixen? Do you think I don't recall what happened between us at Rawley?"

She was confused—why wasn't their brief but passionate interlude a *pleasant* memory? "Of course I expected you to remember me. And frankly, I expected you to be pleased, knowing that our encounter in Rawley was only a taste of what's to come."

"That part you have right, vixen," he said, his voice going deeper, and sounding almost like a threat.

They'd started walking again—him pulling her along was more like it—and since the caravan loomed closer, she knew she must speak plainly, for she wished to get to the bottom of this *now*. "I should think you'd be happy to know you have a bride who desires you. Deeply," she added, figuring there was no cause to hide the truth. "I should think that would bode well for our marriage."

"How many other men have you desired deeply, Teesia? How many men have you lifted your skirts for in back hallways?"

She gasped at the accusation. How dare he? "Only you, I swear it!"

His sideways glance said he didn't believe her. "I have no qualms with pretty girls who want to play, vixen. But *you* are royalty. With duties to your family. You possess a bride price. Or at least I *hope* you still have it."

"Of course I do! I—"

"Royal girls do not let down their hair and tell lies to entice the nearest available man in a darkened corridor. It was a betrayal to your father. In fact, you've made him look foolish to have traded your supposed chasteness in marriage—for one cannot trade what does not exist."

"But I—"

"Had I wanted to marry a common girl with common sexual habits, I would have. But I wanted a chaste, inexperienced virgin, Teesia. I wanted a girl who would belong to me alone."

"I *am* a virgin, and I *do* belong to you, Ralen—I promise."

He stopped walking again to cast her a glance, as if considering her words—but then chose to disregard them. "Yet chaste and inexperienced you are not, Teesia. As for your claim of being mine, why should I believe you've not offered that ripe little pussy of yours to every interested suitor who might have come sniffing around? You knew me not at all when I stroked you to ecstasy. And then, by chance, not knowing who you were, I bargained with your father to wed you. Do you realize the coincidence involved here, vixen?" He paused for a dry chuckle that held no humor. "But even more amazing to me is that you expect me to believe your silly story. I might not have gotten what I paid for in you, but I won't be made a fool of by my wanton bride."

Teesia was incensed. She'd quickly grown tired of his accusations and had gone from saddened to angry in a few pounding heartbeats. "Has it occurred to you, you big brute, that it was *not* a coincidence? That perhaps the reason my father chose you was because he knew I fancied you?"

He let out a scalding laugh. "Am I to believe his virgin daughter told him she spread her legs for my touch before a viewing glass and would have eagerly taken my cock if I'd offered it, as well?"

She drew in her breath at having her most thrilling memory transformed into one of regret. "There is no shame in what I did!"

"For a common farmgirl or a villager, no—they may spread their legs for one and all, as is their right. But a girl of royal descent knows good and well she must keep her desires at bay."

"And for your information, what my father *does* know is that you and I exchanged glances at Dane's feast. My sisters witnessed it. My mother, too. And though I know you are an apt choice for a husband for other reasons, it's my belief that he took my wishes into consideration because he knew I was attracted to you and would find you a pleasing choice."

The caravan was but a few hundred yards away now and cheers began to go up as Ralen and Teesia approached. It seemed to end their conversation, much to her dismay—she *had* to make him see the truth!

Girls in frocks of leather offered gaily colored flowers to Teesia as she and Ralen passed through the two lines forming at either side of the path they took. People waved colorful streamers in the air and shouts were raised. "A cheer for Ralen and his lovely bride!" "To a long and happy marriage!" "Welcome, Teesia, new lady of Charelton Fortress!"

For a brief moment, the fanfare made Teesia believe she'd simply imagined the horrible exchange with Ralen just now. *This* was how the days leading up to her wedding were supposed to be! A welcome from his people. A welcome into his life. Around her, carts stood at the ready—and dear Ares, she'd never seen so many horses in one place! All the wagons were drawn by the rare and expensive animals. The conveyances were painted in bright hues, strung with more of the colored streamers and flowers that befitted a royal bride. One young girl lifted a wreath of daisies onto Teesia's head— matching perfectly the flowing silk dress of pale yellow made by Bella especially for this day, for the Giving Ceremony and the departure to her new existence.

Overcome, she dared smile up at Ralen, her hand still wrapped tightly in his.

He did not return it. Her heart sank.

Thankful when he led her to a particularly grand cart the color of ripe red apples, she stared up at him. "So this is how we are to be? We are to have an unhappy union because you doubt my virtue?"

"We are to have an unhappy marriage because I have discovered my wife-to-be is a liar with no regard to duty or loyalty. How can I put any trust in such a woman?"

"Look into my eyes," she said earnestly, "and you'll see that my desire for you is real and my claims true."

"I looked into your eyes in that dark hallway, vixen, and what I saw there was uncontained lust."

"For *you*."

"I could have been any man."

She shook her head. "From the moment I saw you, I wanted you in a way I wanted no one else."

"You should save your pretty lies, vixen." His eyes narrowed into thin slits. "In fact, you should save *all* your strength, in every way."

She swallowed, feeling threatened by his forbidding tone. "What do you mean?"

"You're going to *need* strength after we wed."

"For?"

"I have plans for you, my little wanton. Wanton you may be, but before I'm through with your punishment, you shall understand that you will be a wanton only for your husband."

"You *are* the only man I wish to be with, Ralen!" Why couldn't the insufferable brute get that through his head?

"No, my vixen bride, you don't understand."

That was true—she didn't understand *any* of this. "What are you talking about?"

"When I am through with your training," he said slowly, his dark eyes gleaming with menace beneath the morning sun, "you will know of no other lust than for me. You will be able to conceive of pleasing no one else. You will do whatever I wish, whenever I wish it. You will no longer be capable of having sexual thoughts or desires that are not brought about solely by me. I will be your master, Teesia, and you will be my slave. My sex slave."

Teesia felt faint. At once, her stomach roiled with revulsion and fear even as her nerve endings stood on end, prickling with a left-over hint of anticipation.

"Now, into the cart with you," he said, motioning toward the red conveyance that sported a leather awning for shade.

She could barely speak around the lump that had grown in her throat. "Will you be riding with me?"

He gave his head a short shake as a wry chuckle left him. "I think not, vixen. I don't desire your company, I'm afraid."

* * * * *

The ride in the horse-drawn cart was lonely, even with various members of Ralen's party occasionally happening past to greet her, some giving her more flowers, others bringing snacks of cheeses and sweet breads for sustenance on the journey.

One handsome young man who introduced himself as Laene explained to her that they would arrive in Charelton by midday tomorrow.

"So soon?" she exclaimed. She could have sworn Charelton lay farther away.

"Horses make the travel much faster, Lady Teesia." He motioned slightly to the mount he rode alongside her wagon.

She felt silly, for it was so obvious. But she'd never traveled in a caravan with so many horses that the speed of movement was increased. "Of course," she said, rather flattered by the way he'd addressed her, and wondering if Ralen would appreciate the designation as much.

Laene smiled, his pale blue eyes striking beneath a swatch of messy blond hair. "So you shall be Ralen's bride by tomorrow eve."

"Oh," she said on a heavy breath, trying to appear happy rather than horrified. She still couldn't believe how catastrophically her betrothal had turned out. What yesterday had seemed dreamlike had now become a hideous nightmare of the unknown. She'd counted on having a much longer journey to absorb all that had happened, and to somehow try to prepare herself for the sexual punishment her husband-to-be planned to deal out. She had no idea how one could even *turn* sex into punishment. According to Bella, sex was always a wondrous, joyful thing shared between willing participants who wished to experience pleasure together. Could sex ever be a *bad* thing?

Then she shivered with the thought that Ralen had certainly succeeded in making it *sound* rather ominous.

"Breeze chilling you?" Laene asked from his mount.

In her terror, she'd nearly forgotten his presence.

"The roof can be removed if you'd prefer the sun."

She glanced up to the awning and forced a pleasant shake of her head at the handsome Laene. "No, no, I prefer the shade. Thank you, though."

That night, when the caravan stopped to camp, Teesia had no idea what to expect.

She soon got her answer, however, when a young woman with silky chestnut-colored tresses approached and announced she was to accompany Teesia to her tent. Teesia followed and found a sizable space with a bed erected, as well as a dressing table complete with a small viewing glass. Under other circumstances, she'd have thought it very luxurious traveling accommodations.

"My name is Shaena," the woman said, offering a friendly smile within the shadows of the tent, "and I am to be your maid."

Teesia worked to return a smile. It wasn't Shaena's fault her employer was an ogre. "I'm happy to meet you, Shaena."

"I cannot tell you how honored I was when Ralen appointed me to this position. I shall work hard to please you in every way."

"I'm sure you shall." Teesia liked the young woman's earnest brown eyes and ready grin. The leather frock that wrapped Shaena's thin frame revealed soft cleavage darkened by the sun, and her arms and legs were tanned, as well, but there was something very natural about the girl that made Teesia think the look attractive on her, even if not fully in fashion — well, at least not in Myrtell. It suddenly occurred to her how little she knew of the world beyond her homeland — the world she was set to become a part of.

"Shall I undress you now?" Shaena asked.

Teesia nodded. She loved her yellow silk frock, but the day it had been made for had not turned out as she'd expected and she was well-ready to shed it.

Approaching, Shaena untied the gold cord that circled Teesia's waist, then drew the yellow silk off over her head. The maid's eyes gravitated toward Teesia's breasts and it briefly reminded her of all she'd learned from Bella yesterday — perhaps because Shaena's gaze held the same sense of sensuality as her friend's. "Do you wish a bath this evening? We did not bring a bathing tub on the journey, but I would be happy to give you a cool sponge bath if you like."

"That sounds refreshing, yes."

Teesia sat naked in the chair at the dressing table waiting for Shaena to return with a sponge, the softening night air of the coast wafting through the tent to make her skin prickle and nipples pucker. When the tent flap opened, for a brief second she thought — even hoped — it might be Ralen, coming to mend things with her. She had the instant thought that maybe seeing her like this, bare from head to toe, might excite him and even somehow endear her to him, making him forget all this silly sex slave business.

But, of course, it was only her new maid bearing a ewer of water and a sea sponge. She came to stand behind Teesia so that their eyes met in the viewing glass as Shaena began to run the cool brownish sponge over Teesia's skin.

"How is it that Ralen has so many horses?" she found herself asking. She'd been wondering about it since meeting the caravan early this morning, but until now, graver topics had kept her mind fully occupied.

Shaena smoothed the sponge down the length of Teesia's arm. "Ralen believes horses are the future of travel, not to mention warfare. He is breeding them with great success on his estate."

Despite herself, Teesia was fascinated. She'd always loved horses, but even her father — the ruler of all Caralon — only owned a stable of ten or so of the expensive animals. The idea of living in a place so rich with them appealed immensely. Perhaps they would provide her with some much-needed cheer.

"Forgive me if this is out of line," Shaena said, "but you look sad. Especially for a woman who's marrying a strong, wealthy man like Ralen." When Teesia didn't answer — unable to come up with any simple way to explain, Shaena went on. "Ralen's fortress is very fine, filled with every luxury. And we are all pleased that he's taking a bride, so you shall be very welcomed."

Teesia tried for a smile in the jagged viewing glass as Shaena's sponge circled one round breast, sending a slight shiver through her. "Yes, I already feel welcome," she said, knowing that, despite her words, she still sounded distressed. Her new maid would probably think her quite odd.

"Then why so sad?" Shaena's expression spilled true concern. She tilted her head behind Teesia, and added in a softened tone, "Is it because you have heard rumors about Ralen? About his…well, I shouldn't say this, but about his tastes in fucking? Don't fear them, Teesia, for he will be gentle with you."

Teesia blinked and drew in her breath sharply. "How can you say that? I mean, how can you know what he plans?"

Shaena abandoned the sponge and drew up a nearby stool to sit next to her. Reaching out, she took Teesia's hands. "Ralen and I are the same age—twenty-nine. I grew up on his estate—my parents served his parents, and now *I* serve *him*. We played together as children and I know him well, better than most mere servants. He has spoken to me about your impending marriage and I know he wishes to please you, in bed and out. He can be very fierce, yes—but there are other sides to him, as well."

"You don't understand," Teesia said, shaking her head. "Any wish Ralen had to please me died this morning."

Shaena's back straightened. "Oh?"

Embarrassed, but seeing no reason not to tell Shaena the tale, she relayed the story of her first meeting with her bridegroom, getting so caught up in the pleasant memory that she spared no details about how wild Ralen's touch had made her feel, how she had come for him in front of the enormous viewing glass in her brother-in-law's fortress to the north. "Now he says he intends to punish me," she concluded, "to make sure I know I belong to him. He wishes to make me his sexual slave."

Shaena's brows knitted with concern, and even as she used her thumbs to caress the sensitive skin atop Teesia's hands, she seemed unable to find words of comfort.

"Then it's as bad as I suspect," Teesia concluded.

Shaena sighed. "As I said, Ralen can be very ferocious, and I fear you've roused that part of him. You have to understand, he's not had an easy life."

Ralen? She hardly believed *that*. "But he's rich. As rich as my father, from what I can tell. I would suppose his life has been much like mine, but better—since he is a man, with all the advantages that entails." Although her mother had taught Teesia and her sisters to respect themselves, and though her father treated Jalal as his peer, women in Caralon were often considered possessions to their husbands—which was, perhaps, why many simply chose not to marry. Although seen as equals in sexual play, women were not always shown the same respect in other aspects of life.

"Sometimes money does not mean happiness, Teesia."

"What was so horrible for Ralen?" The question came out sounding like an accusation, but she didn't care—what could have been so awful to make him treat her so terribly?

"He once loved a girl. Another maid, a friend of mine named Banya. But when he announced his intent to marry her, his father, Granick, paid her a great sum not to, thinking her far below his son. She left Charelton without even saying goodbye. Ralen had expected as much from his father—it was *Banya's* betrayal that wounded him so deeply. Since then…well, I'm afraid it doesn't take much to destroy his faith in someone, especially a woman."

Teesia supposed that explained his overreaction to their previous encounter, but it hardly helped her situation. "I understand his hurt, but I still don't understand his ability to be so cruel to me."

Again, Shaena sighed. "You have to understand, Granick was cruel to *him*. Ralen was taught that any sort of misbehavior must be dealt with harshly, that the offender must be punished in such a way that they will never commit the offense again. His father once beat him nearly to death for telling a silly lie when we were children, for saying he had done a chore he had not. And indeed, after Granick's beating,

Ralen never lied again. His father dealt with misbehaving servants with the same severity."

Charelton was beginning to sound like a terrible place, and Teesia suspected her eyes shone wide with the horror of it. "Why did you stay, Shaena? Why did you continue to work for Granick when you reached adulthood?"

The maid shrugged. "Where else would I go? I know no other place. And I wished to stay with my parents, as I am their only child. They are retired now, living in a cottage in the village near the fort, and they enjoy having me near. And besides, Granick was growing sickly years ago. No one outside the fortress realized it, even some *inside* probably did not know—it was kept a secret. But I knew he would die soon enough and then Ralen would be in power."

"And Ralen is so much better to serve?"

"He is more civil to all. You have seen already how happy his people are. And frankly, Granick rained so much wrath on his staff that, since his death over two years ago, no one has gotten out of line." Now even Shaena looked doubtful, though. "I had thought—hoped—that Ralen would not rule with such severity, and maybe he won't, but if his reaction to your indiscretion is any indication—well, I might be wrong about that."

"You know him well. Do you have any advice for me?" It seemed smart to learn anything she could from her new maid—she was thankful Shaena was so forthcoming and seemed to wish her well.

"From this point forward," the maid said, "I would strive to be as obedient as you can. Even if that obedience is not in your heart, act as though it is. Try to please him until he softens to you."

She nodded. "Anything else?"

"As for sex—well, I cannot say, since I don't know exactly what he has in store for you, but...try not to fear, Teesia. Try to be open-minded." Bella's similar advice came to mind as

Shaena leaned slightly forward, bringing their faces close. "It may not be so horrible as he intends for it to be, if you know what I mean."

"No, I don't know what you mean," Teesia admitted on a sigh of frustration. Here Ralen thought she knew so much about sex, but clearly she remained completely ignorant about it.

Shaena smiled. "I won't lie to you, Teesia—I have been in Ralen's bed before. And things I once thought distasteful are now pleasing to me because of what he taught me there."

A short shock of jealousy struck, however insane, followed by more confusion. "Do you still...you and he?" In Caralon, it was within a man's rights, even a married one, to fuck whomever he wished.

"Not for a while now," Shaena said with a reassuring smile. "Except for Banya, Ralen has not been a man to confine himself to one woman, ever. But I know he intends to be faithful within his marriage, so now it would seem that you alone shall reap the pleasures he can impart."

Teesia shivered. "Pleasures? Or tortures?"

The maid cast a knowing smile. "I can only say that perhaps you will find being his slave is not such an unsavory thing."

Chapter Three

ဢ

Ralen stood, dressed in black, watching as his bride approached. The sun set over the hills behind her, the shock of late daylight making her seem to glow as she crossed the sand toward him in bare feet. The red silk wedding gown he'd chosen for her clung deliciously to her curves, reminding him of a frock of sea green that had fit her just as well. Wanton she may be, but she was undeniably comely, making his cock perk to attention within his leather pants even now. Her raven hair still fell in a long braid down her back, a gold cord wound about it to match the thicker sash that bound her from just below her breasts to the flare of her hips.

Bound, he thought. Did the sash make her feel bound? Did it hold her as tightly, mold to her flesh as warmly as he liked to think? Did it somehow give her even the slightest arousal? He narrowed his gaze on her. *You'd best hope so, vixen, for there's much more of that to come.*

Part of him wished things were different—that he'd never recognized her, that some other foolish man had fallen prey to her seductive charms in the hallway, so that he'd never know what a wanton little royal she was. Had he never met her before yesterday, he'd be very pleased with the thought of spending the rest of his life with Enrick's middle daughter.

And despite her transgressions, a girl so pretty would make any man's bed a warmer place. Once her punishment was over, she would warm his nicely, too. Once he felt certain she would never stray from him.

"You selected a lovely spot for our marriage rites," she said, smiling up at him as if they were a happy couple in love. "As a child of Myrtell, I love the ocean."

He replied dryly, making sure not to look into her crystal blue eyes. "Chosen before I knew who you were, I assure you."

The priest behind him let out a sigh of dismay, but Ralen ignored him.

The ceremony was the drudgery he'd expected, although thankfully short. When the priest asked Teesia if she had a gift for her groom, she held out the bit of cloth he'd noticed in her hand, fluttering in the sea breeze. Surprised she had anything—given that she'd had only a day's warning before leaving home—he took it from her, smoothing in his hands. *To my husband. Yours forever, Teesia.* The words were embroidered in thread dyed indigo, the edges of the cloth embellished with flowers of yellow, red and fuchsia. He was surprised to find his heart softened—only slightly—by the feminine offering.

"For you to carry with you when you must leave home, or if you are called to battle," she explained. "A remembrance. A token of my affection."

He didn't plan to meet her sparkling eyes, but once he found her staring up at him so earnestly, he was trapped within her gaze—just for a brief moment before stuffing the cloth into his waistband and turning back to the priest.

"Have you a gift for your bride?" the older man asked, the breeze ruffling what remained of his grayed hair.

In response, Ralen reached down to a small leather bag next to him on the sand, extracting the extravagant jewelry he'd commissioned. Before he'd known he was wedding a woman in need of training and punishment, he'd intended the gifts to be seen as merely that—jewelry—figuring he'd reveal their real use sometime later in the marriage when he felt his new wife was ready for a taste of his darker appetites. Teesia, however, would discover the true purpose of the gift *tonight.*

"Your wrists," he said, indicating that she should hold them out. He locked first one thick, bejeweled bracelet around her arm, then the other.

She gasped. "They're exquisite, Ralen."

"Indeed," he murmured tightly. But he did like the look of them on her, feeling they made her *his* in a way mere words spoken by a man of Ares could not. "There's more," he said, then stooped to clasp the matching ankle cuffs just above her feet. Valuable stones of red, green, blue and gold glittered beneath the rays of the setting sun.

He almost felt sorry for the naïve little wanton as they left the beach to return to the fort. She was smiling, happy, thinking somehow that his expensive gifts spelled love, or forgiveness. But soon enough she would understand that nothing had been forgiven, that her indiscretion could only be forgotten through punishment, learning to obey.

The feast was grand, every person in Charelton there to celebrate his marriage. Ralen made an effort to smile through it all, to pretend he was as happy as he'd hoped to be on this night. No one knew his stomach churned with a fear of betrayal—a betrayal that might take place if he didn't quickly get his vixen bride in line.

How many men have touched you already, my little wanton? He cast her a sideways glance as they dined on every manner of beast and fowl, fruit and sweets—then swallowed back his disappointment along with a swig of dark wine, deciding it was of no matter. Soon enough she would know only him. *Only him.* Nothing else would exist in her world.

As usual for a wedding of such circumstance, the region's residents had turned out in their most revealing garments of fur and leather, awaiting the Rituals of Passion they thought were to come. He caught Laene's eye, where he stood flirting with a girl who wore only two strategically placed strips of thick brown leather, and waved him over.

"We are dispensing with the Rituals of Passion this evening," he said when Laene arrived.

His servant and friend of ten years blinked his shock. "What did you just say?"

"You heard me. There will be no Rituals of Passion following the feast."

Laene gave his messy blond mane a short shake, his eyes narrowing in confusion. "Then how shall she be made ready, Ralen? She is more than just a virgin, you recall — she's a *royal* virgin. You know full well how clueless such girls are kept."

Ralen shook his head and spoke with low confidence. "Not *this* girl. She knows more than she's supposed to, trust me on this. She's ready enough for what I have in store. So carry forth with whatever entertainment was planned and if that does not please the crowd enough, find some willing females who might engage in a seductive dance for them. They expected Rituals of Passion, give them at least *some* passion, whatever you can devise to excite them."

Laene still persisted in questioning him. "It's unheard of to forsake such tradition, Ralen."

Ralen's reply came in a matter-of-fact tone. "My bride does not need the rituals, my friend. She needs to be punished. No rituals necessary for that — I can handle it on my own."

* * * * *

Teesia flinched as Ralen's hand latched tight onto hers, his large fingers squeezing her smaller ones. "Let us go, bride." His piercing look, along with his sharp delivery of the words, stunned her. Who *was* this man? He'd seemed so content during dinner — happy even — but now, in the time it took to blink, he'd turned cold and harsh once more.

As he pulled her up from her seat, her emotions swung from pleasant to fearful — again. The dress he'd commissioned for her was lovely, as were the extravagant wedding jewels that adorned her, yet his fluctuating moods made it impossible to know if he had perhaps started to forgive her — or if he simply hated her.

As he practically dragged her toward the great hall's exit, she realized the crowd looked stunned to see them departing so soon. "Where are we going?" she asked. The large wooden doors fell shut behind them, leaving her alone with him in a wide hallway — much like the one where they'd first met. Even now, she shivered at the memory, her pussy tingling.

"To begin your training," he said, never slowing their stride.

Her chest went hollow. "*Sexual* training," she said to clarify.

"Yes, vixen." He didn't bother looking at her.

"But what about the Maran tiles?" she asked as he pulled her up a wide stone staircase. "Is it not time for me to play the Maran tiles?" Perhaps that explained the crowd's dismay.

He drew to a rough halt on the steps, turning to glare down at her. "You seem awfully eager about that. Most royal girls fear it, from what I'm told. Perhaps, like everything else, you know more about it than you should."

She cowered, feeling tiny beneath his accusing gaze. "No."

A humorless laugh echoed through the fort around her. "Well, no Rituals of Passion for you, wanton."

She swallowed as they proceeded up the stairs. "Rituals...of Passion?"

Only once they reached the top did he pause long enough to turn his dark, narrowed eyes on her again. "I'm sure you've heard of the pleasures to be had after the Maran game."

She could barely breathe. "Only...that, yes, there *are* pleasures."

"And you'd like that, wouldn't you, naughty Teesia?" His expression hovered somewhere between aroused and threatening — then tipped entirely toward the latter. "Well, too bad, I'm afraid. For I have a whole different sort of training in mind for you."

* * * * *

Teesia held her breath as Ralen led her into a large room filled with…Ares, so many exotic, erotic things that she could barely absorb it all!

First, a large, ornate bed—unlike any she'd ever seen. Large posts rose from its four corners, the wood carved so that it appeared to twist 'round and 'round. Some six feet up, each post curved inward, the four winding cylinders of wood meeting in the center and then wrapping around one another until finally coming to a sharp point at the top. Above the bed—dear Ares—she saw a large viewing glass pieced together and mounted on the ceiling!

Another spot in the room contained a small table, two chairs on either side. Nothing too heinous about that, but then came the next, larger table—or she guessed it was a table anyway. But it was covered, padded with soft, brushed leather. Expensive metal chains extended from the table's four corners—she had no idea why, only the faint sensation that it looked forbidding.

Beyond that lay a wall mounted with countless pegs and shelves and cabinetry, on which were displayed leather riding crops of various sizes and styles, and—oh my!—an assortment of the clay cocks Bella had introduced her to, and other items she didn't even recognize. The sight of the play cocks tightened her chest and, Ares help her, her cunt. The entire chamber, hung and covered with rich silks and leathers, seemed made for a sort of fucking she could not quite comprehend—yet somehow she already felt it seeping into her. She knew instinctively that whatever happened in this room would change her, become a part of her forever. Her next shiver was not one of arousal, but of cold, stark fear. Fear of her new husband.

It was then that he drew her firmly to him, his large hand closing over her bottom as he pressed a long, hard kiss across her lips. Her practice with Bella seemed useless in this instance as there was nothing to do but succumb to Ralen's demanding mouth. Despite herself, his kiss and the very power behind it poured down through her like a rush of warm wine, and when his other hand closed over her breast, it was pleasure that shot to her cunt and made her gasp beneath him. He ended the passionate meeting of mouths with a soft, sensual bite on her lower lip that seared her—and seemed to promise more to come.

She felt dizzy by the time he stepped back to loosen the sash at her waist, slowly untwining it until the flowing red silk spilled straight down her body, no longer highlighting her curves. She felt almost chaste for a moment—until he reached for the shoulder straps, drawing them swiftly down until the whole dress dropped in a red heap at her feet.

She suddenly stood naked before him, wearing only the colorful wrist and ankle bracelets he'd given her. Her skin prickled with the shocking sense of being put bluntly on display. She was torn between desperately wanting to cover herself and brazenly wanting him to see her. He drew back to look his fill, his eyes like flames, burning her skin.

"As lovely as I imagined," he said, but his voice was void of emotion, leaving her as uncertain as she'd felt since discovering his rancor toward her. "And now, your hair, wanton."

She swallowed nervously. She'd wanted it down so badly for so long, yet now, as he stepped behind her to unbraid it, his fingers in her tresses felt ominous.

"You showed me your unbound hair on our first meeting," he purred near her ear. "Do you remember?"

She merely nodded, feeling her nudity—and fearing the loss of her braid would somehow add to it, making her even more vulnerable.

"This time it will *stay* down," he said firmly, reminding her that after tonight, no one need ever think her a virgin again.

Once it had been freed, Ralen turned her to face him, then lifted his hands to fan his large fingers through her hair, spreading it across her shoulders. "Yes," he said. "No one will be fooled into thinking you innocent any longer."

Taking her hand, he led her to the padded table with the chains. She drew in her breath, wondering what awaited her—but even in fear, her pussy began to warm with a strange, indecipherable longing.

How could she want whatever tortures her barbarian husband would dish out to her? How could she desire him even now? Perhaps it was the dark mane of hair, or the eyes that seemed to match. Perhaps it was the raw virility that hung about him. Or maybe, maybe…it was even the *danger*.

She'd seen it instantly on the night they'd met, had somehow instinctively known he was a dangerous man, and she'd wanted him *because* of it. It almost frightened her to think she wanted that even now—his danger, his punishment, whatever he had to give. But the truth was…she did. She wanted Ralen of Charelton, her beast husband. She wanted him however she could have him.

"Lie down," he told her, his voice as dark as the rest of him.

Her nipples beaded under his scrutiny as she climbed up on the table, her pussy as hungry as ever. A glance down reminded her it was as bare as the day she'd been born, and—dear Ares—the soft skin was parted of its own accord, revealing the pink flesh inside. She'd been yearning for him for two long years, and it would seem it took more than a little fear to squelch such deep-seated want.

As she lay back on the soft leather, Ralen instructed her, "Raise your arms above your head."

She did as she was told, unflinchingly. Shaena had told her to obey, so she didn't even think about protesting. Even when she heard two firm clicks and looked back over her shoulder to see that the chains had been attached to her jeweled bracelets. Which, she suddenly understood, weren't really bracelets in the traditional sense at all. He'd given her gifts to aid him in chaining her up.

Her heart seemed to sink to her stomach and it was difficult to breathe.

Chaining her. He was chaining her to the table.

All desire fled and her next impulse was to try to break away, somehow try to slip free of the bracelets and escape from the brute she'd just wed. But she knew already the bracelets were too tight—she was not a small-boned girl and they'd clasped snugly about her wrists when he'd put them on. Same for those at her ankles.

She was trapped. Chained to a table, and Ares only knew what he intended to do to her—only that she would be totally at his mercy when he did it.

Two more loud clicks and her ankles were locked as well, her legs spread toward the corners, her body making a perfect X shape on the platform. When she tugged slightly at her wrists, she discovered she couldn't move them at all—she lay utterly helpless before him.

Her heart beat wildly as she watched Ralen pull his black silk wedding shirt over his head to reveal broad shoulders, a strong chest and arms more muscular than any she'd ever seen. He looked as if he could crush her with one small embrace and the thought made her thankful he'd not done so—at least not yet.

Offering a short, speculative glance in her direction, he walked to the pegboard and selected a small riding crop. Her stomach churned—was he going to beat her? He'd spoken of punishment. Making her a sex slave. A beating, she feared, might seem an effective way to start both processes.

She tensed as he stepped to the end of the table, dropping his gaze to her parted thighs. She wondered if her pussy glistened, even amid her brittle fear.

Please, please, let me loose! Let me go! Don't hurt me! The desperate pleas lay on the tip of her tongue, and it was a struggle to hold them back, but she did—because of Shaena's advice. *Obey him. Difficult as it is. Take whatever he metes out.* And even had she begged, she didn't think Ralen was the sort of man to show mercy.

When he held the black leather crop over her, she closed her eyes and waited for the first strike to cut into her tender flesh. When, instead, the thick fringing at the end was dragged gently, almost caressingly, between her breasts, she opened them again, peering down, and let out the breath she'd been holding.

Her gaze followed the trail of the small whipping device as Ralen drew it across her stomach—making circles, curves, then one long line that stretched from neck to navel and extended—in sensation only—down into her cunt. *What are you doing to me? What is this all about?* she wanted to ask, but bit her tongue once more.

As her husband glided the soft tip of the crop slowly from her shoulder to her wrist, then gently up her arm, the touch echoing pleasurably through her, something in her began to relax. Relax and almost even enjoy. She had not known the same leather they made clothing and bedding and household items from could be so...sensuous.

Moving the crop's fringed end to the center of her chest, Ralen dragged it slowly around the edge of one breast in a wide arc, then circled it slightly inward, in soft, tightening curves that grew closer to her nipple with each orbit. She drew in her breath, watching, feeling the slow pleasure begin to escalate.

When he reached the pink bud, he nudged it, once, twice, then raked the hard end of the crop, hidden beneath the fringe, around the stiff point. Teesia wondered if her arousal would leak from her pussy to the leather beneath her as darts of delight spread outward from her breast.

Ralen soon began the same exquisite torture on the other breast, and though Teesia still watched, she tried to hide her emotion. Perhaps because Ralen, this day, had been so emotionless with *her*. Suddenly, she didn't want to let him witness her feeling anything, didn't want to let him know he had any power over her in any way.

Even if she was chained to a table by his hand. And even if hiding her response got harder with every second. She pressed her tongue to the roof of her mouth to keep from sighing her enjoyment, but the erotic sight of the crop pleasuring her receptive breast only added to her reaction.

"What is my name, vixen?" he asked without warning, his voice menacingly low.

She flinched beneath the crop and got an unexpected burst of pleasure in her pussy as a result. "R-Ralen," she managed to eke out, then realized she'd been holding her breath again. *Not* holding it made her feel every nuance of the crop's touch even more.

"Say it again," he commanded in a deep voice as the crop reached her turgid nipple.

"Ralen." Smoother this time. But it was a miracle, given that he now nudged her nipple back and forth with the tip of the riding tool.

"Good," he said, still flicking the crop over the puckered tip of her breast. The pleasure, at once both cool and hot, burst through her with each and every graze.

Next, he lay the length of the crop flat against the same rounded mound of flesh he already teased, dragging the strip of hard, braided leather across her nipple until the pink peak popped free on the other side. She let out a small cry—against her will, drat!

Pleasure or pain? She wasn't even sure what she was responding to. A bit of both?

She refused to look him directly in the eye, but sensed his gaze turning darker, his expression more feral, at the sound.

"My name is the answer for all questions tonight, wanton," he said slowly. "Nod if you understand that."

Pulling in her breath, she gave him the silent reply he sought, then flinched when the braiding raked across her sensitive nipple once more. Ares in heaven, how much of this lingering, heated torment could she take?

"Who do you desire?" he asked.

She clenched her teeth slightly, hating the truth behind the answer as much as she hated obeying his stark command — but she said it quickly, lest she anger him. "Ralen."

She watched her husband's well-muscled arm as he slid the crop downward, gliding the fringe over her sensitive stomach again. "Who do you crave?"

"Ralen." It came easier this time, just part of his game.

The crop next moved in a tantalizing line over her hip, making her cunt spasm slightly as he asked, "Who do you belong to, vixen?"

"Ralen."

"Whose cock belongs in your pussy?"

"Ralen." It came out huskier this time, drat it all. The mention of his cock and her pussy left her a bit breathless.

"Who do you worship?" He dragged the riding crop's fringed end down her outer thigh, calf, in one long, even stroke that seemed to radiate through her entire body.

"Ralen," she said, then softer, "Ralen." Why twice? She didn't know — it had simply come out.

"Who is your master, my wanton bride?"

"Ralen."

"And whom do you serve?"

Now he moved the crop slowly up her *inner* thigh. "Ralen." It was a quivery whisper, her cunt tickling with desire as a wave of harsh delight raced up her leg.

"Whose cock will fuck your mouth?"

She flinched, that particular question catching her off guard. She had the foreboding sense that his cock was going to be much bigger than anything hanging on the wall, and she found herself wondering if it would even be possible for her to do what he'd just said. And indeed, *fuck* her mouth? The same way she'd fucked Bella's pussy with the clay cock? Bella had never referred to pleasures given by the mouth in exactly that way before and Teesia hadn't imagined Ralen's shaft moving between her lips of *his* volition.

When she didn't answer right away, the crop came down in a stinging snap at her hip. She let out a yowl, her entire body jerking.

Their eyes met, her teeth clenched.

"Whose cock will fuck your mouth, wanton?"

She unclenched, both teeth and body, nipples still tight with pleasure, pussy still weeping with it. "Yours," she whispered meekly, then, remembering, "Ralen. *Ralen.*"

"Better," he murmured, seemingly more to himself than to her, as he resumed gliding the crop down her other leg. "Who is your ruler, vixen?"

Her father was the Ruler of all Caralon, of all who lived here—but she knew that, truly, this man *did* rule her now. "Ralen."

The crop slid sensually back up her inner calf, her inner thigh. Oh, the severe pleasure of it! It was all she could do not to moan.

"Who does your pussy throb for?"

"Ralen," she replied shakily, unable to deny that truth even to herself.

When he raked the soft fringed end of the tool up through her open cunt, she let out a trembling cry, the sensation skittering all through her like nothing she'd ever felt—a tiny earthquake inside her body.

"Who is your husband?" he asked, gliding the crop across her clit.

She let out another short, hot sigh of pleasure. "Ralen."

"Your master?" He moved the tip of the crop in little circles around the anxious nub, forcing her to lift slightly from the table, pressing against it. There was no choice—simply her body's hungry response.

"Ralen."

"Your new god, vixen?"

Ares forgive her for the blasphemy. "Ralen." Even if she could have resisted answering without fear of being whipped, she could *not* have without fear of him taking the crop away from her pussy—which, at the moment, was unthinkable. She'd never given herself permission to move against the torturous tool, but her body had taken over—her cunt yearned too badly for stimulation, and the crop delivered it so delightfully in Ralen's skilled hand.

"Who do you wish to fuck?" he asked.

"Ralen." The answer came weakly, for it was growing hard to speak.

"Whose bidding will you do, now and forever?"

A fresh burst of heat made her cry out. "Ralen!" The pleasure grew, her pussy turning swollen, anxious—pleading for release. The sweet crop stroked her, stroked her, hard and soft at the same time.

"Whose commands will you follow?"

"Ralen. Ralen!"

He moved the crop so quickly now, lightning fast, at a feverish pace, making her crazy—and so very near to the orgasm she ached for. She thrust up against it, driving her pelvis in the same fast little lunges. "Say your master's name, vixen," he demanded harshly.

"Ralen!"

"Say it. Again."

"Ralen! Ralen is my master!"

"Again, wanton!"

She drew in a great gulp of air—once, swiftly—and then cried out his name on each breath as the ultimate pleasure crashed down over her, through her. *"Ralen...Ralen...Ralen."* Her whole body shuddered as the waves of heat vibrated through every limb to the very tips of her fingers and toes—a *true* earthquake inside her body, racking her entire being. "Ralen," she whispered one last time in wearied conclusion, her eyes falling shut.

She wanted to curl into his arms after such a wrenching event—a shame she was chained across a table, and married to a man who would probably never wish to hold her anyway. Thank Ares she'd closed her eyes before he could see such emotion passing through them.

She opened them again only when she realized he was *joining* her on the table. Indeed, they bolted open at that, especially when he climbed astride her, one leather-clad knee planted aside each hip, and reached down to begin unlacing his pants.

Her voice quivered when she gave way to fear and asked, "What are you going to do to me?"

In a flash, he took up the crop and snapped it against the curve of her breast. The slight sting didn't hurt so much as she would have expected, and somehow she felt the strike in her cunt, as well. As intended, she went silent, waiting...fearing...anticipating what was to come. *Ares help me.*

Ralen was much more aroused than he'd expected to be at this point. Touching and exploring Teesia with the crop—watching her body respond, then watching her give herself over to ecstasy—had set his loins blazing.

He refused to care for the girl in any way—to him, she was still a reckless wanton who couldn't be trusted to understand her place in the world—but he couldn't deny the pleasure he would take with her, and *in* her, either. Somehow, in his fury, he'd forgotten just how deeply he enjoyed mastering a woman, bending her to his will. Already, he knew instinctively he would find an even greater satisfaction in mastering *this* little vixen—and not only because she was his wife and clearly *needed* to be mastered, but for the same reason he'd allowed himself to dip his fingers into the honey-sweet moisture of her pussy that night at Dane's fortress. There was something invisible but tangible between them. Some magnetic heat, an attraction that pulled at him, hard and deep.

It had nothing to do with caring, or any sort of true affection. But it existed just the same, and it turned him wild inside—wild to pleasure her even as he tamed her, wild to use her to pleasure himself.

Now, he wanted her to feel his power, to understand what he had in store for her and understand it well. As he finished undoing the lacings of his pants, his cock sprung free.

She flinched—at the mere sight of it or at its massive size, he didn't know. But he took a cruel, controlling sort of delight in the fear and awe that shone in her eyes as she studied his hard shaft, shooting up some ten thick inches from root to tip. The strength in his rod, the very dimensions of it, filled him with an arrogant pleasure—the pleasure of knowing how intimidating it looked and the intense joy it could bring. If ever he had occasion to doubt his power, in sex, in battle, in governing Charelton, he need only glance down at the very mass of the tool between his legs to be reminded he was a mighty and dominant man.

"Take a long look at my cock, vixen, for soon it will be inside you."

She let out a small gasp as he leaned forward just slightly, enough that the weight of his shaft balanced on her chest.

"I will *own* you with this cock," he said, his voice going warm and dark with the anticipation of sinking into her tight, wet passage below.

Reaching down, he molded his hands around the outer curves of her plump, pretty breasts, drawing them up around his erection. His low sigh of pleasure mingled with her higher one of surprise.

"Watch me fuck them," he instructed, then sank with slow passion into the task. The soft flesh hugged his hardness, forming a perfect valley to slide in and out of. The fluid on the tip of his shaft wet her inner curves, making for a moist, warm path between. For a long moment, he allowed himself to sink fully into the raw pleasure of gliding between the two delectable mounds, raking his thumbs over the delightfully stiff nipples with each long, thorough stroke, leaning his head back, breathing heavier, audibly.

It was then that he realized she sighed deeper beneath him, as well, in time with his strokes between her breasts—taking joy from it just as he was. "You *already* worship this cock," he accused with a devilish hint of a smile.

She didn't reply. Good for her, as anything other than his name would have earned her a crack of the riding crop. But their eyes met, heat simmering between, and he whispered lowly, "Whose cock do you crave, vixen?"

"Ralen's," she whispered back, her voice surprisingly soft and sweet—almost docile. Yes, very good.

He almost could have come that way, fucking her lovely breasts, but was far from ready yet—he had a virgin bride to deflower, after all.

She'd *better* be a virgin, anyway.

Leaving her ripe breasts, he wrapped his hand about his length and leaned in toward her face to drag the head across the seam of her lush lips. She looked nervous—her mouth trembled. He was utterly tempted to push his way inside and show her what it was to have her pretty little mouth thoroughly fucked.

But for a reason he couldn't explain, he held steady, just letting the tip of his cock play about her dark, berry-colored lips, watching her fearful expression fade slightly as she grew used to the sensation. "You will worship it with your mouth soon enough, wanton," he told her before drawing away.

For now, though, *she* was to be feasted on—the urge to know her body better grew inside him with each passing second.

So he eased down her curves until he lay slanted across her, her breasts jutting into his bare chest, his cock pressing into her hip. As he lowered his mouth to her neck for a tender kiss, then a bite, he whispered, "Who do you desire?"

Her answer came breathily, making him even harder. "You, Ralen, you."

He kissed her mouth then, firm, deep, as he kneaded the globes of her breasts in both hands. He kept telling himself he didn't particularly wish to pleasure her so much just yet, but he wanted to take the lovely pink beads of her nipples into his mouth. He wanted to touch her everywhere. That much giving, pleasing, this soon, risked the lesson he intended to teach—but damn it all, her curves were too enticing to resist.

He sank down, lowering his mouth over one nipple, beautifully hard on his tongue as he explored the curves of her waist, hips, thighs, with eager hands below. He licked, suckled lightly, played and teased with his mouth, making her whimper and moan above him. He lifted one hand to the other breast, molding it warmly, then lightly pinching and rolling the delectably pointed peak. She possessed long, prominent nipples that seemed made for play with fingers, teeth, tongue, lips.

At this moment, he thought he could take joy in his vixen's breasts for hours, never tiring of the soft, malleable flesh or their hard, jutting centers. Her little cries of pleasure told him she would not tire of it, either, and the odd concept— of pleasuring the both of them in only that one way, for such a long time—hardened his already rigid cock even further.

But this was not that time—no, this was the time for much, much more than mere breast play. As he continued caressing one of the hot mounds, with his other hand he reached below, pressing eager fingertips into the warm moisture of her cunt. So smooth outside, so wet and swallowing within the sweet folds. Her cries of heat echoed upward, growing as he began to stroke the damp, fleshy ridges and valleys within her slit.

He kissed her neck—a chain of kisses from one side to the other. He molded her breast, petted her pussy.

Then he *parted* her pussy, using his first two fingers, and shifted so the length of his hungry cock rested in the wet valley of her cunt.

He rubbed his rod against her, watching her throw her head back in passion, her arms pulling instinctively at their shackles as she writhed beneath him. Ares help him, he took profound, unflinching delight in seeing her chained and pleasured—it was a measure of the beast within him and he'd never tried to fight it, for the satisfaction it delivered ran too deep. It was his lot in life, the way Ares had made him, a man born to make a woman obey.

He rubbed his length deep into her warm, hugging pussy, aware of her clit, swollen and seeking ecstasy once again. Hungry little wanton.

He dipped to nip his teeth across her nipple, then lightly bit her neck and slid against her until he could tell she was getting close once more, moaning, whimpering, lifting her body to his, dirty girl—so he glided his cock more deeply against her seeking cunt, until her desperate little cries grew faster, faster, and then he whispered in her ear, "You'd better hope you're a virgin, my naughty bride, or there will be a whole new hell for you to pay."

As she cried out her ecstasy in beautiful high-pitched shrieks that fueled his desire, he rammed his cock inside her.

Warm. Deep. Her anguished cries—the pleasure of coming or the pain of entry, he wasn't sure—permeated him. But she was a virgin. His bride was a virgin. Lucky for her. And shockingly satisfying for him. No cock but his had ever sunk into this cunt before.

She belonged to him already, and she would come to understand the depth of that belonging much more—but this was something separate and apart from that. Her pussy was his, only his. Forever.

Chapter Four

ॐ

Teesia lay shocked and wrenched beneath Ralen. Her lips trembled, but she would not cry — she simply would not. The orgasm had been…well, painful, given the mighty thrust inside her, and yet, still joyfully satisfying even amid the pain. Just like when he snapped the crop against her. Just like when he bit her nipple, or her lip. Joy and pain at once.

Now she went still, waiting, wondering what was next.

Oh, drat it all, tears threatened. She closed her eyes to ward them off, then turned her head to one side so he wouldn't see, but she still felt one lone tear leak free to roll down her cheek.

Her husband stayed still within her, and when she felt the tender swipe of his thumb blotting away the tear, she opened her eyes in surprise. She caught the hint of a tender look before he shifted his gaze from hers, and to her further shock, her heart warmed toward him just slightly.

When his teeth closed gently over her collarbone, she couldn't hold in her soft moan, and when he started to move inside her she realized that — oh Ares! — the pain was gone. Incredible fullness replaced it. *Impossible* fullness. A tightness that made her grit her teeth as he began delivering short, slow thrusts.

Despite such unimaginable tightness, she no longer suffered the blinding pain that had sliced into her in that first moment. Now, she wanted him in her body, welcomed him. Had her arms been free, she'd have wrapped them around him, pulled him as close as she could. Her husband, the brute.

As his thrusts lengthened slightly, pressing deeper into her cunt, she began to cry out again with each. Pleasure? Pain?

Ares above, she was beginning to wonder if there was a difference.

"Say the name of your master, the name of the man who fucks you and owns you, the man who owns your ripe little pussy."

"Ralen," she breathed. Somehow, as his name left her, she felt her cunt contract around him. "Ralen. Ralen."

He fucked her deeper, and she wanted to say his name yet again. "Ralen. Oh, Ralen. Yes, Ralen. *Ralen.*"

When she least expected it, his massive cock left her body and she looked up to see it in his hand, still pointing toward her cunt. As he let his head drop back with a deep, guttural groan, a stream of white-hot fluid shot onto her bared pussy, making her gasp in surprise. Another followed, and another, and a fourth, the last arcing onto her belly.

She peered down at it as best she could given her chains, her lips trembling in awe. Oh Ares—Bella had told her about this, but mere words could not describe it. So wet on her, a tangible part of him, a pleasurable assault she hadn't seen coming, and it left her feeling a strange, binding sort of intimacy with him that she hadn't up to now. Even if he hated her.

And then—oh, yes—Ralen's big hands came, his fingers firmly rubbing, massaging the warm wetness into her skin, into her cunt. The sensation moved all through her like a living thing, and a moan echoed from deep inside her.

His large hands continued to press into her, fingertips smoothing the white fluid into her clit as she watched, making her hot, hotter, with each circular motion, until her breath came heavy again and she was rising, lifting herself from the table to meet his touch, thinking of this amazing liquid part of him being massaged into her body until...oh Ares—yes, yes, yes! "*Ralen!*" she cried as yet another powerful orgasm pumped through her, racking her within her chains, sending her into uncontrollable spasms, until finally she dropped limp and exhausted onto the padded table once more.

* * * * *

When Teesia awoke, she was surprised she'd actually slept. Looking to her right, she found Ralen slumbering on the ornate bed across the room. To her consternation, she remained fastened to the table, arms and legs outstretched. She couldn't help snarling at her sleeping husband while he couldn't see her doing so. Merciless barbarian!

He'd re-laced his pants, so that unbelievable cock of his was once again hidden. Her stomach went hollow remembering the sheer size of it. And that he'd managed to get it inside her! And that—dear Ares—the brute had actually made her come three incredible times. Even amid the punishment she'd taken so valiantly.

Maybe because there were moments when it didn't exactly *feel* like punishment? Certainly, his control over her *was* punishment—turning her head to look from one bound wrist to the other, she could scarcely believe her husband had chained her to a table on their wedding night! But, despite her anger, she had experienced undeniable pleasure.

And she had said his name. Every time he asked. Sometimes when he *hadn't* asked. She supposed she'd done everything exactly as he wished.

Which was good, she reminded herself, for to refuse might have brought much more brutal treatment, such as she couldn't even fathom. *This* was bearable.

Maybe. If he unchained her soon. If he took her to his bed.

The truth was, she'd say his name and be his slave and willingly submit to him over and over again if he'd free her from the table and treat her just a little as a husband should treat a wife. She gazed back at him across the candlelit room, wishing.

Then she lay her head back, tired, her muscles sore and stretched. She yanked helplessly at her bracelets and ankle cuffs—such pretty and deceptive torture devices—rattling the chains that held her.

A stirring across the room drew her attention back to her husband—she watched as he gave a leisurely stretch, drawing her gaze to all the hard muscles on his arms and chest before he rose and padded toward her.

"Lift your ass." No greeting, no surprise she was awake and waiting for his next instruction.

With little choice, she obeyed.

Reaching to one of the pegs on the wall, he drew down a slender almost delicate-looking chain, constructed of wide links formed from ultra-thin gold. He slid it around her waist, then hooked it in front, just below her navel. She lowered herself back to the table, as it was difficult to lift at all, let alone stay that way. Just as she noticed that a considerable length of the gold links remained after being hooked around her torso, the excess falling ticklishly between her thighs, Ralen said, "Again," leaving her no choice but to comply.

When she lifted this time, he stretched the remaining chain between her legs, through her pussy, and up the valley of her rear, attaching it to the links that crossed her lower back. She tensed at the pressure it delivered. It was not painfully tight, but rubbed against every exposed part of her cunt, as well as her anus, at even the slightest move. She quickly realized that drawing in her breath alleviated the awareness, but letting it out immediately brought it back, even accentuating the sensation. Dear Ares, what was the man doing to her?

Next, he went to the shelves on the wall and returned with two little rings, made of the same thin gold as the chain— only these rings were smaller in circumference than the chain links, and they were connected by a much thinner, tightly linked chain, the sort artisans might use to fashion a necklace. Only then did it hit her—Ralen was so wealthy that even his sexual tools were made of the finest, most expensive materials known to man! It somehow made her tense further to realize the value of what stretched across her cunt.

She watched as he bent over her with the tiny gold rings. He used his fingers to pry one of them apart—allowing her to see it was not a true circle, the thin gold not soldered together. He then pressed the open ring around her nipple—grown shamefully erect from the chain stretched between her thighs. She nearly held her breath, waiting for whatever would come next, then flinched when he squeezed the gold back into a tighter, tinier circle at the base of the pink bud. Her nipple grew even stiffer in response and she felt the ring's tight caress deep within her breast. She bit her lip, watching as he attached the other ring in the same manner, leaving the thin chain connecting them to droop slightly between the peaks.

When Ralen moved to one corner of the table, working at the thick chain that held her wrist, she thought—finally, sweet release! She'd been bound to the table for only a few hours, but it felt much longer and she yearned to be free.

As he stepped away, to the other wrist, she lowered her aching arm, thinking it had indeed been unbound. But not so. He'd only *loosened* the chain, adding slack and length so that she could move more freely—yet she was still shackled to the table, his captive.

She pulled in her breath, trying not to explode in rage or crumple in tears. Her heart yearned desperately for home. For her mother. Or her sisters. For Bella. Another woman who would feel her anguish, understand her pain.

She thought of them as she sadly lowered her other arm to her side, trying to ease the tight ache in her muscles, her thoughts centering particularly on her mother. Everyone knew how strong and smart Jalal was. And everyone always said Teesia took after her. So she imagined her mother's voice whispering in her ear. *You must be strong now, daughter. You must persevere. You can do this.*

As Ralen went about loosening the chains at her ankles the same way, she gathered her courage and asked a question she hoped would not anger him. "The links between my legs," she said softly. "And the rings at my breasts. What are they for?"

He didn't bother looking up from his adjustment of the last chain. "They will keep you in a state of arousal until I decide your training is through."

She sucked in her breath, then let it back out, suffering a fresh awareness of the thin circles of metal stretching through her pussy — the very arousal he ordained for her. She tried to sound calm as she asked, "How shall I sleep?"

This time he met her gaze, his glimmering wickedly. "With dirty dreams, vixen."

"And I am to *stay* chained?"

"I wouldn't want you running away when we've only just begun," he said, then picked up his earlier discarded shirt, walked to the door, and left her there without even a goodbye or a goodnight.

* * * * *

The next morning, Ralen visited the stables to check on two mares soon to deliver foals, and spoke to his stablemaster about current breeding plans for some of the horses in his carefully pieced-together herd.

He went for a short ride on his beloved black stallion, Charger, taking the horse down to the beach to gallop along the shore. The sounds of seabirds and the rolling tide always relaxed him. Well, as much as a man with a raging erection could be relaxed. Thoughts of his brazen little bride buffeted him as dependably as the waves buffeted the shore below Charelton Fortress.

Ares, but she was an orgasmic little thing — he'd nearly lost count of how many times he'd made her come. It didn't take much — a thought which at once aroused and disturbed him.

Disturbed him because it made him remember the night of their first meeting — she'd come easily then, too. It forced him to wonder how many *other* men she'd come for. Even having kept her virginity intact, how could a girl so sensual and excitable have possibly kept herself from other men, given her eagerness in Rawley? He still had no choice but to draw the same conclusion — she hadn't.

I will control you. I will. There was no other alternative in Ralen's mind. For if he did not control the things and people in his midst, mightn't they somehow control *him*? He sighed, drawn back to a much darker place in time, where he'd lived in fear and anger, where a leather strap had been his punishment for any and every offense, slicing into his skin, making him feel trapped, caged, crazed to escape. The rush of memories barreled down through him, settling low in his belly, until he pushed them away. That was the past. *Keep it there.*

He supposed disciplining his young bride had brought it to mind.

Good for her, he thought, letting a wicked grin form, that he chose to mete out discipline in a much more pleasurable manner.

He headed back toward the stables, thinking it was near time for the midday meal. His bride would be hungry, too. And he could make that work for him — he could use every human need she possessed to continue transforming her into his perfect submissive.

Some time later, he walked into the room where she lay chained, a tray of food in his grasp. Cheese, bread, red berries, peach pudding, a leg of turkey and a large goblet of wine made a hearty meal.

He lowered the tray onto the end of the padded platform where she lay on her side sleeping. The very sight of her added to the stiffness in his pants. He wondered how many times the chain had stimulated her clit and tiny asshole through the night, and felt deeply pleased to see that her nipples remained hard and pointed even as she slept, thanks to the tight rings that would not allow them to escape, nor allow their sensitivity to fade.

The jeweled cuffs he'd commissioned for her from an artisan south of Caralon shimmered prettily, reminding him of their wedding yesterday, and that she belonged to him now.

In body anyway. In soul—soon enough.

"Wake up, my wanton little bride," he said, running a hand up her thigh and onto her round ass. He squeezed lightly and she opened her eyes, dark blue in the pale daylight drifting through the windows, almost the color of the blue stones in her bracelets, and a striking contrast to her long, dark billows of hair. "Time for a snack."

She blinked repeatedly, as if trying to come awake, and finally pushed to a sitting position, which the slack in the chains allowed. "Wh-what time is it?" she asked groggily.

"Midday. Did you sleep well?"

She gave him a look of disbelief. "Not exactly, no."

He quirked a half-smile in her direction. "Perhaps not. But your training period is not about sleep, vixen."

"No, I didn't figure it was."

He gave a wry laugh, then sat up on the table beside her and reached for a wedge of cheese. When he held it up toward her mouth, she reached to take it from him, but he pulled it back. "No," he said softly, and again moved it to her lips until she understood she was not to feed herself.

Meeting his gaze briefly, she opened her mouth and bit off a chunk of the pale yellow cheese, chewing then swallowing, after which he reached for the goblet. He held it carefully to her mouth until she took a sip, then he ate a bit of cheese and took a gulp of wine himself.

"Lie down," he told her.

She looked aghast. "That's all I get? One bite of food?"

"Lie down."

Letting out a sigh, she obeyed, and he took a long moment to study her lovely nude body before he parted her legs to kneel between them. "Be a good girl and maybe I won't have to tighten the chains. Can you do that?"

She looked uncertain for a brief moment, then gave a short nod. Good. Acquiescing on her own was a promising start toward total submission.

"Raise your ass," he instructed, eyes on her cunt. It looked wet and inviting, even with the sizable gold links curving through the pink flesh. When she lifted, he reached around to unhook the chain from the back, at the same time unable to resist raking his tongue quickly through the moisture between her thighs.

She moaned and seemed unable to keep her ass off the table any longer, even given the loose bindings that allowed for easy movement, quickly dropping back to the leather padding with a sigh.

He felt her gaze as he released his cock from his leather lacings, and liked when he sensed her tensing at the sight of it, even now, as if she hadn't seen it before.

"Part your legs wider."

She bit her lip nervously, then followed the instruction. At that, he reached under her, his hands closing warm around her ass and pulling her toward him until her pussy met the hard ridge of his shaft. "Oh!" she said on a rough groan.

"Tell me you want it inside you."

She nodded, her lips trembling prettily. "Yes. I want it inside me."

He contained a cynical chuckle as he playfully asked, "Is it big enough for my wanton little bride?"

This nod came more vigorously. "So big. *Unbelievably* big. I couldn't have imagined…"

He let the laughter out, pleased by her answer. Then he used his hand to guide the shaft to her opening, pushing, pushing, not one swift drive like last night, but instead prodding her body to accept his cock on its own. She moaned at each thrust, and moaned deeper when he slid all the way in.

Their eyes met darkly at the joining and he bent to deliver a firm lick to one ringed nipple. She shuddered her delight, and when he used his fingers to loosen the ring, she let out a sound of dismay. He felt it deep within his cock because, already, she was missing what he'd forced on her.

"You're taking those off me, too?" she asked, soft and innocent.

He nodded, freeing the other nipple. "Don't worry — they'll return to your hungry little body."

She simply nodded and waited, looking expectant, and he liked knowing that, this quickly, she was curious rather than frightened to see what would come next.

Reaching around to the tray, he found one of the rare Before Times spoons he'd bartered for with traders. Dipping it into the pudding, he held it to her mouth, thrusting gently into her below even as she swallowed the sweet treat.

"Mmm," she said, and if he wasn't imagining things, she lifted her hips a little higher, affording him easier entry.

Still moving inside her, he spooned a dollop of pudding onto one of her nipples, then bent to lick and lave her breast clean. Her lovely whimper was like music as he worked.

Ralen fucked her a bit harder then, unable to resist as her body became more pliant, her pussy more accepting of his cock. "More to eat?" he asked between strokes.

"Yes, please."

Good girl. He reached for the slab of cheese, this time pinching off a bite in his fingers and feeding it to her as he slid his stiff shaft in and out below. He helped himself to the cheese, as well, and then the fowl, after which he held the turkey leg up to her mouth.

She parted her lips in response and he fucked her and fed her at the same time, watching her bite the meat from the bone, taking it into her mouth even as she took his rod in her tight, royal cunt.

He continued the game—feeding and fucking, fucking and feeding, hopeful that she'd soon associate the basic need to eat with the need for sex, that she'd require one as much as the other, and that she'd realize she obtained them both from *him*, that he was the giver of all things in her world.

"Who fucks you, Teesia?"

"Ralen," she said.

Like a little reward, he pushed a berry into her mouth. "And who feeds you?"

"Ralen," she said, swallowing.

"That's right, vixen. I give you all the things you need." He concluded the dark, binding words by squeezing her breasts tight and bending to kiss her with his tongue. Hers twined with his and he increased the depths of his thrusts, thinking—*Feel it, vixen. Feel it!*

"More," she begged.

"More food or more cock?"

She laughed lightly—the first time he'd seen such a phenomenon. It lit up her eyes. "Both," she admitted.

He spooned more pudding into her waiting mouth, this time dropping a globule on her other breast for himself. He moved in her—long, slow strokes—as he suckled her clean. Dropping a few small berries on her chest, he lifted her breasts like dams to keep them from rolling away until he could lightly grasp one with his teeth before dropping it into her mouth with a kiss.

He scooped the next berry up for himself, then delivered the last one to her waiting mouth the same way.

She licked her lips as he began fucking her a bit harder, and she clutched at the table on both sides of her, clearly forgetting about the food.

"Who fucks you, Teesia?" he asked harshly, to match the increased rhythm of his strokes.

"Ralen."

"Whose cock fills you?"

"Mmm, Ralen's."

Still driving into her sweet, warm pussy, he lowered one thumb between them to her clit and began rubbing, fast. She groaned and moved harder against him, meeting the pressure there, as hungry for it as she had been for the meal. "Who makes you come, vixen?" he asked in a low, determined voice.

"Ralen," she replied, and quick as that, her hands left the table, rising to mold desperately to her breasts as she leaned her head back and let her eyes fall shut. "Oh Ares!" she cried. "Ralen! Ralen! Oh, Ralen! Yes!"

He never slowed the strokes delivered by both shaft and thumb, not as she exploded in ecstasy beneath him, and not even afterward. He was like a charging stallion—no stopping now. Seeing her clutch onto her breasts so unexpectedly had pushed him past a point of control and he fucked her as hard as he could until the pleasure mounted, mounted, until... "Ares," he murmured through clenched teeth. "Ah, yes!"

He thrust hard, hard, hard, spilling his semen deep inside her pussy for the first time, inexorably thrilled by knowing he was leaving part of himself inside her.

"Oh, Ralen—me, too!" she cried when he least expected it. And, coming down from his grand release, he watched, stunned, as his dirty little wife came yet again, only a minute at most after her last climax.

Ares, her proclivity for reaching ecstasy was amazing! Thrilling, and—as he'd thought earlier—worrisome, too. *Are you mine alone, little wanton?* he wondered, peering down at her. Then silently asked the more burning question — *How will I ever know for sure?*

* * * * *

Teesia lay on her table, staring at the ceiling…waiting, waiting. He'd left her there alone, again. She'd discovered she could sit comfortably on the edge of either side of the platform, but could not step down — the chains prevented movement that far.

She'd also found the covered pot on the shelf mounted just beneath the table, within her reach — which she assumed was for certain practical needs. She cynically thought she was probably lucky he'd at least provided some way to relieve herself when necessary, given his general disregard for her comfort.

Was this table to be her home now? she wondered futilely. How long would he keep her this way, tied like an animal? She let out a sigh, supposing perhaps she should just be happy he'd loosened the chains and given her something to eat.

The gold chain was fastened back through her cunt now, and the rings tightened again around her nipples. And to her shame, she was glad. She was horrified to remember the moment she'd seized her own breasts in her hands during sex, but it had been an instinctive move — since last night, they'd been the recipients of constant stimulation. As her orgasm had neared, the poor mounds of flesh had felt empty, neglected, needy. She'd simply followed an urge — and in response saw a flare of heat in her husband's eyes more powerful than ever before. Frighteningly so.

Be strong. She heard her mother's voice again, whispering in her ear.

Yes, yes, Mother, I will. I'll survive this.

And soon it would all be nothing more than a memory.

She hoped.

Surely Ralen would release her from the table and allow her to live normally.

What did he want from her that she hadn't freely given, after all? She'd possessed her virginity, and she'd willingly submitted to everything he'd done to her here. She'd complained very little, and despite it all, she still loved being fucked by him. She loved it as much as she'd ever suspected she would. It was nothing at all like what she'd anticipated, of course, given the various chains involved and his constant questions and demands—but she still wanted him. Why wouldn't he set her free now so they could behave as a normal married couple?

It was nightfall when the door opened again to admit her husband. He found her sitting up, as if awaiting him, and she supposed she *had* been.

Won't you please unchain me now? She bit her tongue. Asking would likely only earn her a longer sentence.

It took a moment before she realized he'd brought another tray of food—the delay probably due to the fact that the mere sight of him set her blood to humming. Her pussy pulsed against its chain as he neared her, tonight wearing his usual black—soft leather pants and a leather vest.

She had not touched him during sex today when she'd had the chance, and when he sat down on the table next to her, lowering the tray there, she instinctively reached her hand up, splaying it across his stomach. His skin was warm over hard muscles, a smattering of ebony curls sprinkled across his chest, then narrowing into a tight vee that led downward to where his cock lay concealed.

He looked down at her hand. "What are you doing?"

She liked the idea that *she'd* actually surprised *him* for a change. "I have not touched you. Your body."

He met her gaze with his dark, penetrating one, then glanced down at her fingers once more. "I'm surprised you want to."

She blinked and sat up next to him. "Why? You've known from the start of my desire for you."

His eyebrows knitted. "Even now? I assumed you would hold me in contempt by now." He reached down and tugged lightly on the chain that hung between her breasts. "All things considered."

She gasped at the sensual pull and said, "I wish to do whatever you wish me to do. I wish to be whatever you wish me to be." She didn't exactly *mean* the words, but she thought it might earn her a quicker release.

In reply, he dipped his fingers between her legs and lifted a chunk of ham to her mouth. She bit into it as he stroked her around and through the thin gold links, parting her legs without forethought. Another bite of the sweetened ham came with more of his fingers, playing in her pussy, fondling her clit—made so needy by the ever-present chain. He fed her the entire portion of ham that way and she ate it hungrily.

Next, he molded her breast in one hand as he lifted the wine goblet to her mouth with the other. She drank heartily, arching into his touch. Then, at his urging, she lay back on the table.

When he used the antique metal spoon—among only a few such artifacts she'd ever seen—to transport peas into her mouth, one dropped free and settled directly in her navel. Ralen didn't hesitate to dip down and scoop it out with his tongue.

Together, they shared a thick slice of sweet cornbread, him holding it to her mouth, then his own, then pausing for a firm kiss or a lick to her breast. "Enough for you," he said, his voice thick with teasing, as he swallowed the last bite, then repositioned himself until he knelt between her spread thighs, pressing berries into the folds of her cunt and the links that stretched across it, then using his tongue to extract them.

She sat up and leaned back on her hands, watching him feast on her, unaccountably filled with hot joy. His mouth at her pussy was among the grandest delights he'd yet dealt out, rivaling the thrust of his cock deep within her. She actually purred her pleasure, watching him, her only other wish at the moment that she not be chained to a dratted table.

Yet soon pleasure surpassed the wish and any other worries, until it was all she knew. She lifted her cunt against his teasing licks, now coming through the chain without the presence of berries, until she breathed, "I shall come soon."

"No, vixen, you shall not," he replied, abruptly leaving her pussy behind and rising to face her.

She gasped her shock, her cunt pulsing with desperate, abandoned need. It was nearly unbearable. "You would...you would...leave me like...?" What was she saying? Of course he would leave her on the edge of ecstasy. He *wished* her there, *always*! He gave orgasms frequently, yes, but he bound her with titillating devices designed to keep her exactly where she resided now—on the very rim of pleasure, but not quite able to topple over.

"Turn over," he said. "On your hands and knees."

Sighing her agonizing frustration, she followed the order, her pussy aching with wild desire. And as she waited for him to go to the pegboard and come back with his instrument of choice, she began to wonder—what if she *had* meant the words? What if she really did wish to please him, whatever it took? For she didn't even question his commands now—she simply followed them.

But then, what choice did she have? She'd accepted from the start that as long as she was chained, she *had* to obey. And she still feared finding out the consequences if she did not.

He returned with a familiar riding crop—only it seemed much longer ago than last night that he'd used it on her.

"Wh-what now?" she asked over her shoulder, her cunt still pulsing madly.

He snapped the crop across her ass—a sting that shocked...yet echoed through her body in an oddly pleasurable way, intensifying the raging fire between her legs. "You shall see 'what now' when I choose to reveal it," he replied in a harsh voice.

When he fed her, it seemed he turned softer for some reason, but now he'd transformed back into his more severe self again, ready to remind her who was in charge—as if she might have somehow forgotten.

Starting at the inside of one knee, her captor dragged the length of the braided crop slowly up her sensitive thigh. She hissed her pleasure when it pressed against her cunt, or at least against the chain that stretched through it.

"Your pussy looks so pretty bound for me," he said from behind her, almost as if reading her mind.

Are you going to keep me tied up forever? No, she still couldn't ask. She was certain she'd pay for the question if she did. Instead, she formulated the *correct* answer. "I'm glad it pleases you."

"Mmm, indeed," he said on a hot little growl that, amazingly, made her cunt throb against the thin links, as well as the crop, even more than it already was.

Next, he ran the fringed tip of the crop from her neck slowly down the arch of her back and up onto her ass, where it collided with the center chain, adding even more pressure, especially when he reached her anus. She bit her lip at the unanticipated sensation, holding back her moan. She hadn't known...or ever even *thought* about that part of the body bringing pleasure. She'd thought it had one not-particularly-sensual use and that was all. Why did it suddenly feel so *good*, and so much like it wanted even *more* attention?

Ignore it. Your senses are on overload. He's got you so sexually wound up that your poor body doesn't even know anymore which parts are supposed to be the pleasure-seeking ones.

"Does your little asshole feel good, vixen?" As he asked, he—dear Ares!—pushed the tip of one finger inside it.

She clenched her teeth against the sensation as she tried to fight back her shock. "No."

Quick as that, his finger left and he swatted her ass with the crop. She flinched as the confusing pleasure-pain vibrated through her. "Ow! What was that for?"

She looked over her shoulder in time to see him bend forward and bestow a small bite on her bottom. Stunning, piercing pleasure echoed outward as their eyes met. "Lying," he said.

She turned back away from him and swallowed. He *knew* it felt good? She must be even worse at hiding her reactions than she thought. And did he *want* it to feel good? Was it *supposed* to?

"May I ...ask a question?" she asked, still poised on hands and knees.

"All right." He drew little circles on her ass with the tip of the crop.

"That particular spot," she began uncertainly, "it...it is a spot of pleasure? A...*normal* spot of pleasure? For many people?"

His rich, mocking laughter washed over her, making her feel like an idiot. "Well, at least now I know of another orifice on your body that has not been breached."

"*Nothing* on me has been *breached*!" she snapped, anger getting the best of her. "Before you, anyway!"

This time the crop came down hard on her rear, making her squeal in pain. "*Quiet*," he said. "I'll decide your innocence in my own way, vixen. You are not to comment on it. Do you understand?"

She let out a sigh. Oh, the insufferable man! She feared he would be the death of her.

"I said, *do you understand*?" Another—lighter—snap of the riding tool came, this one vibrating through her more like usual—a bit of pain, a burst of pleasant heat.

"Yes," she whispered.

"Good." His voice came softer, too, and he rubbed the length of the crop in the crack of her ass as if giving her a little reward. The stimulation felt so wonderful that she found herself arching her bottom against it, longing to feel the pressure deeper, wanting the crop to rub the chain more vigorously across the tiny fissure there.

The next thing she knew, Ralen was climbing up on the table behind her, balancing on his knees, bending to deliver a shockingly gentle kiss to the side of her ass that had not yet been swatted or bitten or rubbed at all. A sharp moan left her—how could it feel so delicious, coursing through her like a river of delight? Then his fingers played at the center of her rear, raking the chain aside from the opening, a move which pulled it tighter against her cunt. She battled the urge to rock against it, to stimulate her pussy against the links, and barely managed to resist.

But she couldn't hold back the question that now nagged at her, because—drat it all—she missed, *desperately* missed, the press of the chain up the valley of her ass. "What are you going to do to me now?" she asked over her shoulder.

His dark gaze met hers. "I'm going to fuck your pretty ass with the crop."

Abject shock sliced through her. He was going to do *what* with the crop? Put it inside her? *There*?

She knew horror shone in her eyes, but he didn't smile, didn't frown, simply lowered another little bite to her ass and said, "Turn back around, vixen."

Chapter Five

ဢ

For a moment, she felt like she couldn't breathe. This was impossible. She'd been stunned enough when he'd pushed the tip of his finger in there—he couldn't put an *object* in. Could he?

Oh Ares, as he pressed it against her anus, a pleasure and need heretofore unknown erupted inside her, spreading through her body like a shockingly intense heat. She wanted more, there was no denying that, yet she still couldn't quite accept—fathom—the possibility. Despite her desire, she wasn't sure she was ready for something so unanticipated.

When he began to push, she said, "Wait!" peering back over her shoulder.

"No waiting," he said simply, "and if I wasn't so intent on getting the handle of this crop in your ass, I'd whip you with it."

She sucked in her breath. The handle. Yes, she could see the fringed end of the crop pointing away from her. As she turned her head back to face forward, she recalled that the handle, covered with smooth black leather, was rounded, not braided. Somewhat, she thought speculatively, like a thin little cock.

"Ohhh!" she cried deeply as the crop slipped inside her, then deeper, deeper. "Oh! Oh Ares!" How could it be? So different than the pussy, not the same sort of pleasure at all and yet…still pleasure. *Strange* and *astounding* pleasure because it seemed so impossible, the idea so utterly new. It was as if Ralen had discovered an entirely unknown region of her body, as if it had been hidden from her all this time and suddenly, in the blink of an eye, he was delivering deep delights to her in this unforeseen way.

"Fuck it, vixen," he said softly, and when she dared move lightly, carefully, against the crop in her ass, her husband groaned his approval.

She moaned, too, in a mixture of disbelief and joy at this new sensation she'd never even imagined.

"Yes, fuck it," he commanded again, and she continued, still a bit wary, yet sinking into a slow comfort at the idea of having something inside that part of her.

When she dared glance back over her shoulder, she found Ralen's gaze glued hotly to his task, and she wondered what it looked like to see her ass swallowing the crop. Her pussy went wetter at the image in her mind. Or maybe it was because she was moving and every movement brought the chain between her legs into scintillating contact with her clit.

Too much pleasure, too much pleasure. She began to feel lost in it, almost overwhelmed. Her arms were tired, her knees, too—yet nothing mattered but the sensations at her ass and cunt. She moaned, sinking deeper, deeper into the raw heat of it, the stimulation of the thin gold links, the shockingly good insertion of the riding tool, the lovely pleasure gained with each little thrust of her ass. She would come soon, *yes, yes…*

Only then he withdrew the crop!

She whimpered at the loss and thought she'd never felt emptier in her life. *"Wh-why?"*

That fast, he managed to snap the fringed end of the leather against the softest part of her ass. The result was a ferocious echoing sensation through her poor pussy and bottom that nearly made her collapse with the intensity of her longing. "Because there's more, vixen," he said sharply. "Which you will not get if you continue to question me. Understand?"

Her mouth quivered. "Yes."

"That's better. Now," he began, leaving her in order to return to the peg board, "let's try this."

She looked up to see in his hand a smallish clay cock—bigger than the crop, smaller than the cock she and Bella had played with during Orientation. Smaller, but...it was to go inside her ass? She at once longed for it but dreaded it—it was too big for that newly opened spot. And it was all she could do not to protest, but she struggled to keep her mouth clamped tightly shut. She watched over her shoulder as he dipped his fingers into a jar of something wet, then smoothed them over the tool, making it glisten.

Her teeth chattered nervously when the blunt end of the toy cock nudged her anus—then, dear Ares, he pushed firmly, making her cry out as it sunk deep. "Ohhh!" She thought she was crying out from pain, but just as quickly, discomfort abated, leaving her with a stunning sense of fullness in a place she'd never expected to be filled, and a sense of her own sexuality so hot and dirty that she'd never experienced anything like it. In that strange, transforming instant, she became wild and hungry, *truly* wanting to be everything he wanted her to be, wanting to do his every bidding, please his darkest whim.

"How does that feel, vixen?" he asked from behind her.

Her lips trembled from the overwhelming pleasure of being his slave. "Brutally good," she said on a shaky voice.

Her husband's deep sigh was all she needed to hear to know the answer had pleased him. As he began to move the clay cock slowly in and out of her ass, she clenched her teeth at the pure sexual being she'd just become. Nothing mattered but sensation. She ceased to think, to reason, to worry, to wish or to plan. Nothing mattered but the tool in her ass and the incredible knowledge that she was genuinely succumbing, becoming what he wanted her to be. Hot, so hot. Everything inside her burned with an unrefined lust and desire so deep and dark that she'd never imagined it could exist.

She moved against the clay cock, amazed when it began to glide more freely in the orifice, even more amazed when the pleasure deepened, threatening to swallow her. The thin gold links between her thighs rubbed deliciously through her pussy, chafing her clit, centering all she was in the region of her ass and cunt. She was nothing else but those parts of her body in that moment, lost in the sensations, drowning there—a most *wonderful, powerful* drowning.

She cried out at the raw pleasure. It was tinged with pain—she felt it somewhere around the edges of her anus—but the pleasure was so great that it *embraced* the pain. The hint of pain made it even *better*. She wanted to hurt for him.

Behind her, he growled in clear response to her mewling cries, and she found herself languidly licking her lips, sinking, sinking, knowing ecstasy was near. *Rub me, my little gold chain. Rub my clit.* It was swollen—she could sense that—swollen and protruding through one of the thick links, making the contact all the sweeter.

Soon. So soon. Any second now. Closer…closer…

Then Ralen's hand was at her back—and he unhooked the chain so that its end dropped free from her belly onto the table below her.

She howled her frustration as the loss roared through her—and Ralen answered by slapping her ass, hard.

She cried out again, angered, but was forced to bite her lip at the jolt of pleasure the hot blow sent crashing through her nether region. *Everything* was pleasure and arousal now—*everything*.

And then—oh Ares!—he was suddenly in her, thrusting his thick, solid cock into her hungry pussy, making her cry out yet again. This time all pleasure, no pain. She was impossibly full—filled in both cunt and ass—and if she'd thought the sensations were overwhelming before, they were nothing compared to this.

"Oh, Ralen!"

"That's right, vixen," he uttered through clenched teeth. "Say my name. Tell me who fucks you hard and deep."

"Ralen," she whimpered. "Ralen."

Her arms went weak — too much pressure on them for too long and too much pleasure from behind — and she sank down toward the table. She waited for him to complain, or smack her ass, but he simply kept fucking her, his strokes thorough and reaching, perhaps deeper than she'd ever felt him in her before. Amazingly, while he looped one arm around her waist, he continued to deliver small thrusts of the clay cock with his free hand, in time with the drives in her pussy, filling her to overflowing with each plunge of both. Her whole body shuddered with the crushing pleasure.

Her cries were wild — she was lost to Ralen and heat and sex, and the spell was broken only when he said, "Spread your legs."

She wasn't sure exactly what he meant, given her position on her knees, but she tried, parting them as much as she could across the table as he fucked her.

He bent over her then, his warm hard chest grazing her back, and the hand around her waist dropped to her cunt. Two big fingers began to stroke the right spot — rubbing in hot circles over her poor, swollen clit. Her pussy and ass were still full, and this added sensation took her to a place of instant perfection.

She yelled out with heated abandon, aware of nothing but brazen joy and the man who delivered it so shockingly well. And this time he *wanted* her to come — she knew. He wouldn't stop, or take anything away. This time he wanted to draw the pleasure from her with his thrusting cock and skilled fingers turning in hot little circles…turning, turning…so sweet — sweet and hot and making the sensation gather in a tight ball just beneath his touch…and then… Oh! It broke over her like a fury, raining down from the sky. Her whole body was swept into the tumult of pulsing pleasure, and the sounds that left her were no longer just mere cries, but his name. She was yelling it. Screaming it. "*Ralen! Ralen! Ralen!*"

When the storm inside her subsided she collapsed beneath him completely, and just as quickly he pulled out of her—both her ass and her pussy—leaving her to feel agonizingly empty with the sudden departures...until he growled his own release and the sweet hot bursts of his fluid warmed her ass.

Even in exhaustion, she instinctually thrust it higher for him, and then came his hands, rubbing it in, into her rear, and into the opening at its center. Again, she found herself wondering what it looked like *now*, now that it had been so thoroughly fucked by Ralen's toy. Open, she thought—she could tell because as he rubbed the warm liquid in, his fingers sank inside in short but full thrusts, at least two of his large fingers, with room to spare.

"My ass is open wide for you," she heard herself murmur without forethought.

His low groan was rife with heat. "Yes, vixen. So very open, your sweet little ass."

Still resting in front of him, her knees drawn up to her chest, she sighed, feeling a lazy smile of satiation form on her lips as she licked them. So pleasured. She was so very pleasured and so very pleased to have given such pleasure to her man.

But then—oh Ares! What was happening *now*?

Something *else* was slipping into her ass, something new and different.

She began to moan softly as it slid in with relative ease. She wasn't sure she could take anymore at the moment, yet at the same time, she desired it. "Wh-what...?" she mumbled mindlessly.

"Another toy for your ass." He pushed it deeper, and when it began to meet resistance, he pushed more.

She yowled at the burst of pain—and then it ceased, that quickly. It was as if the object had suddenly sunk home, slid into place somehow, found purchase. In fact, she became aware that Ralen no longer pushed, and if she wasn't mistaken, his hand no longer held the anal toy in place. But something tickled her below, on her ass and the backs of her legs, drawn up beneath her as they were.

She peeked over her shoulder and, unable to see anything from there, was forced to push back up on her hands, stiffening her elbows.

A cluster of thin leather strips appeared to protrude from her ass, a large tuft of thick fringe hanging down. She gasped, then met Ralen's dark, feral eyes behind her.

Stepping down off the table to take in the profile of her body, he looked supremely pleased. "Would you like a better view?"

She nodded, her breath coming a bit labored from confusion...as well as the fact that she was, in effect, still being fucked in her ass.

He stepped to the wall and drew down a swath of black silk that had hung unnoticed, up to now, near the pegboard—to reveal a large viewing glass. Its sharp, jagged pieces revealed a shocking sight, especially given that she was situated on hands and knees. "It looks like a horse's tail," she said, a bit breathless.

"That must be why I enjoy the way it looks on you so much."

His confirmation was as shocking as her appearance at the moment. She darted her gaze to his, and as usual, the look in his eyes was enough to bury her, make her forget everything but sex...and an ounce of fear and intimidation. An oddly stirring combination.

He moved forward, smoothing his palm from her shoulder down the arch of her back and up onto her bottom.

"You're my lovely little filly, Teesia," he purred darkly. "My little filly who I love to ride."

Her mouth went dry. She wanted to hate him for this. But her pussy tingled with heat and her nipples felt as tight and sensitive as ever, locked as they were within their rings.

She *didn't* hate him. Despite herself, she loved that she pleased him.

He moved in to deliver a long, firm kiss and she kissed him back with all that was in her, meeting his tongue, tasting his mouth, drinking in the scent of him.

When the kiss was through, he reached for the gold chain dangling from her stomach, stretching it between her legs and reattaching it in back. "Goodnight, vixen," he said when he was done.

She bit her lip, suddenly distressed. "I am to sleep with this thing inside me?"

"Yes," he said on a short nod. "And don't even think about removing it or you will sleep prone, with your limbs stretched. I think you'd much rather have your ass stretched instead."

* * * * *

The next day held activities she was beginning to become accustomed to. The first thing her husband did was extract the tool from her ass and insert a slightly larger one—this one, too, sporting the tail of fringe, and fashioned in such a way that it stayed in place on its own.

When she asked about that, he showed her the one he'd just removed—it grew slightly wider toward the base in a coned shape, then curved drastically inward so that once the base was pushed inside, her anus closed around the thinner part, trapping the toy inside until removed by the handle, which was wrapped with the leather fringe.

He fed her again, and fucked her again—taking turns with the two and keeping her on hands and knees so he could enter her without removing the tail.

He also brought in a basin of water and a sea sponge, with which he bathed her. This was a new addition to their encounters and the moist sponge gliding over her already so-very-sensitized skin only added to her arousal.

Her nipple rings stayed on the whole time, seeming to tighten around her further, making her always aware of the puckered peaks of her breasts, always in a state of excitement—and the chain, too, stayed hooked except for when he entered her.

When he fucked her, as always with Ralen, supreme pleasure became her reward, and it seemed worth all she endured—like the prize at the end of a game.

When he was away, Teesia sometimes came back to herself a little—able to shut out the memories of sex, and his searing eyes and the touches that made her melt inside. She could lie on the table, eyes closed, and think about home, her sisters, her parents, Bella—a life that had seemed normal.

Yet having to always lie on her side was a constant reminder of the tool in her ass, and the tickling fringe kept in her mind the thought of being his "filly," his…pet. The constant fullness there, when added to the nipple rings and the chain on her pussy, turned her arousal into something she could never fully escape, even in sleep.

Ralen had been correct when he'd predicted dirty dreams for her—she had them constantly, in waves, so that fucking and lust for more were truly becoming her whole world. In sleep, she saw her lover's face, his cock, she felt his touch, his kiss. Sometimes she thought she even orgasmed while asleep, and was left to wonder—if you came in a dream, were you really coming physically or was it only in your mind? And did it even matter? For the pleasure was just the same.

When she opened her eyes, she was surrounded by whips and clay cocks and chains, the sinfully ornate bed across the room, and the oversized viewing glass on the wall that now reflected her state of sexual helplessness whenever she glanced in that direction.

So when Ralen returned that evening, and said, "If you'll be a good little filly, I will unchain you for a while," it never occurred to her to run. The very idea of getting off the table was so pleasing that she wanted only to luxuriate in that comfort—to stretch her legs, walk about the room.

No, she thought of running only as she padded slowly across the floor on weakened legs, bracelets and ankle cuffs still in place, the object in her ass feeling more prominent as she moved. The notion came when she caught sight of the big wooden doors, and the idea passed through her mind only fleetingly—because it would be foolish, because she didn't *want* to leave.

She would enjoy having a more normal sort of life again, yes, but only if Ralen *wanted* her to have it.

A shocking notion, and she knew she should hate herself for feeling that way, but she couldn't fight it. Everything he'd done to train her had worked. With stunning ease. She was his now—his sex slave.

Ralen sat in a chair, watching his vixen bride walk quietly about the room. He enjoyed the sight of her tail, not only because he knew it was stretching her ass for him, but because she wore it so docilely, like it was a part of her now. His naughty little filly. He loosened the lacings on his pants so that he could stroke his hardened cock as she walked.

The sight of her beautiful breasts, the nipples held taut in their rings, and her pussy, bound by the chain at her waist, added to his stiffness. Even the jewels at her wrists and ankles continued to excite him. It all reminded him that she was his, and her pure beauty pleased him all the more.

When she stilled across the room to look at him, he said, "Keep walking about for me, wanton." Her eyes dropped briefly to his erection and he saw the spark of desire glitter in her gaze as she turned to pace away from him once more, her sensual tail swaying behind.

Had she been this beautiful all along? In the hallway at Rawley? At the Giving Ceremony? At their seaside wedding? Perhaps, for he'd always been drawn to her, from the first moment he'd seen her two years ago—but somehow he couldn't help thinking her even more beautiful now. Her eyes held fire, blue flames.

She would like what he had planned for her this night. A few days ago, he'd enjoyed injecting fear into their relationship. Now, though, he enjoyed her pleasure, her eagerness to please him, and he knew instinctively that his hungry bride would relish learning this new task.

Had she done it to anyone else before? He didn't think so. And he was trying very hard to start believing she'd never done *anything* with anyone else before. He still found it a challenging conclusion to draw, given how easy it would have been for her to lift her dress for a man's hand or mouth at any time—just as she had for him, but he *wanted* to believe she was his alone, as she should be.

"I had the cook prepare a dessert for you today," he told her.

She came to stand before him, noticing for the first time, it seemed, the one bowl on the tray behind him that remained untouched from their earlier fucking and feeding session. "What is it?"

"Chocolate."

"Choc-lut?"

He grinned. "You've never had chocolate before, vixen?" In truth, he wasn't surprised. It was a recent import this far north, brought by boats, at a great price, from tropical regions far south. He'd discovered it while traveling to the islands

150

beyond Floridan—an island empress had shared it with him, and despite the outrageous cost, he'd ordered a small supply of his own. He'd been saving it, although he hadn't been certain why—and now he knew. He couldn't think of a better way to initiate his vixen wife into one of man's deepest pleasures.

She shook her head, and he reached to the table behind him and swept one finger through the dark, creamy mixture, then held it up to her mouth.

She stepped forward cautiously, then gave a soft, delicate lick to his finger. He was surprised when he shuddered from the small touch, but perhaps his training was having an effect on *him*, too—perhaps his bride wasn't the only one in a state of constant arousal.

She tasted, swallowed, then smiled. "Very sweet."

He nodded. "A great delicacy."

She boldly took his hand in hers, and proceeded to lick the rest of the dark chocolate from it, even taking his finger inside her mouth. His cock tensed even more and he held back a groan, thinking it wouldn't be wise to let her know it took so little these days to excite him.

"May I have more…master?"

He smiled darkly up into her eyes. He didn't know if she was addressing him from the heart or if she wanted the chocolate so badly she was pretending in order to get it, but it didn't matter much. Either way, he liked the sound of the word on her tongue.

"Yes, you may, vixen. Kneel between my legs."

Pleased that she didn't even flinch at the request, he parted the lacings of his pants farther, pushing them down so that his whole length, along with his balls, was freed. He spread his legs and watched as she dropped to her knees before him while he shrugged from his leather vest. Then he reached for the bowl and carefully spooned the creamy chocolate over the length of his cock. "You may lick it off, Teesia."

The dark-haired girl before him bit her berry-colored lip as she studied his rod. Even her eyes, planted there, kept him fully aroused.

He didn't have to wait long, though, before she leaned in and boldly licked up the length of his cock where it lay rigid against his stomach, taking the chocolate onto her tongue and making him groan at the sight, not to mention the sensation.

Their eyes met as she made a show of thoroughly licking her upper lip — pleasure raged in her gaze.

"You like it," he said.

"Very much."

Chocolate or cock? Hopefully both.

He spooned more onto his length. "Have some more."

This time, she didn't hesitate, licking her way up his hard shaft, even using the tip of her tongue to rake the chocolate from the indention just under the head. He moaned and decided his eager bride was ready to go further. This time, he held his cock away from his stomach and spooned the creamy chocolate onto the head, then used the spoon to smear it downward on all sides. "Now suck it, vixen," he whispered darkly.

Ralen watched as she studied his cock a moment more, then opened her mouth and leaned over him. Slowly, slowly, she went down, taking him inside, sucking away the chocolate as instructed. He let out a deep sigh as the pleasure radiated through him from the workings of her soft mouth. "That's right, my little wanton. Suck all the chocolate away, just like that." This quickly, she was eager and thorough — indeed, the chocolate had been a very good idea.

When finally she backed off, her gaze was purely sexual, and her lips, laced with remnants of the sweet treat, looked delightfully swollen from her task. On impulse, he leaned over and kissed her hard, tasting the chocolate, reveling in his bride's sensuality.

The next time she took his chocolate-laden cock between her pretty lips, he watched her work, sucking at the dark, liquid delicacy, driving him wild with desire until he pushed, just slightly. She looked up at him, the first time she'd done so with his shaft buried in her mouth, and he nearly exploded into the soft recesses that caressed his hardness. He forgot the chocolate and cupped her face in his hands. "Take more of me, vixen." Not a command, a request. He almost regretted the tenderness in his voice.

But below him, she closed her eyes and eased her mouth deeper onto him—impossibly deep, he thought, for an inexperienced girl. *But that doesn't mean she's sucked another man's cock before.* He wasn't sure why, but he just didn't believe she had. In ways *this* intimate, she truly seemed innocent to him. No, he couldn't help believing that her slow skill was the result of how deeply aroused she was, and how much she desired him, even how much she desired pleasing him.

"Yes, Teesia," he whispered. She moved her mouth only a little now, she'd taken him so deep, and it was simply being there, having her hold him there, so immersed in her mouth, that spurred his excitement. "You are lovely, my naughty bride," he breathed, his voice actually coming out shaky. "Lovely with your mouth stretched around me, lovely sucking me with those pretty, swollen lips."

After what seemed a long while, she backed off, releasing him, then let out a harsh breath and closed her eyes. When she opened them, she smiled up at him and said, "Shall I do it some more?"

He returned a slow grin. "Oh yes, sweet wanton, suck my cock some more."

She bit her lip coquettishly. "May I have more chocolate?"

This time, he actually laughed. "As much as you like."

Reaching up, she generously slathered his cock with the dark creamy liquid, then vigorously went down. She sucked with great enthusiasm and even reached up to fondle his balls as she worked. He pumped softly into her accepting mouth, the sensations running through him as dark and sweet as the chocolate itself—and again, he nearly came when she lifted her blue gaze to him.

When she seemed to have sucked her fill, he told her to clean him off especially well, getting every remnant of chocolate, so she used her tongue and lips to great advantage until he deemed his cock clean enough and stood, pulling her to feet as well.

"Walk to one corner of the bed for me," he said, and as she went, he felt nearly drunk on her—the sway of her ass and fringy tail, the enthusiasm with his cock, it was almost too much for him to take.

But no, he *could* take it, *would* take it, because he wasn't ready to come yet. Not even close.

"Grab onto the post with both hands and arch your pretty round ass toward me."

She did so, peeking enticingly over her shoulder at him, then wiggling her bottom just slightly. It nearly undid him. "Naughty little filly," he purred in her ear as he approached from behind to warmly cup her breasts, rub his cock in her horse's tail.

He reached one hand to pull back her long tresses so that he could kiss her slender, arching neck, then lowered his hands to her hips. "Do you still feel this in your ass?" he whispered, grabbing onto the leather tail to swish it back and forth.

"Ooooh…mmm, yes." His vixen's reply came breathy hot.

Using one hand to push the tail aside, he used the other to unhook her chain and position his cock at her pussy—already warm and wet on his swollen tip. One smooth, enveloping slide of his shaft and he was in her. She moaned the same deep pleasure that assaulted him and he couldn't help asking, "And do you feel *this* in your cunt?" He thrust short and hard.

"Oh yes, master! Yes!"

Master again. It turned his loins all the warmer and made it impossible to keep from driving into her, hard, harder. She let out lovely little cries with each hot plunge, and his heated groans mingled with them.

"Say my name, my hungry little filly."

"Ralen! Oh, Ralen!"

He pounded in to her with growing force, unable to control it.

"Oh Ares—yes! Ralen! Fuck me, Ralen! Fuck me!"

He recalled that she'd made that same demand on the night they'd met, and he'd been unable to oblige her. Now, he wanted to be angry with her for issuing *any* demand, but instead, he only did as she asked—he fucked her, and fucked her, and fucked her.

She arched into him, meeting his strokes, her soft tail falling around where he entered her. "Such a naughty girl," he found himself breathing in her ear as he moved in her warmth. "Such a naughty little vixen. I should give you a spanking."

"Yes, you should," she breathed without hesitation.

In rhythm with his next plunge into her wet depths, he brought the flat of his hand down on her creamy round ass. Her cry was deeper than usual, and he relished the raw delight of knowing he'd taught her to love a bit of pain with her pleasure, then slapped her bottom again, and again, as they fucked.

More of her, he needed more of her somehow. He longed to explode inside the warm, wicked little cave of her cunt, yet he desired some further connection. He wanted to touch her more, kiss her, find other ways to be close.

On impulse, he withdrew his cock and spun her to face him. She looked slightly alarmed at the sudden change, but he only said, "Come here, vixen," as he backed toward the chair, her hands in his. As he sat down, he tugged at the chain between her breasts to pull her nearer. She cried out, but he had no regrets, knowing with confidence now that she *loved* those blessed bits of pain he could deliver. Nothing but heat and unadulterated longing shone on her face as she straddled him in the chair.

He didn't want to go slowly now, so he gave a hard yank on the breast chain and the rings popped free. She shrieked again, her expression filled with anguish, and he worried he'd really hurt her—until he bent to suckle her and she moaned and arched against his mouth in response.

Stopping to reach for the chocolate, he haphazardly smeared it across both her round breasts, then feverishly licked and sucked it from the lush mounds. Hands at her ass, mouth at her chocolaty nipples, he pulled her down, smoothly sheathing his cock with her warm, slick pussy. They both moaned, and though they'd never fucked this way before— he'd never deigned to let her be up on top of him in any way until this unplanned moment—she moved on him with instinctive, rhythmic moves, as if performing an erotic dance.

He suckled and she fucked, he licked and she writhed. When the chocolate was mostly gone, she raked her breasts against his chest and he kissed her shoulders, her neck. Need stampeded through him, the all-consuming lust taking over his entire being. He said, "Come, my dirty little wanton wife. Come for me. *Now.*"

The cry tore from her throat without warning and she rode him so hard—her head dropping back, eyes shut, breasts bouncing—that he couldn't hold in his eruption another second. He exploded inside her, all the while envisioning his fluids drenching the inner walls of her cunt.

He hated thinking she was amazing, hated thinking she was everything he could have ever wanted in a wife. He hated giving her that power, even only in his mind.

But as he emptied his hot semen up inside her, it was a pleasure unsurpassed by anything he'd ever known. She'd become his perfect, willing sex slave. And indeed, she *was* everything he'd ever dreamed a woman could be.

* * * * *

The coming days were filled with more hot fucking for Teesia. Sometimes she pranced about the room for Ralen, swishing her tail this way and that. Sometimes he even took the tail out for a while and tied her back to the table, tightly, just like that first night, arms and legs outstretched, and slowly moved one of the clay cocks in and out of her, watching carefully as it entered and exited her pussy, seeming as aroused by it as she was. Afterward, he would bend over the table, down between her thighs, and lick her until she climaxed.

Rather than fear him as she had at first, she now relished his arrivals, wondering what new treats and experiences he had in store. She didn't even balk on the day he inserted yet a larger fringed cone in her ass—moreover, she'd ended up howling with pleasure when he'd bent her over the padded table to do it and commenced spanking her at the same time.

He still kept her loosely chained at night to sleep, and never once took her in the bed or deigned to sleep next to her. Yet, even so, she knew it was complete. She had surrendered— utterly, totally. He was her whole world.

She knew this was what he'd wanted, this total submission of body and soul. And she didn't even mind, because she'd never known her devotion and dependence on someone could run so deep. She loved belonging to him. It was that simple.

"You're ready for more, vixen," he said one afternoon as she sat in his lap, naked but for her jeweled bracelets, free even of her nipple rings and pussy chain. He had just relieved her of them, pulling her down atop his thighs to feed her the midday meal.

But she was confused. More? "What more could there be?"

In reply, her dark husband flashed the most wicked smile she'd ever seen him wear. "There are things I wish to do to you that I cannot accomplish alone."

Chapter Six

ಐ

Teesia swallowed. "I...don't understand."

"There are things, Teesia, that I wish to *watch* be done to you."

She knit her brows, wondering what he meant.

"Now, stand up," he said, and she complied, waiting as he crossed the room to a cabinet next to the shelves and pegboard where he kept all his sexual toys. A moment later, he returned bearing a heaping handful of small gold disks — they resembled the ancient Before Times coins she'd seen on occasion, but shone smoother and shinier.

Lowering the pile to the table, Ralen separated some of them from the rest and Teesia realized they were not single disks, but bound together by cording so that one disk slightly overlapped another to make long strings of them. The lines of disks were connected to one another in various places, though, as if forming some sort of puzzle or maze. Ralen held up the stringed disks and told her to hold her arms out to him, then he slipped the corded gold over her arms and up onto her shoulders. Moving behind her, he fastened it all together somehow in back. In the front, the disks dipped from her shoulders down under her breasts, hugging them snuggly, lifting them higher.

Next, he took up the remaining disks, also strung to overlap one another, and soon had her stepping between the lines of gold until he was pulling them up to settle at her hips in a circle that went around her, much like her pussy chain. Only no disks stretched directly through her cunt. Instead, dual strands of disks extended down on both sides of her slit before curving into the valley of her ass to connect to the line of disks spanning her lower back.

"What...are these?" she asked, looking at her husband.

"Gifts. Body jewelry. To draw attention to your breasts and pussy, make them even lovelier than they already are. They should also serve to make you feel pleasantly bound. Come," he said, taking her hand and leading her to the viewing glass near the padded table. "Look at yourself."

Teesia peered into the pieces of uneven glass in wonder. Added to the bejeweled bracelets she'd worn since their wedding, she couldn't deny that she looked exquisitely sexual. She felt that way, too. "Thank you," she said, turning to gaze up into her husband's dark eyes.

"Now, return to your platform," he said, taking both of her hands and motioning to the table. "Lie on your back."

Today, he chained her somewhat tightly—not so much that her arms and legs suffered that stretched feeling that was sometimes oddly pleasurable, but enough that she could not move her hands or feet more than an inch or two in any direction.

After visiting his shelves, Ralen returned with a small strip of black leather. Moving up to the end of the table where her wrists were chained, he pressed the soft leather over her eyes and said, "Lift your head, vixen." When she did, he tied the leather in place, leaving her unable to see.

Well, this was new. And not wholly welcome.

Her stomach fluttered with nervousness and uncertainty.

It had been a long time since such feelings had assaulted her, as she'd grown to trust Ralen. Even in pain, he brought her pleasure, and anything she endured for him had held ultimate rewards, so all her fear had slowly dissipated over the days and nights of her confinement—until now.

"Wh-what is happening?"

No answer.

"Ralen?"

Again, nothing. Everything in the room was completely still, no sound.

Had he left her there, like this?

He had. He was gone!

Her heart beat madly in her chest as she wondered what would happen next. She knew he hadn't tied her and covered her eyes for nothing. What in Ares' name was her big brute of a husband planning for her?

Serves you right for having the confidence to relax, to think the worst was over.

Just then, she heard the door open across the room.

"Ralen?"

"Yes, vixen."

It was as if she could breathe again. Relief rushed through her body. "You're here. Thank Ares."

"I left for only a moment."

"Why? What...what's going to happen now?"

Ralen's warm mouth pressed over hers, his tongue dipping past her lips. She wished she could hug him, run her fingers through his dark, beautiful mane of hair—she'd grown used to being able to do that when he unchained her. But she kissed him back anyway, trying to make the connection of their mouths be enough for her. When the kiss was through, she whispered to him softly. "Will you tell me what's happening?"

His hand curved warm and full over her breast, caressing softly as his breath came hot in her ear. "Trust me, my little sex slave."

Trust him. Just as she had grown to do. She took a deep breath. "All right, master. I shall."

All went quiet after that, the room feeling unbelievably still once more. Yet she felt his presence, knew he remained near her, and her awareness of him brought a semblance of peace in her newly darkened world. She tried to hear him breathing, having heard that being blinded heightened other senses.

She could *not* hear him, but when, a few moments later, a soft kiss met her hip, it set her skin tingling. "Mmm," she purred. The mouth moved to her stomach, its touch scintillatingly sweet—and at the same time, lips closed over one nipple.

She drew in her breath at the shocking realization that two people were kissing her! *Two!* And she didn't know who the second person was!

Oh Ares, this was insanity—how could it be? Why was her husband doing this to her?

Had she not endured enough, been as submissive as he could wish? Her breast continued being lightly suckled as more unfamiliar kisses arced across her belly and up toward the other breast. She tensed, her hands knotting into fists above her head in their cuffs. The sensations were at once delicious and unthinkably outrageous. Why? *Why?*

"Relax, my naughty wife," Ralen's warm voice said near her ear. She'd never heard it sound so soothing. "Relax, enjoy, and let the pleasure consume you."

And then she realized that if Ralen was talking, he was not even one of the people kissing her!

As a mouth moved warmly onto her other nipple, closing gently around it, the first was released, that pair of lips rising to kiss the curving ridge of her breast, then her neck. She let out a sigh of distress, despite the undeniably glorious physical delights being bestowed. Why would Ralen give her to someone else like this? *Two* someone elses!

"I want to watch you be pleasured, vixen," he said from the foot of the table, his voice still strong, calm, reassuring. "I want you to feel how deeply it pleasures *me* to watch this. And I want to hear you say my name."

"But who—?"

A light snap of the crop stung her hip when she least expected it, but his voice remained low and even. "Say my name. Tells me whose pleasure brings about your own. Whose eyes watch you."

Teesia trembled beneath the kisses from unknown mouths. "Ralen."

"Again."

"Ralen."

"Keep saying it."

She let out a sigh, her entire body tingling, and whispered his name. "Ralen. Oh, Ralen."

The kisses seemed to buffet her body like waves that crashed from both sides.

"Ralen."

One person's mouth climbed her arm, the other licked rhythmically at her taut, sensitive nipple.

"Ralen."

Kisses came from everywhere—moving down her inner thigh, across her shoulder. Low on her stomach—just above her pulsing cunt—and high on her chest.

"Ralen." Forehead. "Ralen." Breast. "Ralen." A tongue in her navel. "Ralen, oh Ralen!"

The pleasure was consuming and...irresistible. She couldn't *not* feel it. *And* Ralen's gaze. She couldn't see his eyes, but she could feel those, too, burning through her, watching this decadent act as his cock filled with stiff lust.

When a kiss came on her mouth, shockingly soft, she instinctively kissed back. A hand on her breast cupped and caressed. Another kiss touched her lips, this one slightly rougher—being delivered from the other party, she thought. Another hand on her other breast, again firmer and larger, kneaded her hungry flesh.

"Oh Ralen," she purred, almost as if it were *his* kisses, *his* hands.

Her sensual tormentors took turns kissing her, lulling her until she all she knew was their touch and their warm mouths—and Ralen's hot gaze, even hidden from her as it was.

And then came *both* mouths, kissing her together, engaging her tongue with theirs as they continued massaging her breasts, tweaking the points of her nipples, driving her wild. Where was her pussy chain when she needed it?

Like an answer to a silent plea, one of her new lovers descended, leaving her lips, his mouth sweeping across breast and belly until he was kissing her inner thigh, then letting a warm, wet tongue sink into her aching cunt. She cried out at the needed joy, pulling at her chains, wishing she could see, but captive to the darkness her husband had foisted upon her. "Ralen," she sobbed. "Dear Ares, Ralen."

The other mouth returned to her nipple, licking, suckling with a sweet, gentle quality she couldn't quite comprehend. A small hand closed on her other breast, massaging tenderly. And the tongue between her thighs laved her wet, needy slit until she was raising it to him as much as she could given the chains, moaning her delight with each thorough lick. "Ralen. Yes, Ralen," she breathed. "Oh *yes*, Ralen."

She thrust her cunt at the giving tongue, her movements more wild as orgasm threatened. The mouth at her breast responded in kind, suckling harder, making her feel it more deeply. "Oh Ares," she murmured through clenched teeth. "Oh yes. Ralen...Ralen...Ralen..." She said his name in time with the pulses that vibrated through her body, centering in her cunt—and then, sweet heaven, the glorious release broke, the ecstasy washing over her like great sheets of rain, and she cried Ralen's name again and again as it echoed through her like a mighty thunderstorm.

And even as the torrent washed through her, a hand was in her hair, pulling the strip of leather away, giving back her vision so that she found Shaena at her breasts, Laene at her cunt.

It was the first time she'd seen anyone but Ralen in a long while. Both the pretty maid and the handsome man were naked and smiling at her. She could only stare, stunned.

"Ralen asked us to pleasure you for him, lady," Laene said. "A pleasure for us, as well."

Shaena leaned over to bestow a short kiss to her mouth, their breasts brushing gently, nipples grazing each other's skin, inexorably soft. She whispered in Teesia's ear, "By now I'm sure you know that being Ralen's slave is not so horrible."

Teesia swallowed nervously, taken aback even amid the mind-numbing pleasure.

She failed to summon an answer for Shaena, but suspected her orgasm confirmed the maid's suspicions well enough. While it was, in one sense, odd and awkward to have Laene and Shaena see her naked and chained—and writhing with pleasure beneath them, for Ares' sake—the fact that it had already happened, along with their sensual, friendly smiles, somehow took all embarrassment away.

"Shaena," Ralen said, "move onto the table, behind her, so that her head rests in your lap."

Shaena did as Ralen instructed, folding her legs so that Teesia's head lay in the "v" formed by the maid's slender calves. She watched as Shaena's feminine hands reached out to gently stroke and massage her breasts, sucking in her breath at the soft pleasure. "So pretty," Shaena murmured, gazing down at them.

Teesia bit her lip, then utterly softly, "Yours, too." For she'd noticed, despite herself, that the maid's breasts were pert and lovely, the skin there not quite as tanned as the rest of her, and tipped with coral peaks that had grazed so deliciously over hers just moments ago.

They exchanged smiles as Shaena's caresses kept Teesia deeply aroused, despite the orgasm that had just flooded her senses. When she dared shift her gaze to the men, both standing at the foot of the table, they grinned, too.

Ralen's eyes glittered darkly on hers as he said to Laene, "Choose a cock for her cunt."

"Not my own, I presume," Laene said, his gaze sparkling with a hint of amusement as he looked to Ralen.

Ralen's eyes responded in kind, even as he said, "From the wall, Laene. Choose a cock from the shelves."

Legs still spread by the chains shackling her ankles, Teesia's pussy fluttered and wept as she waited for Laene to return. Despite her orgasm, she was desperately hungry for more stimulation within this new situation. He chose a fairly large toy—not at big as Ralen's shaft, but she yearned to have it inside her the second she saw it.

She tensed slightly as Laene positioned it at her opening—it felt strange that anyone but her husband would be inserting something into her—but she groaned deeply at the clay cock's entry.

"Now in and out," Ralen instructed, both men's eyes seeming glued to her cunt.

Laene slid the large rod deep, then eased it halfway out, and at the next slow drive, she met the thrust and enjoyed knowing she'd caused the growl that had just escaped her husband's throat.

Both men continued watching, looking almost drunk on her as Laene glided the toy into her pussy. Above, Shaena's sweet hands molded and caressed, her fingertips occasionally rising to tweak Teesia's pink nipples just as the cock reached its deepest point inside her. Her body sizzled to know she was the center of all this touching and fucking, all this giving of pleasure—it emphasized for her what a purely sexual being she had become under Ralen's tutelage. She met the clay cock again, pushing back, wanting it in her deeper, for both Ralen's delight and her own.

Ralen left the table briefly, returning a moment later with a small viewing glass, which he held propped between her widespread legs so that she and Shaena could see what the men saw. "Watch," Ralen said deeply. "Watch the way it slides so smoothly in and out of you, vixen."

She drew in her breath as they *all* watched. Her pussy was parted to reveal pink folds of flesh, the tiny knob of pleasure at the top, the stretched opening below that accepted the cock with comfortable ease.

"My master is fascinated with watching my cunt," she observed, and everyone laughed softly.

Even Ralen, and she couldn't help thinking that he seemed...*softer* with his friends here. Still her well-muscled master with the dark, dangerous eyes, but his expression had grown more relaxed than she'd ever seen it before.

"That's Shaena's fault," he said to Teesia. "When we were children, she dragged me to the village one day to show me a discovery. We peered in the window of a cottage where a woman fucked herself with a dildo, just like Laene fucks you now."

"We became obsessed," Shaena added, laughing at the memory. "We returned every day at the same time, for she kept a regular schedule. We couldn't seem to stop watching her."

"I will admit," Ralen said, his eyes still focused between her legs, his countenance going a bit more serious, "that ever since that day as a boy of twelve, I have been captivated by the pussy. I never grow less amazed at its lush pinkness, the way it so smoothly swallows a cock."

"Or anything else one wishes to put inside it," Laene said on a laugh, and Teesia caught a sensual glance exchanged between him and Shaena that made her wonder exactly what Laene had pushed into her maid's cunt.

"Let's remove the cock and unchain my wanton little vixen," Ralen said, his eyes glittering with a lust that made Teesia hungry for whatever came next. Would it be only Ralen? Or would the play involve all three of them? It didn't matter—all that mattered was sensation, and the knowledge that however it came, it was by Ralen's bidding.

She was pleased, as always, to leave the table, swept up in dark warmth when Ralen pulled her naked body down with him into a chair so that she sat sideways across his lap.

Before them, Shaena braced her hands on one of the bedposts, licked her lips and looked over her shoulder at Laene, her eyes issuing a heated invitation. Watching Laene place his hands firmly at the swell of her hips and listening to them both moan as he eased his handsome cock smoothly inside made Teesia even wetter.

Her husband kissed her neck as they both observed, and Teesia got caught up in the visual pleasure. She'd never have guessed that watching someone *else* fuck could fill her with so much excitement. Laene's shaft was not as large as Ralen's, but was still a lovely sight, pleasingly stiff as he moved in and out of a moisture they could all hear.

And Shaena's body was not quite as curvy as her own, but more slender and sleek. She found herself thinking that if she was lush valleys and mountains, then Shaena was a windswept beach with tanned slopes and gentle waves. Her deep moans thrilled Teesia to the core and reminded her of her Orientation with dear Bella.

When Ralen began to play at her bare breasts, she glanced down to see him re-attaching her nipple rings. "Keep watching Laene and Shaena," he instructed her.

Thin metal closed tightly around one erect nipple, sending a brutal bite of pleasure to her cunt. She hissed in her breath, then whispered, "But why are you—?"

"Your breasts are beautiful without them," he returned softly, "but I love the sight of them captured within the rings, too."

His large fingertips curved the ring at the other end of the thin chain about her opposite nipple, making her feel delightfully bound once more, yet at the same time still free.

168

She cast him her naughtiest smile. "Whatever *you* wish, *I* wish."

Nothing could have pleased her more than his wicked grin and the dark gleam in his eyes when they met hers.

When he bent to deliver tiny licks to her taut and re-sensitized nipples, it was all she could do not to watch *him* instead of the couple before her. She switched her gaze from her husband's wet tongue to the arousing site of Shaena and Laene groaning their heat. She was surprised to find Shaena's eyes turned on *her*.

When the pretty maid spoke, her voice took on a desperate quality. "Ralen, I wish to kiss her. I want more of her breasts."

Ralen caught the tip end of one nipple between his teeth, looking up at the other woman only as he released it. "*I'm* playing with them right now, Shaena."

Shaena whined further, even as Laene continued thrusting into her from behind. "You have them all the time. Let me have them now, this once."

Teesia was certain Ralen would respond with anger to the girl's commands, but to her surprise, his look slowly softened. "All right," he said, clearly grudgingly, then murmured, "Suppose it will make a lovely sight, now that I think about it."

Teesia blinked, looking at him. "You wish me to be with her further?" For some reason, she'd presumed the sharing was over, yet Ralen nodded.

A shiver of anticipation ran up Teesia's spine. She hadn't quite known she wanted this, but suddenly, now, it appealed in more ways than she could fully comprehend. "Then I wish it, too."

Leaving her husband's lap and stepping up to the foot of the bed, Teesia watched as Shaena released her hold on the tall, thick wooden post and curled the fingertips of one hand around the chain that dipped between Teesia's breasts.

A little yank pulled Teesia closer, made her cry out quickly, made her pussy hum with unexpected delight.

Shaena's eyes were wild on Teesia's breasts before she raised her passionate gaze to her face. "Rub them against mine," she said, her voice echoing a low, thick heat.

Giving her lip a sensual bite, Teesia moved even closer, closer, until Laene's thrusts from behind drove Shaena's arched breasts softly against Teesia's own. There was no need to rub, for Laene's rough plunges managed that for them. Their nipples jutted into each other's breasts and Teesia imagined the rings around hers must deliver a slightly abrading sensation. With each gentle crush of their chests, Teesia's pussy spasmed with a fresh, undeniable heat that left her in pure wonder.

When she'd been with Bella, somehow, despite the pleasure, it had seemed as if it were pretend, because it was practice, and she'd been thinking of Ralen, rehearsing to be with *him*. It hadn't occurred to her that two women could seek pleasure together for no other purpose than pleasure itself.

But then, this *did* hold another purpose, at least for Teesia. Her husband's eyes burned through her like fire. She looked at Shaena, at their breasts bouncing together, but she *felt* Ralen's hard, hot stare. So intense, she had no doubt that the same hardness and hotness echoed to his cock below.

She wanted to please him in every way, even wanted to find ways to *surprise* him—so she followed her instincts and kissed Shaena's mouth.

Both women moaned at the sensation the kiss sent skittering through them, and Ralen's low growl could be heard across the room. "So pretty, ladies," Laene purred from his spot at Shaena's rear.

Teesia knew Shaena had kissed her before, back on the table when her eyes had been hidden, and this was the same as that but also different. Same soft meeting of mouths, but by her decision. And the thrill she felt flowing through her

170

husband's veins flowed through hers, as well, as she quickly came to understand how erotic he found the sight of her with another woman.

So she was slightly shocked when Ralen crossed the room, looped an arm around her waist and pulled her away from Shaena. "Enough," he said gruffly. "I must have you myself."

With that, he pushed her to her back across the big bed, pried her legs wide with strong hands that bit roughly into her inner thighs, and sank his mouth to her cunt. She cried out at the delicious shock of delight. He was not gentle, but she didn't wish him to be—she wanted to feel his passion pulsing resoundingly through her pussy, through all of her.

The freedom to sink her hands into his thick hair was heavenly—she splayed her fingers over his scalp, pressed down to let him know she wanted him to taste her even more deeply. The knowledge that Shaena and Laene witnessed her pleasure only added to the fire racing through her limbs and she moaned her intense joy. "Oh yes, master, yes," she sobbed deeply, loving the sight of his face buried between her thighs.

That's when she glanced up for the first time—and found the long-forgotten viewing glass mounted above the bed. Given her array of body jewelry, she looked like what she was—a sexual plaything, a slave to his every whim. And Ralen looked like what *he* was, too—a man vigorously pleasuring his wife, his head moving back and forth as his mouth devoured her eager cunt. She didn't shy away from looking—doubly pleased not only by the ultra-erotic vision they made together, but also by the fact that she'd finally been taken to the bed, *his* bed, a place that had begun to seem unattainable. The ornate bed, the jagged glass placed above it—they were finally hers. She didn't know whether Ralen even realized it, or if she'd get to stay here, but for this moment, it felt like a grand triumph in her heart.

She continued watching them in the glass, her desire heightened by the rough grunts and moans echoing from the couple to her right. A glance revealed that Shaena gripped the corner bedpost with both hands again, arching her ass toward her lover. Laene pounded into her in mighty, unforgiving strokes for which she clearly had to brace herself.

Teesia lifted her pussy to Ralen's hungry mouth, thrusting, thrusting, then reaching for his hands, guiding them up to mold to her breasts. He massaged the flesh deeply, seeming to eat at her with still more power, and her clit vibrated and swelled with pleasure, so much pleasure — until, *yes, yes, yes*, it exploded through her like a starburst in the night sky.

She screamed her release, letting her eyes fall shut as she lost herself in the consuming joy — only to find her husband pinning her arms next to her head as he thrust his enormous cock inside her. She cried out, but the entry was shockingly smooth given the power of his lunge. And then he was driving, driving, deep and thorough, leaving her capable of no other thought but how completely he filled her. Her legs curled instinctively around his broad back, and they both groaned at each hot stroke he delivered.

She could still hear Shaena and Laene fucking next to them, but all she saw was Ralen. His dark, possessive eyes, his lush mouth, wet with her juices, his muscled body taking her, owning her, filling her with a sense of pure awe she'd never known could exist.

"Yes, fuck me, master," she breathed up at him. "Fuck me."

"I'm fucking you so deeply, vixen, so deeply." His voice was a dark, hungry purr.

She met each thrust. "So big, so wonderful. Possessing me."

He growled, thrusting into her even harder, and she loved knowing her words had fueled him.

At the foot of the bed, Shaena's groans turned to hot whimpers, and from the corner of her eye, Teesia could see that Laene had reached one hand around to stroke her clit. Within seconds, Shaena was crying out, "I'm coming! I'm coming!" just before Laene let out a low groan that told Teesia he'd reached his ecstasy, too.

Above her, Ralen's mighty plunges continued, and she reached up to kiss his neck, his muscular shoulder, whatever parts of him she could reach. He brought his mouth down on hers, hard, and she tasted her own cunt—tangy, salty, like the sea. "I want to make you come," she murmured against his lips.

And oh, the supreme joy that filled her when she learned that was all it took—her words, her desire—to make him spill his hot semen inside her. His groans were deep and long, to match the thrusts that nailed her to the bed. They were so ferocious they almost hurt—but as she'd learned, experiencing a bit of pain for her man had a scrumptious way of heightening her pleasure, so her cries were ones of pure delight as he drove his last inside her, then sank heavy and warm atop her in the bed.

Chapter Seven

හ

That night they slept together in Ralen's bed, Teesia wrapped snugly in his strong arms. It was as simple as him crawling in and pulling her beneath the thin fur covering after Shaena and Laene departed, hand in hand.

They did not speak, merely fell asleep together—although sleep gave way to sex several times through the night. It was a sweet passage of time during which sleeping and fucking and touching all blended together into one great comfort.

Teesia awoke the next morning, amazed to open her eyes and see the two of them side by side in the viewing glass above the bed, the fur pulled to their waists. The sight of the rings on her nipples and the bejeweled cuffs still at her wrists were reminders that she remained his sex slave, but she thought she could be a very *happy* sex slave like this, in his bed, in his arms, unchained. After all, she'd already become content with the idea of her sensual enslavement, so mixing that with the freedom to sleep unbound and with *him* only made it all the sweeter.

Upon falling back asleep and awakening again some time later, she grew disheartened to find him gone from the bed—and the room. It had been too much to hope, she supposed, that he was going to stay with her, like a real husband to a real wife, and not leave her abandoned and alone.

She lay fretting over it, but trying not to, when the chamber's door opened to admit him. He carried a tray of food, and what appeared to be apparel lay draped over one arm. "Help me, vixen," he said, looking surprisingly merry, "before I drop something."

She scurried naked from the bed to take the tray from his hands, amazed at his demeanor. She'd suspected—feared—that the softer nature she'd witnessed in him last night would fade with the morning, given that Shaena and Laene seemed to bring it out in him and they were no longer present. But when her foot snagged in the pile of gold disks discarded to the floor at some point during the night and she nearly tripped, she caught herself and laughed—and looked up to find her husband chuckling along with her.

"Sit," he said, motioning to a chair next to the small table where she lowered the tray. She obeyed, eager as ever to please him.

His usual wicked grin held an air of playfulness. "If I let you eat by your own hand this day, you will not forget who is your master, will you?"

"No, master, of course not." And it was true. She liked being fed by him and felt a bit stunned that she was suddenly to feed herself.

"Not that I wouldn't enjoy doing it myself, wanton, for I love to watch your mouth when it wraps around a spoon, or a slice of bread—or my cock," he stopped to flash another brazen smile that warmed her pussy, "but I have business to attend to. After you eat, you may dress." He pointed to the clothing he'd placed on the bed.

She couldn't have been more surprised. "Dress?" She hadn't been dressed since their wedding.

He nodded shortly. "I thought you might enjoy a walk outside, to see the grounds."

Her heartbeat sped up, even if cautiously. Despite her devotion to him, getting out of this room sounded like a gift from Ares. "If you wish it, I do, too."

"Keep the bracelets on, though," he instructed.

She told him the truth she was just now admitting to herself. "I never want to take them off, for they allow me to somehow feel you against me even when you're not there."

His eyes lit with a dark fire. "Does the tail do that, as well, my wanton?"

"Yes. Very much."

He smiled in earnest. "I should have put it back in before we slept last night, but I forgot. And I would do it now, but it wouldn't work beneath your skirt. Later, though, you shall get to wear it for me again."

The fissure of her ass spasmed at the promise, and she realized how much she missed the fullness there.

"Ready yourself to go out and I shall be back soon."

* * * * *

When Shaena breezed into the chamber a little while later, you'd never have known that just the previous night the two women had kissed and touched and rubbed their breasts together. Dressed in a pale leather frock, the maid wore the same smile as always as she carried in items to decorate Teesia's hair.

Teesia laughed, though, when she saw the sprigs of summer flowers in Shaena's hand, saying, "Look at how simply I'm dressed." She wore the clothes Ralen had brought to her, a short brown leather skirt and a thin fur vest of chestnut and cream that hugged her breasts and below. "No need for flowers in my hair."

But Shaena only grinned. "There is *always* need for flowers, in my opinion. They brighten everything around us."

True enough, Teesia thought. In a world where most things were the dull brown of ground and gray of stone, color indeed turned the air more vibrant. She'd never taken for granted the fact that she was born into enough wealth to provide her with dyes for her silk gowns and even for some of her leather garments, as well.

She took a seat at the table where she and Ralen often ate, facing Shaena while the maid worked on her hair, smoothing it with a brush and twining some of the tiny yellow-gold flowers through her long, ebony locks. "Besides," Shaena added, "your bracelets and ankle cuffs are certainly not simple, and the flowers rather match the amber stone."

It reminded her, once more, that Ralen was wealthy, too. Flowers and sunsets were among the only color that came freely in Caralon—in their world, most such vibrant hues had to be bought. Shaena's words also drew her thoughts back to the cuffs themselves. She'd actually forgotten she was wearing them—they seemed like such a natural part of her now.

"You seemed well-pleasured last night," Shaena said kindly.

At this point, Teesia had thought the maid wouldn't mention the previous evening, but she didn't mind. "Very much. And you were right, Shaena. I feared being Ralen's slave, but turns out that now I relish it." She tilted her head, thinking. "Although I cannot deny how thrilled I am that he is taking me from this room today. I'd begun to think I might never leave, and a more normal life would be welcome."

Shaena smiled into her eyes. "He is gruff, but I saw real affection for you in him last night, Teesia. I sense things changing for you."

Teesia nodded. "I do, too." The thought warmed her heart.

Soon after Shaena departed, Ralen returned. "Shall we go?" he said, his voice echoing good cheer as he took her hand. Just that simple touch, paired with the tenderness in his eyes, nearly turned her inside out. It was just as Shaena had said— things seemed different between them now.

Stepping out into the bright Caralon sunshine was like swallowing a warm drink of wine that oozed all through Teesia, body and soul. She turned her face up to the blue sky to soak in the comforting rays.

"A beautiful day," Ralen commented, clearly seeing her enjoyment.

"Indeed." She raised her gaze to her husband, whose dark hair shone like silk in the sunlight. "Thank you. For bringing me outside. It feels wonderful."

If she wasn't mistaken, a hint of guilt flashed through his expression—something she'd never thought to see in Ralen. "I'm glad to share a walk with you, Teesia." He squeezed her hand tighter in his large one. "I thought you might like to visit my stables."

"Oh yes," she said, her spirits lifting even higher. "Nothing would make me happier."

The walk to the stables from the main fortress was a short one, and Teesia enjoyed seeing the elaborate stone exterior of her new home. The coast was visible in the near distance over ancient battlements that still existed from the Before Times. "I miss the sea," she murmured without forethought as she drank in the scent of an ocean breeze.

"I shall take you there," he promised. "Would you like that?"

She smiled up at him, nodding. "Very much, master."

As usual, the endearment filled his expression with the dark heat she'd learned to love so dearly.

Nearing the stables, they approached a small corral where a number of frisky horses frolicked. Teesia was immediately drawn to a lovely little sorrel with a white star on her forehead who came directly to the fencing when they grew close, allowing Teesia to feed her a palmful of grass. She stroked the animal's neck and cooed to her, "What a pretty, friendly girl you are."

It warmed Ralen's heart unexpectedly to see how taken Teesia was with the horse, the very horse he'd thought of for her. "If you'd like her," he said, "she's yours."

His bride's eyes lit with a pure joy that trickled all through him. Ares, but she was captivating. In her sexuality. And in her purity, as well.

Was she pure? he wondered, shocked by his own thought. Had she been as pure upon coming to him as she claimed? He'd asked himself the question less and less lately, and when he did ask it, he realized he'd slowly begun to believe in her. Deeply.

"What's her name?" Teesia asked, scratching the sorrel's nose.

Ralen couldn't resist grinning down at her. "Vixen."

Her pretty, trilling laughter filled the air around him and he bent to kiss her as automatically as if they'd been married for fifty years. The mere meeting of their mouths stirred him to excitement, making his cock twitch between his thighs. There was something oddly...*freeing* about being out in the warm sun with her, kissing her while fresh air and the salty scent of the sea surrounded them.

When the kiss ended, she gave her chin a saucy tilt. "What's *your* horse's name? *Master?*"

He chuckled. She *was* a little vixen, in more ways than one. "No—actually it's the very uninspired Charger. That's him there," he said, pointing to the shiny black stallion that trotted on the far side of the fenced area.

She cast a coquettish grin. "Perhaps we could nickname your *cock* Charger. It does charge into me so..."

Growing harder, just from that—his wanton making a dirty joke—he leaned in to her hip to let her feel the evidence of his arousal. "That it does," he purred near her ear. "And do you love it, my little vixen?"

She awarded him with another tantalizing grin, her blue eyes filled with the heat he adored. "You know I do, master," she said softly. Then she looked back to the corral. Vixen had sauntered away and now shared a trough of grain with Charger nearby. "They make nearly as handsome a couple as you and I."

"Perhaps I shall consider breeding the two next year when Vixen is of the right age," he said, the thought just occurring to him. "See what sort of lovely little colt they produce together."

She bit her lip, peering up at him. "I have no doubt their offspring would be very fine."

And quick as that, he found himself bending to give her yet another kiss—this one slight, only on the forehead—but it happened without his quite deciding to do it, which took him aback.

"Shall we go for a ride together?" he asked to cover his unease. "We could take the horses up the beach if you'd like."

Again, her eyes lit and it was like the first burst of sunlight beaming over the horizon at dawn. "Yes, that sounds wonderful!"

Ralen instructed one of his stablemen to bring the two mounts out, and soon he and Teesia were riding up the coastline, the horses' hooves leaving two soft trails in the sand. "You ride well," he said, taking note of the way her body swayed comfortably with the horse's movements, and also remembering the fearless way she'd climbed up on the mounting block outside the corral.

"I've not ridden *much*," she admitted, glancing over at him. "The horses my father owns are used primarily by he and his men, but I've relished the opportunities I've had, often begging my father to give me lessons when he's had the time. I'm very fond of horses."

"As am I," he agreed with a smile, thinking how fortuitous it was that he should end up with a wife who possessed that particular affinity. Horses were so rare in most parts of Caralon that many viewed them as animals best left in the hands of warriors. Few realized how gentle horses could be, and Ralen had always appreciated the animals' ability to be both docile and strong.

Without quite making the conscious decision to do so, Ralen found himself sharing with Teesia his vision for breeding enough horses to supply his entire army with them, and others to sell. "I wouldn't want to let them get into the hands of our enemies to the north, of course, but your father, or men like Dane of Rawley, could strengthen their forces mightily."

"Is it possible to breed that many horses? I mean, they *are* rare."

"It takes care to breed them, certainly," he explained. "But I believe that in the Before Times there were possibly a great many more horses than we might expect. By working to breed them in a controlled atmosphere, I believe I can produce a bounty of strong, healthy animals. It may sound unlikely, but I don't believe anyone has ever tried before, at least not in *our* age—and that *this* is why they remain rare. I intend to prove it can be done, and to make the horse a powerful force in keeping Caralon intact always."

His wife's admiring expression filled him with unexpected pride. He didn't need her veneration to hold up his sense of dignity, and yet...he simply *liked* it. Liked knowing she might think he was intelligent, industrious...strong...brave.

"Can you gallop?" he asked, feeling the urge to take Charger racing up the beach with Teesia at his side.

She smiled. "Yes, I'm not afraid."

He gave her a playful look. "Never for long anyway," he said, thinking of their sex.

Her answering smile seemed to say she understood where his thoughts had gone. "Race you," she challenged, then put heels to Vixen's side as she slapped the reins against the sorrel's neck.

He could have easily overtaken her at any time, but for some reason did not—he simply came up even with her and enjoyed the wind in his hair and his wife's presence as they sped up the beach, side by side.

It was only when they'd slowed the horses back to a gentle trot that he saw the coquettish way his wanton bit her lip as she stole a glance at him. He couldn't help thinking it meant she was hungry for him, which set his skin prickling with fresh lust. "What are you thinking about, vixen?" he asked, his voice going slightly deeper.

"That I forgot what happens whenever I ride at a gallop."

He tilted his head, puzzled. "What's that?"

She might be young, but when her blue eyes met his, she wore the determined expression of a full-fledged woman. "My pussy begins to tingle."

He grinned as his cock stiffened in response. "This happens often, does it?"

"Well, I've not had the chance to ride at a gallop *often*, but on the occasions I have…"

"And what did you do about it?" It was not an accusation—he simply wondered what she would say.

She softly shook her head. "Nothing. I suffered. And wished."

"And later touched yourself when you were alone?" he offered softly.

Looking halfway between sheepish and aroused, she nodded. "Once, last summer, the need was so great that I simply snuck off to a corner of my father's stables."

"And now?"

"The need is great again, my husband. My master." Her voice grew warmer with each word. "My pussy is so swollen, wet. It aches for you."

"Show me," he said as they continued riding side by side up the quiet, empty beach, the only other sound that of the rolling tide. "Lift your skirt."

Closing her hand around the leather that already rode high on her thigh, she raised it until he could see her cunt, pressed against the horse's spine. As if anticipating his next command, she leaned back to give him a much better view, and indeed, her lovely flesh was parted, the inner pink folds glistening for him. His cock went so hard he feared it would burst the lacings on his pants.

"Do not fear, my wanton," he told her, casting his most devilish smile. "I shall take care of that hungry little ache on the ride back to the fort."

Being her master was a powerful and fulfilling indulgence, but mutual lust was good, too, and the look they exchanged indicated they both wanted the same thing—badly. Ralen instructed Teesia to join him on Charger's back, and once she was straddling the horse between his thighs, he tied Vixen's reins to his, so the pretty sorrel would follow along.

"Lean," he told her as Charger walked slowly up the coastline, heading toward home. He smoothed his hands up her thighs, under her skirt, and onto her ass, urging her forward. She arched her body against the horse's mane, locking her feet around Ralen's leather-clad calves until the enticing inner flesh of her cunt was visible to him.

Something inside him shuddered at the sight. This part of her body was certainly not new to him, so his reaction struck him as odd—but perhaps it was the *giving*, the way she so freely *wanted*, the notion that this particular liaison had been of her instigation. That had never happened before. He'd never given it a *chance* to happen.

"So lovely," he murmured without forethought. He meant her pussy, but also all of her. Every hair on her head, every inch of her flesh. The way her fingers curled into the shiny black fur on Charger's neck. The soft, pretty sigh that met his words.

"You *do* like the way I look there," she purred, reminding him of their conversation about his cunt obsession just last night with Shaena and Laene.

"I like the way you look *everywhere*, wanton," he assured her, "but yes, I do like the way you look *there*."

With one hand, he began to loosen the lacings that would free his hungry cock and with the other he began to touch her.

183

Two fingers slipped easily into her wet, warm passage, making her let out a deep, heated moan. He relished watching her pussy clench around them, her widened asshole spreading slightly as she moved against him.

As soon as his shaft sprang free, he replaced his fingers with it, sliding it slow, smooth, deep into his vixen's welcoming cunt. They both groaned at the connection and he found a pleasing rhythm that matched the horse's gait. He looked down between them, watching the eager way her body took him, all of him, every hard inch, and longed to fuck her even deeper.

That was impossible, but he *could* fuck her *more*, in another way. Very easily. He slid two fingers into the open fissure of her ass and she cried out, "Oh master, yes!"

"Like that, do you?"

"So much." Her voice was a mere breath on the wind. "I even…"

"What, vixen? You what?"

"I even miss my tail."

He felt the words deep in his gut as he continued the slow, firm fuck in both openings. "Miss being my filly, do you?" he said, more gratified than he could have imagined.

"Yes," she admitted. "I miss the way you watch me when I walk about the room wearing it. I miss the hot look in your eyes. When you look at me that way, the tail feels better and better, making me want to be filled there even fuller."

Her words sizzled through his blood and for a moment, he feared he would come. But he hissed in a deep breath and got hold of himself, even as he slid his fingers deeply in her anus, even as he resumed the slow drive of his cock. He leaned near to whisper low in her ear. "We shall remedy that, vixen, for your ass is well stretched now, stretched enough for me to fuck you there."

She looked over her shoulder, clearly stunned. "With your cock? You can fuck me there with your cock?"

He couldn't help kissing her, bringing his mouth down hard on hers before moving it back to her delicate ear. "Yes, wanton, with my cock. That's what we've been working toward, stretching your ass, opening it for me. My cock will stretch it even farther, but you can take it now."

Her eyes shone with heated wonder. "I would love that, master."

"Then you shall love it *now*," he whispered and, withdrawing both fingers and shaft from her, he repositioned slightly until the tip of his rod poked at her ass. Already, her breath trembled with anticipation, so he didn't hesitate — taking his wet cock in hand, he pushed and guided it until he sank partway in.

"Oh Ares!" she cried, her eyes falling shut before him.

"Does it feel good?" Although he'd succeeded in teaching her that sometimes pain was an aid to sex, on this particular occasion, he wanted to bring her nothing but pleasure. Intense, overwhelming pleasure.

Her answer was little more than a moan, but her nod told him what he needed to know, and also urged him deeper into her, feeling the tight, tight walls of her anal passage hug him as it accepted his entry.

Ares, so tight, so snug — he could climax in a heartbeat if he desired. But he *didn't* desire it — he wanted to fuck her, wanted to make her feel it deep, make her scream, deliver her to an ecstasy so profound that she lost herself in it.

More than half of his length in her now, he drew back slightly, aroused by the warm slide of cock against flesh, that welcoming, embracing flesh. When he drove firmly back in, she cried out once more, her body prone against the horse now, arms wrapping about its thick withers, head pressed fully into the mane.

He drove again — slick, warm, tight — and she screamed with a joy he felt shuddering through her body.

No more going slow, for he knew they both needed it faster now, harder. His vixen's ass was ready for him, ready for what he wanted to give her, so he began to fuck her in earnest, both of them moaning at each plunge into that once-tiny opening that now took his giant cock so amazingly well.

Charger's gait increased—he didn't trot, but moved faster, driven by *their* moves. As Ralen wished, she was lost in it—he could see it in her face, hear it in her cries—and Ares help him, he was lost, too. Pleasure saturated him from head to toe, and thank Ares the horse knew his way, for Ralen had long since forgotten to guide him. His hands curled around to massage her breasts through the thin fur that covered them as she lifted her ass to meet each thrust until she was moving faster, faster—and he realized only a second before she screamed that she was on the verge of coming from rubbing her pussy against Charger's back.

The spasms moved through her body like an earthquake he could feel rumbling against his thighs, hands, shaft. "Ah, Vixen, you're making me come, too!" he yelled, then let it go, his hot semen emptying deep inside her perfect ass as the depth of pleasure forced his eyes shut, shook his body just as it had shaken hers, left him weak and replete with it in a way he'd never been before.

He lay warm against her back for a long moment after the tremors had passed, then finally leaned to whisper playfully in her ear, "I think Charger made you come."

She turned to look in time for him to catch her blush. "No, master, believe me when I say it was all you."

* * * * *

That night, back in their chamber, Teesia paraded about the room, her tail swaying proudly behind her, swishing against her ass.

Ralen lay on the bed on his side, propped on one elbow, watching. Both were naked and his cock stood at full attention, drawing Teesia's eyes. She wanted him like never before.

Today, on the horse, their sex had been...something new, something so powerful she couldn't have imagined it had she not experienced it. She'd known she loved her big brute of a husband before today, but she'd never felt such love *coming back* to her as she had when they'd climbed onto Charger together.

Now, the culmination of love and want and raw, feral lust roared through her, somehow only strengthened by what they'd shared on the beach, like a storm that gains power the more it swirls.

"Bend over," he told her when her back faced him, and she did so. "Now wiggle your ass."

It was a game they played and it excited her as much as it pleased him. She shimmied her bottom just as he'd asked.

"Very good. Now raise back up—slowly."

She rose and turned to face him, sensually running her hands over her body, feeling her own soft curves, tweaking her stiff nipples. He smiled darkly in response. "Very nice, wanton. Pinch them again."

She pinched and twirled for him, letting the sensation melt through her flesh and down between her thighs.

"Is your pussy wet?"

She nodded. "Yes, master. Very. I'm afraid my juices will roll down my thighs soon."

He chuckled lustfully. "Now *that* I would like to see." Then he met her gaze. "Drag your middle finger up through your cunt, then come and let me suck it dry."

Another blaze of hunger burned through her as she stroked herself while he watched, then padded to the bed. He reached for her hand and she suffered a new, brutal rush of heat as his warm, wet mouth closed around her dampened finger.

It was then that a knock came on the door, and Teesia flinched. No one *ever* knocked on their door, let alone late at night. Her first thought was that something must be wrong, Ralen must be needed for something important—but his expression never wavered as he said, "Answer the door, slave."

She blinked, then glanced down at her nudity. "Like this?"

He nodded, delivering his usual wicked grin. "Yes. Like that."

Teesia didn't know what to think, her skin prickling with nervousness as she walked slowly to the door. She pulled in her breath warily—until she saw Laene on the other side.

His eyes glittered with lust. "You look as tantalizing as ever, Lady Teesia."

Given her high degree of arousal, his hungry gaze only added to it, making her nipples seem to pucker tighter, her cunt seem to weep still more freely.

As Laene stepped in and closed the door, then started to unlace his brown leather pants, Teesia began to understand, but she still looked to Ralen for confirmation.

"I have one last longing to fulfill with you, vixen," he said.

"And it is?"

He smiled, dark and determined. "I want to see you take two cocks. I want to see you with every lovely opening on your body...filled."

Chapter Eight

ஒ

The suggestion at once thrilled and frightened Teesia. She should not be afraid, she knew—for Ralen had never brought her anything but pleasure, even when it came with a bit of pain—and yet, the notion took her aback. Both Ralen's cock and Laene's? Ralen's was so powerful that sometimes it seemed amazing to her that she could take his alone.

"Come to me, vixen," he said, looking as if he saw her mixed emotions. "Lie down with me."

She went to the bed as instructed, joining Ralen there, letting his big, masculine body curve around hers. His breath warmed her ear as he spoke low and potent. "Do not fear it. You shall relish it."

When he drew back, locking his dark gaze on hers, she asked the question that burned in her mind. "Is that a command?"

"It's a promise." With that, he kissed her, one large hand closing possessively over her breast, the other snaking around her waist to wrench her to him so that his shaft nestled hard against her clit, stretching prominently upward between them.

"Oh Ares, I crave your cock," she purred without planning, then opened her eyes to find his twinkling with pleasure. Their faces were not an inch apart. "But another?" she whispered, lips trembling. She didn't want to hurt Laene's feelings—the memory of his touches and kisses still burned hot in her mind—yet her trepidation stayed in place.

"Yes, vixen, another." Her husband's voice came as warm and dark as the chocolate he'd given her days ago. "Trust me."

Her husband was asking for her trust. Seeking her faith. Not simply ordering her to do something.

Perhaps it *was* still an order and she was hearing it wrongly, or perhaps she read too much into his voice, but she couldn't help feeling that he wanted her to enter into this freely, believing in him to bring her only pleasure.

And so she did, for how could she not?

With the simple decision, everything inside Teesia seemed to open—her mind, her body—and all worries dissipated. "Oh Ralen, I do. I trust you."

His small, warm smile was her reward.

And it was only after Ralen resumed his hot, deep kisses, only after she was so consumed by them that she'd nearly forgotten what was to happen...that she felt new hands, touching her from behind. Laene's hands.

One caressed her bare hip and slid smoothly up her side as the other warmly began to massage her shoulder, then her neck. As Ralen pulled her leg up, urging her knee over his waist, he reached to stroke the round flesh of her ass as Laene's palm moved around to cup her breast, the nipple fitting neatly between his first two fingers.

When Ralen's fingertips dipped down into her pussy from behind, she moaned at the raw pleasure. And when Laene's kiss pressed soft on her shoulder, his cock coming to rest in the crevice of her ass, jutting up into the root of her tail, she knew, that quickly, that she was lost to the overpowering delights the two men would deliver. So she gave herself into it, body and soul. No more thoughts—only actions, only sensation.

Instinct led her to kiss her way down her husband's broad chest and stomach until she was able to flick the tip of her tongue over his majestic cock. She smiled up at Ralen, and when Laene's hands came into her hair, holding the tresses back so they could both watch her, she shifted her gaze to him, utterly unafraid now. Already, as Ralen had promised, relishing it.

She took her husband's shaft full in her mouth, as deeply as her throat would allow. She wanted to fuck him that way as well as she could, and delighted in the groans he issued from above. "Yes, sweet vixen," he said darkly, "suck your master's cock."

She worked vigorously, looking up at both men from time to time, making sure they watched her, for she wanted their eyes on her, wanted them to see how much joy she took in her task. She'd grown more skilled with sucking him in the past days and hoped he could feel that as well as see it.

The awareness of Laene's shaft, jutting into her shoulder as she slid her lips up and down Ralen's length, filled her with an unexpected longing that took over much quicker than she could have imagined. So, after smiling up at her husband, she turned in the bed to face her other companion and didn't hesitate to lick a long, wet path from the base of Laene's rod to the tip.

As Laene moaned deeply, Ralen murmured, "Ares, vixen, you are lovely." Now her husband's hands sank into her hair, pulling it back, massaging her scalp, a sensation that added shockingly to her arousal.

She took Laene's warm cock in hand, gently licking the tip, taking the bit of wetness gathered there onto her tongue. She sought Ralen's gaze, her desire blazing, until he said, "Yes, Teesia, suck him, too."

The command from her husband drove her mouth down around the other man's rod. Pleasantly large without being nearly as sizable as Ralen's, it was a much easier fit in her mouth. But she didn't attempt to take as much as she could, somehow wanting to save such efforts for her master. Laene she sucked easily, delighting even further when Ralen moved down in the bed with her, curling in close behind her, kissing her neck, shoulder, caressing her breasts and nudging his cock at her cunt from the back.

She arched her ass to welcome him and he slid into her warmth beneath the tail, a full, tight fit that made her groan around Laene's shaft.

Ralen began to move in her, strokes that matched the ones she delivered with her mouth, and then his voice came hot in her ear. "Just as I desired for you, my lovely wanton, all your holes are filled."

Oh Ares, were they! Ralen's cock moved deep in her pussy, and inside her it pushed up next to the toy that connected to her tail. Laene's cock, sliding into her mouth, completed it, making her feel more well and fully fucked than she'd known a woman could.

"Let's rise to our knees," Ralen breathed in instruction and they all shifted until she was on her hands and knees between them, Laene kneeling before her, Ralen behind. He could fuck her deeper that way, she realized, and she experienced the faint wish to see the leather strands of her tail falling around his cock, where it entered her just beneath.

As Ralen's thrusts grew harder, so did Laene's, between her lips. As the men's groans buffeted her from each end, she moaned around Laene's cock, lost in the pure pleasure of being fucked.

But she wanted more somehow — and yet, how *could* there be more?

"Fuck my ass," she pulled away from Laene to plead over her shoulder to her husband. "Please fuck my ass. I want to feel you there."

A low growl rumbled from him as his fingertips dug slightly into the sensitive flesh of her bottom. "No, vixen."

"No?" For some reason, just now, she'd not expected his refusal.

"That's mine alone, for later, when we're by ourselves. This, now, is about filling you until you forget everything else but being filled."

She almost told him she *had* forgotten everything else, but she supposed if she was still begging, she hadn't been *totally* swept away by it all.

"Right now I want to fuck your warm, wet pussy," he said, plunging into her, "while I watch Laene fuck your eager, pretty mouth, and while I know your filly's tail fucks you just as deeply. I want you to feel *everything*."

Just then, his hand dipped past her hip and underneath, his fingers catching around her clit and—oh! That, she realized, was the one more thing she needed so badly, the one other way she could be fucked. And as her husband rubbed her there, as she was fucked from the front and behind, the top and the bottom, fucked in every way she could conceive of, she got truly lost in it, deeply overwhelmed. Her world was, as Ralen had desired, about being filled. Stroked. Caressed. And now Laene even bent to massage her dangling breasts.

She moved against the two men's cocks and hands, met everything they delivered, hungered for more. She closed her eyes, gave her body over to it in a whole new sort of surrender, and felt almost as if she were somewhere entirely new, being lifted to a higher plane. Maybe this was heaven. Ares knew it was the closest she'd ever come on earth.

And as Ralen's hot fingers continued to stroke, stroke, in time with each driving thrust from the two cocks that entered her, she fell. She could have sworn her body physically toppled as she released Laene's cock in time to scream the pleasure that pounded through her in great, engulfing waves of heat.

She collapsed to the bed, no longer able to support herself on her weakened arms and legs, but Ralen stayed with her, still inside her, still thrusting, each hot stroke seeming to stretch her orgasm a little longer.

Without speaking, they rolled to their sides, back to their earlier position, and Teesia reached again for Laene's shaft, pulling it back toward her lips. But soon her mouth grew too tired to continue, her body finally beginning to wear out from so much vigorous sex, so she urged him down, nestling the wet rod between her breasts, which she squeezed around him. Both men moaned at the sight and Laene began to slide between. One more way to be fucked.

Sated and exhausted, she still reaped grand pleasure from the two cocks, now crying out louder with each lovely assaulting thrust from both.

Soon, though, Laene's moans overpowered hers, until he pulled back and shot warmly onto her breasts, jagged spurts of hot white fluid that both men immediately began to rub into her. Into the two mounds, caressing, massaging, and into the soft skin of her belly below—and she shut her eyes at the warm pleasure, until she realized Ralen was close to exploding, too.

"Ah, Ares, *now*," he said. "I'm coming for you, my vixen, coming so deep inside you." His breath was ragged as he drove into her, four last brutal thrusts that she accepted with raw delight.

As Ralen slowly withdrew a moment later, she became vaguely aware that he was removing her tail, as well, but she was too exhausted to comment or care. As her eyes began to drift shut, Laene's hands cupped her face and he bent to deliver a gentle kiss to her lips. "Your mouth took me to heaven, lady," he said with a soft, appreciative smile.

She managed a grin back at him, then looked around to find her husband behind her. "You *both* took *me* to heaven. I could have sworn I saw Ares Himself."

She knew nothing more then but the sweet sensation of seeming to sink deeper into the bed as her eyes fell shut and her master's strong arms closed around her from behind.

* * * * *

Later, after a long, luxurious nap, Ralen brought her sweet bread and chocolate and they ate in bed by candlelight. Once the food was gone, they settled into each other's arms, but the candles stayed lit and Teesia found herself peering up at the two of them in the viewing glass above the bed.

"Will you tell me about Laene?"

Her husband leaned in from behind to kiss her neck, his arms circling warm beneath her breasts. The fur coverlet was pulled to their waists. "What would you like to know about him?"

"Is he your friend? Or does he work here at the fortress?"

"Like Shaena, both. Although he was my employee before he became my friend. He hails from inland, the mountain country, and came south to seek a spot in my father's army when he was but sixteen years old. My father doubted a boy so young could be an asset, but the man had no foresight. He was a...well, a narrow-minded, very flawed man." Teesia saw something dark and faraway in his eyes as he spoke of his father, and she remembered what she'd learned about their relationship from Shaena. "I saw immediately that Laene was smart and loyal, and that he could be a leader someday. Over time, we became close, and now he keeps my estate well-run and is my most trusted advisor when it comes to matters of fortification and security."

"And when it comes to sharing your wife," she said, giving him a soft smile over her shoulder.

He grinned. "To be clear, that was not for his benefit—it was for yours. And, I will admit, mine, as well."

"I know. And it was...*exquisite*. Beyond anything I'd ever imagined I could feel."

"As I intended it to be."

She met his gaze and bit her lip. "May I ask you something else?"

"Anything."

She coquettishly lowered her chin, feeling oddly sheepish. "The Rituals of Passion—what you mentioned happens after the Maran Tiles—will you tell me what would have taken place?"

Her husband imparted a small smile. "You truly do not know?"

She shook her head.

"Well, it's interesting you should ask just now, for maybe tonight was partly about that, partly about my fearing I deprived you of something you should have experienced." Ralen went on to explain that the tiles left after the Maran game ended would have indicated a particular number of men, and certain stimulating acts they would have performed on her, all in order to ready her for her husband's bed.

"Ah," she said, surprised, but not shocked. Bella's praise of the rituals had mentally prepared her something so extreme, she supposed.

"Are you sorry?" he asked. "That you did not get to experience it? You may be honest—I won't be angry."

Teesia considered her answer, then gazed lovingly at her husband. "No," she said. "For what I have experienced at your hands has been...all the education or stimulation I could ever need. And I can't imagine feeling the same connection with you if anything had happened differently."

He grinned darkly. "Tonight, with Laene, did that add to the connection, too?"

She returned the smile. "You know it did. But now..." she said, looking into his dark eyes.

"You need not continue, vixen. I know what you want. And I'm hard just knowing how much you want it."

Responding with only a heated smile of anticipation, she turned away from him and arched her ass toward him in the bed. Like a moth drawn to a flame, his cock met instantly with the hungry fissure of her anus and the tip slipped easily inside.

She groaned, and he whispered, "Your ass is so ready for me now, wanton, so welcoming. You have no idea what that does to me."

"Tell me." She wanted — *needed* — to know. For though she knew he desired her, he'd never really told her so in any sort of open, forthright way. She longed to hear it.

He pushed his shaft a little deeper, leaving them both to moan at the intense intimacy. His voice sounded strained. "It sets me on fire, from the inside out. And it reminds me…that I own you."

She closed her eyes, overcome with heat. "Oh yes, my master, you own me."

"Now you. Tell me how it feels, Teesia." He pushed deeper, melding their bodies tighter within the snug confines of her ass.

"It feels," she said, barely able to speak, "as if you are…intruding. As if you are someplace you should not be. Except…how can I explain this? It's a most *delicious* intrusion, so amazing to me that you *can* be there, *are* there, fucking me in a spot I didn't know I could be fucked. It feels…forbidden. But also perfect. This completes it all somehow — I truly could not feel more connected to you, Ralen."

"I could come merely from your words, vixen," he rasped, leaning in to kiss her neck, cup her breast.

"No," she begged. "Please fuck me first. Make me feel you — more. Move in me."

A week ago he would have punished her for the protest, the command, but now he only growled his heat and began to move his thick, hard cock in and out of the tight little passage. She met each impossibly delectable thrust, still awash in wonder that he was inside her there, where he couldn't possibly be, where he couldn't possibly fit — and yet, where he belonged.

They both cried out at the intensity of the sensations and Ralen reached over her hip to press his fingers into her slick cunt. Teesia's pleasure quadrupled, became mindless, boundless — like before, with both men, but somehow easier now, for all she had to do was lie there and receive it, take it into her, let it consume her.

When she came, it echoed through her whole being, her body jolting uncontrollably, and it seemed to take Ralen to the same place, as well. "I can't hold back," he growled.

"On me, not in me," she begged.

And as he swiftly pulled out of her, she rolled to her back, watching—until his semen arced across her belly and breasts in three mighty bursts of white.

Together, they massaged it into her skin, as she murmured, "Yes, rub it into me, make it a part of me, something I can keep, take inside me." The warmth was like a sheath of wetness, something she could wear.

Settling next to her a moment later, he nuzzled close and spoke slowly. "You do get to keep me, vixen, you know."

Stunned at the thoughts suddenly pummeling her, even as she basked in the afterglow of heated sex, she looked up into his eyes. "Do I?"

"What do you mean?" His brows knit.

She shook her head uncertainly, trying to think how to explain. *Be honest. Just tell him how you feel.* She could do that now, without worry. "Somehow, deep inside me, I suppose I feared that…well, the ultimate punishment would be to make me your willing slave and then to…abandon me."

Ralen lay there, shocked by his wife's words. He'd never even thought about… But then, certainly, there'd been a time when such a plan might have sounded like wonderful retribution to him if he *had* thought of it.

The notion took him back to the past, back to his old love, Banya, who'd taught him what true abandonment meant, and he found himself peering down into Teesia's gentle, worried eyes, wanting nothing more than to calm her fears. "No, vixen, I would not do that to you."

Even in dim candlelight, he saw the stark need within her gaze as she curled her fingers into his chest and said, "Really?"

He nodded. "You are mine...forever."

As his young wife clutched at him, he wanted only to keep her safe, wrapped within his arms, until the end of time. Ares, but he'd not expected this—this strength of emotion. Almost like...what he'd once felt for Banya. Such pure, strong need flowing through his veins—only different in that it came with a sureness, a contentment, a knowledge that she felt the same way and that nothing would ever part them. He lifted his thoughts heavenward and gave silent thanks to Ares for bringing this woman to him, and for making of their union so much more than he'd dreamed it could be.

That was his last thought before sleep took him—a good, deep sleep, his wife tucked warmly within his embrace—until the sun glancing through the window urged his eyes open. He gazed down on her sleeping form, so docile and sweet, so willing to please him.

He was sure now. Sure she had never given herself to another in any way. Sure she'd come to him pure of any touches other than his own.

As he ran his fingertips through her dark mane of hair, her blue eyes eased open, meeting with his. They exchanged a gentle smile that seemed to say their hearts were in the same place.

Amazing, he thought. He'd never expected his *heart* to be involved in this relationship. And even if he'd known it would be, he'd never imagined he would want to let her know it.

"What does the day hold?" she asked with a youthful exuberance he'd not seen much of in her before. He supposed he'd never given her the chance to show him such a side of her personality.

He grinned. "What do you desire for the day, my little vixen?"

Her smile held pure devotion. "Whatever *you* desire."

But he shook his head. He loved her sexual obedience and willingness to please him—he'd wanted that desperately and he'd gotten it—but he was just now realizing that he didn't want it to be a way of life for her outside of bed. He wanted the real Teesia. He wanted to *know* the real Teesia. "No, what do *you* wish, my wife?"

She gazed lovingly up at him. "You don't understand. I have no desires independent of you any longer. What you wish for me, I wish for myself. *Your* pleasure is *my* pleasure."

Her words were like thunder rolling through him. Ares, but the depths of her affection, and his possession, went deeper than he'd even understood until now. She was his true, willing slave. And he loved her for it. But he wanted to love her for other things, too. "I treasure your obedience in sex, Teesia," he explained, "but I wish to see other pieces of you, as well. Tell me. Tell me what else you wish other than to please me. Tell me what you wish purely for *yourself.*"

His wife rolled to her back, her delectable dark-tipped breasts settling slightly to either side as she peered upward, thinking. Finally, she turned to face him again, her expression brimming with sincerity. "If I had any wish," she said, "it's that *you* might somehow experience the true, deep, dark delights that I have, at your hand."

He laughed softly. He'd truly created a sexual monster in his little wife. "That's impossible, of course, vixen."

"Is it? Why?"

He blinked, then looked dotingly into her eyes. "I love you, Teesia, and I wish to make you happy in and out of the bedchamber—but in sex, my little vixen, only one can be the master."

* * * * *

Over the coming weeks, life grew a bit more normal for Teesia. Her clothing was finally brought into the bedchamber and unpacked into a large wooden cabinet Ralen had had commissioned from a carpenter in the nearby village. Each morning, she dressed and left the room, learned her way around the fortress, and got acquainted with the staff. For some meals, she and Ralen ate in the great hall, joined by guests — friends or workers in the fort. For others, they returned to their chamber and indulged in their shared joy of combining food and sex.

Ralen spent much time at work, dealing with Laene and others on estate matters, and sometimes in the stables, tending to his beloved horses and meeting with the breeders to discuss plans for the future and care of the mares and colts.

Teesia got into the habit of wandering out to the stables in the late afternoon, as the hottest part of the day waned, to find her husband and share a few kisses or fondles, and occasionally a horseback ride.

Only once did they venture far enough from the fortress that they could fuck on Charger's back again, but it was just as intense and scintillating as it had been the first time.

Nights with Ralen, too, continued to be more than Teesia could have dreamed. Sometimes he shackled her to the table, sometimes she wore her pussy chain and nipple rings, sometimes her tail. Other times she wore nothing but the jeweled cuffs that never left her wrists and ankles and the two of them rolled on the bed beneath the massive viewing glass above, Teesia shrieking and crying her pleasure as Ralen's massive cock pummeled her.

Whenever she wished to excite Ralen, in the bedchamber or out, she need only whisper to him, "Fuck me, master," to make his shaft go hard. No matter what he was busy with during those moments, he always found time to steal away to their chamber for a round of hot passion with his wife. And on one occasion, he pulled her into a tiny room within the confines of the stables, pushing her leather skirt up and fucking her from behind even as his stablehands labored just beyond the wooden door that hid them from view.

One evening as she and Ralen walked on the beach, hand in hand, at sunset, he told her that Shaena and Laene had become betrothed and that he planned to throw a grand wedding feast for his two dearest friends. Teesia was delighted at the news, but said, "I had no idea they were...well, I supposed I thought when they fucked in our chamber that it had been merely a bit of hot fun at your bidding."

Her husband gave a wicked grin at the memory, then stopped walking and wrapped around her from behind as they faced the ocean, the eastern horizon fading from purple to midnight blue. "The two have always been playfully affectionate, so I knew neither would mind indulging with us, yet Laene tells me something happened between them that night—that somehow what they shared with us made them realize they craved each other for life and wished to be bound in marriage."

The thought warmed Teesia's heart, even as her husband's cock grew stiff against the crack of her ass. "Just as I wish to be bound to you, Ralen," she said in a sexy purr.

"Mmm, vixen, I think I shall take you back to the fortress now, chain you to the table, and fuck you senseless," he whispered hotly in her ear as he slipped one hand inside the leather vest she wore, cupping her breast and stroking his thumb over her taut nipple. She shivered with delight. "Or would you prefer being my filly tonight? You could wear your tail and sit in my lap and ride my cock to ecstasy."

She couldn't resist thrusting her ass slightly toward his wonderfully firm shaft even now. "Remember, if I'm the filly," she teased, "*you're* supposed to take *me* for a ride."

He chuckled behind her, twirling her nipple between forefinger and thumb, but then his voice took on the slightly authoritative tone she'd come to cherish. "Perhaps, my little wanton, but let us not forget who is the master here."

"Perhaps I've been impertinent," she suggested playfully, rubbing her ass against him more intently. "Perhaps I should be punished."

Behind her, he released a low growl. "Mmm, as I was saying, perhaps I shall have to take you back to the bedchamber and bend you to my will."

She nearly purred her answer, succumbing to the naughty heat of it all. "Yes, master."

"Perhaps I shall make you suck my cock."

Her pussy spasmed and she licked her lips, wanting him in her mouth already. "Oh, yes, master. You should make me do that."

"Perhaps we shall break out the riding crop, hmm? It's been a while since we've played with that particular toy."

"Indeed it has. Certainly it would keep me in my place, don't you think?"

She smiled coquettishly over her shoulder to find him wearing the wicked grin she loved. "Come, my little slave. I've just grown very anxious to have my way with you."

* * * * *

That night, they indulged in all the forbidden pleasures that had brought them so close, and Teesia savored every second.

First, Ralen chained her to the table, giving her just enough length so that she could rise to her hands and knees when he demanded it. He inserted her tail into her hungry ass, then his cock into her equally eager cunt. He fucked her with brutal strokes that she felt all the way to the tips of her fingers and toes, made even more intense when he snapped the riding crop against her ass, thigh, hip.

"Let me suck your cock, master!" she demanded at one point, wild with a frantic desire that rushed through her uncontrolled—she wanted her man in every way possible and her mouth was as hungry for him as her pussy.

He struck her with the crop for issuing the command, the hot sting reverberating through her cunt, upward through her breasts, down through her ass and thighs. "Oh yes, punish me, master," she breathed, "for I've been very bad."

Soon, though, he unchained her from the table, and instructed her to prance around the room for him, being his little filly. She happily made a grand show of it, swaying her ass, jiggling her breasts, stopping to caress them while he watched.

She lustily kept her gaze on his cock, which jutted prominently from the nest of hair between his legs as he sat watching. He stroked it—the act becoming punishment in itself because *she* wanted to stroke it.

Clearly seeing her eye his rod, he cast a devilish look. "Do you wish to suck it, wanton?"

She started to say yes, to plead with him to let her—but then a better idea struck her. She attempted to look playfully demure as she softly replied, "No. No, I do not. You would have to...force me. It would be a horrible but fitting punishment for such a bad girl as I."

A slow, sure grin spread across her husband's face—he clearly liked her way of extending the game. But then his smile faded, his expression going stern, his eyes thrillingly dark. "Then force you I shall. On your knees, my dirty little wanton—*now*!"

Trying to look frightened, she obeyed, dropping down before him. She could barely wait to take his beautiful shaft between her lips, but she *had* to wait, until he made her do it.

She raised her gaze from his rod to his face, met his eyes. She might want to look demure, might wish to appear frightened, but in that moment, she knew the same heat swam in her gaze as in his—and it was a connection nearly as intense as sex itself. His hands wound in her hair, his grip tight, as he said, "Do it, vixen. Suck me," and pushed her head down.

She took him deep, his enormous cock gloriously filling her mouth, and he held her head, moving her lips up and down on him, and she cherished the sensation of his taking control, even of this. She wanted to suck him into oblivion, but she also loved his power — loved it to a fault, she thought.

And yet, was it a fault if she wasn't sorry for what she'd become? She was both sex slave and true lover to him, and she wouldn't have changed a thing.

"Yes, suck me, Teesia," he purred. "You suck me so good."

His hands stayed in her hair, but over time, his grip lessened, and the movements became her own. When she looked up, his dark gaze had turned softer, more wanting.

Odd, she thought, the slow switch in control, the gradual surrender he perhaps didn't even realize he'd made.

"I want to ride you now," she told him after releasing his wet shaft from her mouth, "just as you wished earlier."

His smile was warm, lusty. "Yes — my filly riding me."

Without hesitation, she climbed into his lap, straddling him, and sank onto his enormous cock with ease. They both moaned at the union, and as she moved on him in sensual circles that stimulated her clit with perfect precision, he suckled her breasts, caressed every inch of her he could reach — and soon they came together, collapsing in one another's arms.

Control, she thought. *So much of our sex is about control.* Being the master. Authority. And also surrender. It was all a decadent delight she wanted to bask in forever.

Before she drifted off into a deeply satiated sleep in Ralen's strong arms, she stared up in the dim lighting at their reflections in the viewing glass.

I want him to know more of what I feel. I want him to understand…

The purity of surrender.

Of submitting.

Of being within someone's power.

And I want to know more of that power. I want us both to know it all.

* * * * *

Over the coming days, Teesia couldn't break free of the desire to take their master-and-slave games even further, to explore the roles even more deeply. There were moments when she could barely comprehend the intensity of the pleasure that being his slave brought her, and she simply knew there had to be even more. She yearned for Ralen to know that same pleasure—she yearned to trade their roles, just for one night.

One afternoon as she sat in the bathing tub, she shared her wish with Shaena as the pretty maid ran a soapy sponge down the length of Teesia's thigh. Shaena frowned, instantly skeptical. "I don't think Ralen is made to be anyone's slave, Teesia—even yours."

Teesia sulked at her friend as the sponge swept over her uplifted calf and then ticklishly onto her toes. "Perhaps there are sides to him he doesn't know about. I want to find out."

Shaena still shook her head doubtfully—but soon enough, she agreed to help Teesia concoct a plan. "I am your maid, after all," she said on a sigh. "I suppose I must do as you wish."

Teesia responded with a smile. "Thank you," she replied, reaching to squeeze Shaena's hand.

"I just hope you know what you're doing."

"Don't worry—I do. And my pussy is throbbing just thinking about it."

Shaena let out a light laugh. "To tell you the truth, mine is, too." Yet then her grin faded. "But I'm still unsure about this, Teesia. The notion might excite you and me, but that doesn't mean it will excite Ralen."

"Trust me, Shaena," she said as she rose to her feet, water sluicing from her curves before she stepped into the drying cloth the other woman held out for her. "He will love it. He will love it more than he could ever imagine—just as I've loved submitting to him more than I could have known before it happened."

He'd loved everything else she'd done, hadn't he? And he seemed to love her sexually adventurous spirit, particularly enjoying when she turned the tables on him just slightly, teasing him or initiating new little twists in one of their sensual games lately.

He would love this, too—she knew it. And he would love *her*, more than ever, by the time it was done.

* * * * *

That night, Teesia put her plan into action with Shaena's reluctant help. At dinner in the great hall, Shaena served Ralen's wine laced with a special herb that would cause him to fall into a deep sleep only to awaken a short while later, refreshed. Once he drifted into slumber, Teesia would have an hour to prepare.

"Let us adjourn to our chamber, Ralen," she suggested quietly, squeezing his thigh beneath the table.

He smiled down at her, looking hungry despite the meal they'd just consumed. But even so, he reminded her, "We have guests, vixen."

For on this night of all nights, he'd invited guests to dinner without having mentioned it to her—some of the artisans from the village. He wished to commission a great mural on one wall of the very hall in which they gathered, and he'd invited them to hear their thoughts on the project.

Yet now that Ralen had drunk his wine, Teesia knew time was of the essence, so she said what she knew she must. She leaned up close to his ear and imparted in the softest whisper, "Fuck me, master."

His expression took on the dark quality she loved, and within a few minutes, he'd made his excuses to the artisans, telling the group of men he would consider their suggestions and invite them back soon for further discussion.

Once in their chamber, they hurriedly stripped off each other's clothing and reclined on the bed, starting to kiss and touch, when Ralen stopped to lay his head back. "Ares, I feel...odd."

"Odd?" Suddenly, a horrible guilt struck her—had she actually stooped to drugging her husband? *But it will be worth it, for both of us*, she promised herself. She had to show him the other side of pleasure.

"Strangely...tired," he said with a sigh. "I...don't know why."

"Perhaps you've been working too hard lately."

He managed a drowsy chuckle. "Perhaps *you* have worked me too hard lately. We fuck like animals, you know."

She smiled warmly. "Yes. So...maybe I should give you the night to rest."

He never answered, for that quickly he fell asleep.

"You will love this," she whispered, stroking a gentle hand through his hair. "You will thank me later, Ralen. I know you will."

Chapter Nine

ð

When Ralen awoke, he thought he must be dreaming.

He lay stretched across the bed, his wrists and ankles bound to the four bedposts with long strips of silk. Teesia stood at the foot of the bed wearing a tight, black leather vest cut to reveal her sumptuous breasts, their tips dark and erect, and—other than her jeweled bracelets and ankle cuffs— nothing else at all. She wielded the riding crop in one hand and her eyes looked...feral. Wild. Filled with something new he'd never seen in them before.

"What in Ares' name..." he began, at a loss, and started to rise toward her, only to be halted in place by the ties he'd already forgotten.

"Tonight," she said sharply, slapping the end of the riding crop down into her palm, "*I* am the master. Or, I suppose, the mistress. And you are the slave."

As understanding began to seep through him, his chest tightened with the anger beginning to seethe inside him. He spoke very clearly, enunciating each word. "You do not want to do this, Teesia. Do you hear me?"

She looked unfazed as she drew the tip of the crop sensually across the upper curve of one breast and down between. "Oh, but I do, Ralen."

"You don't know what you're doing," he said in warning, pulling again at the infuriating ties. What was she thinking? How could she do this to him?

She stepped forward, to the very edge of the bed, and ran the fringed end of the crop gently from his ankle up his inner thigh, stopping just below his balls. An involuntary shudder snaked through him. "I know *exactly* what I'm doing, my husband. I'm going to make you submit to me. I'm going to show you the joys of being my slave."

"Damnation, Teesia," he snapped, "untie me this instant!"

"Or what?" She dragged the tip of the crop up his other thigh, the tingling sensation darting into his cock, turning it visibly hard.

"Or I will make you very sorry, my wanton, I promise you that." His whole body—no longer just his chest—had begun to clench and tighten now in an odd mixture of arousal and rage.

She granted him a pure vixen's smile. "Is that so?"

"Do you hear me, woman? This is no game I'm interested in playing. When I told you there could be only one master, I was deadly serious and you'd best understand that. I am no one's slave, nor will I ever be—even for a night. So you'd best untie me right now before I grow any angrier." He pulled at the sashes again—Ares, but she'd tied them tightly!

Without warning, she slapped the crop against his thigh, making him flinch at the sting as he let out a low sound of pain.

"Stop it, Teesia," he commanded. "Let me up from this bed."

"You are most ill-behaved," she said, swatting him again, this time at his hip. He let out a grunt of discomfort as the sensation moved through him, making him go even more tense with anger while it tightened his cock.

Fury boiled in his chest. "*You* are the ill-behaved one, wanton. And trust me, you will pay for this—and I don't mean with any sort of pleasure game. Do you understand me? *Do you?*"

He glared at her, but she only kept her confident, lusty expression in place.

Ares above—what had gotten into her? What made her think she could do this? Make him her slave? *Never.* "Clearly, you have turned into the evil, wanton whore I thought you in the beginning." He wasn't sure he actually believed that—wasn't sure *what* he believed right now—but he wanted to hurt her, as she was hurting him.

Yet even this, it seemed, did not wound her. "I am no one's whore but yours," she said, her voice filled with pride. Then she struck him again, soundly on the hip, dangerously close to his cock, and the reverberations from it echoed through him, turning him regretfully harder for her. He moaned—then growled his frustration, once again pulling helplessly at the cords that held him down.

He watched, powerless, as she climbed up onto the bed, between his spread legs, rising to her knees. Her beautifully bare cunt gaped slightly, her clit and pink folds swelling from the slit, moist and glistening. She licked her luscious upper lip, then aroused him against his will even more by raking the length of the riding crop through her pussy with a sensual sigh.

He closed his eyes, willing the heated vision away, figuring he could control at least that much—but shutting out the sight of her helped not at all when she ran the fringed end of the crop up the length of his stiff rod. He couldn't hold in his moan.

Next, her mouth replaced the crop at his shaft—he didn't need to see that to know the feeling, either. She was licking him, from base to tip, a slow torture that heated the blood in his veins no matter how he tried not to respond. "Damnable woman, you are *evil*," he bit out.

"No, I am your mistress, and I am going to make you obey me, slave."

"*I will not*," he said through clenched teeth, opening his eyes to glower at her.

Another useless pull at the ties. He needed to be free. He detested this, having his control taken. It made him feel weak...on the inside. Just like Banya had once made him feel.

Like his father had *always* made him feel. He hated the emotion more than anything on the earth.

"You will," she said, her confidence still fully in place.

Who on earth *was* this woman? Not his sweet, obedient, playful Teesia. Certainly not the woman he loved.

She took his cock full in her mouth and as much as he wanted to look away, he couldn't. Her sexuality was too raw, too open and beautiful, not to watch—even now. And Ares above, when she sucked him, he felt it everywhere. He gritted his teeth against the pleasure, wishing it away, but it wouldn't go. He didn't want this to feel good—he would not let it.

But, Ares help him, it *did* feel good. Too horribly good. He even thrust toward her mouth, unable to help himself. *Yes, yes, vixen, suck me. So good. Your mouth is so sweet and hot on me.*

Yet no—he could not want this, could not let her think she controlled him. It took all his might, but he forced himself to stop thrusting. He tried to hold his breath, think of other things, *anything*—anything to quit feeling it.

Only, just like pulling at the silk ties, resistance was useless. She took him so deep, sucked him so well, he couldn't *not* push back against her, couldn't *not* lift his ass from the table to meet her prettily swollen lips.

And then he stopped trying not to thrust—in fact, he thrust hard, harder, thinking to punish her this way. If she wanted to suck his cock so badly, then he would fuck her mouth as severely as he could, until she pulled back, admitting defeat.

Only—for Ares' sake!—she *didn't* pull back. She merely sucked him harder. No matter how he thrust at her tender mouth, she met him with the same intensity, the battle waging onward.

Ah, vixen. Soon he would come. Come so hard. Her ministrations echoed like rolls of thunder through his whole body now, and her ferocious eagerness had only added to the unquenchable fire in his veins. *Going to come. In her mouth. So good. So hard.* That's all he could think of now. Her mouth. His cock. Pleasure. Deep, searing pleasure—out of control. Thrust, thrust. *Yes, yes.* Soon. Almost.

Then she stopped.

His cock dropped heavy against his stomach and he let out a ferocious groan at the loss.

She met his gaze overtop of it, her eyes more than feral now—she was reckless, demanding, an untamed animal. "Call me mistress."

The sound that left him was a growl as he yanked at the ties.

"*Call me mistress,*" she demanded, her upper lip curling slightly, her voice labored. "Beg me. Beg me to make you come."

He wanted her mouth back on his cock so badly that he was writhing against the table, lifting it toward her involuntarily. But he kept his *own* mouth closed, willing himself to get hold of his body, his mind, to get back his control.

"Say it, slave. Beg me."

Dear Ares, now even the harsh tone of her voice was adding to his want. He clenched his teeth tighter, the words on the tip of his tongue. *Please. Suck me, mistress.* It would be so easy—and then he'd have what he wanted, needed, so badly. But he let out a huge breath. "*No.*"

Without warning, she picked up the crop and snapped it against his erect cock. He cried out and glared at her in horror—but then let his head drop back with a forlorn sigh, for even *that* had felt good. *Ares help me.*

"You will," she said, her voice a bit softer now. "You will beg me, Ralen. I promise you, you will beg me."

"No," he said again.

At which point he suffered the agony of watching her straddle him and begin rubbing her cunt back and forth over the ridge of his cock. She looked no less than tantalizing hovering above him that way, her lush breasts beautifully on display, her sweet pink pussy pressing wet and warm around his shaft. "You will beg me," she said, her voice heated with pleasure now. "You will say whatever I tell you to say."

And then she wrapped her fist around him, held his erection upright, and impaled herself on it, so smoothly you'd think she'd been doing it for a lifetime. They both moaned at the thick warmth of the entry.

Oh, but she felt good sheathing him. Riding him. Once more, he couldn't resist driving himself up into her, deeper, harder—he had to have more of her, needed desperately to find his release. She fucked him vigorously, her breasts bouncing, her dark hair falling like clouds the color of midnight over her shoulder, and—yes, yes—soon he would come.

That's when she went still. "Beg me, Ralen. Beg me not to stop."

He pulled in his breath, let it back out. Begged her in his mind—*please, please*—but refused to give it voice. He wouldn't. Couldn't.

Instead, he thrust up into her hard.

She closed her eyes—pleasure shrouded with a sweet bit of pain, if he read her face correctly—and he thought she would not be able to resist either, that she would resume the ride he needed so badly.

So it nearly killed him when she rose neatly off him, leaving his cock so desperately in need as it dropped wetly down to his belly, abandoned by her.

He shuddered uncontrollably and hated that she could see how affected he was by her wicked performance. He closed his eyes, attempting again to come to grips with this, to convince himself this one round of sex didn't matter, that he didn't need it, that his mind could rule his body if he tried hard enough—but when he opened them back, he found his wife turning away from him on the bed, her knees planted on either side of his leg, one slender arm stretched sensually up the swirled wooden post, the other reaching for the crop.

He was instantly riveted—by the sight of her lovely curving ass, her pussy pouting pinkly underneath, and by wondering what would come next. What was she going to do with that crop?

Strike him? He hated himself for hoping she might, for knowing he'd welcome the sensation.

Only she didn't hit him with it—no, her actions were much more sinister. Arching her ass toward him, she positioned the crop's smooth handle at her asshole and slowly, methodically began to ease it inside.

He thought his body would burst apart from the brutal arousal—layer after layer of it, and now *this*! He couldn't take it. "No! No, stop it!"

She pushed the crop deeper, beginning to gently move her ass, fucking herself there. Only then did she peer brazenly over her shoulder. "Why not? You like to watch my ass open, don't you, slave? You like to watch my ass take something inside it."

"You are vicious!" he spat.

She, however, remained brazenly calm. "You will beg."

Ralen watched, entranced, his body ready to ignite. Damn it all, he wanted loose from this bed. *He* wanted to be the one fucking her ass with that crop. *Him*. He had to have control. Had to have it. At all costs.

The ultimate pleasure-pain? It was *this*—being pleasured and having his masculinity dashed at the same time.

Only it wasn't *real* pleasure, like he'd given her. It was not something he wanted to hate but didn't. He *truly* hated it. Hated how excited he was. Hated how hungry his cock remained. Hated his inability to resist her while he was helpless.

Each slide of the crop into the tiny opening of her ass was a torture to him. *He* had to give her that pleasure! *Him and him alone!* Why was she doing this to him?

He enjoyed a small measure of relief when she finally let the crop fall to the stone floor next to the bed, but then she straddled his hips once more—and to his utter amazement, she leaned back, reached down, and slowly began to glide his cock into her ass. He groaned, both from the sensation and the sight of her lowering her anal passage over him, taking inch after inch of his rod inside herself there. He couldn't fathom her ability to do this without his help, and he also couldn't prevent his moans of deep pleasure from leaking out. It was too much. Too much.

And then she moved on him—leaned her weight back on her arms behind her and lifted herself up and down, slowly fucking him with her tight little ass, pushing him closer and closer to explosion, until finally she said, her voice wrenched with intensity, "Beg me. Beg me or I will stop right now."

He couldn't let her stop. He couldn't bear it. He could barely breathe under the weight of his excitement. The words came in a slow, painful whisper. "I'm begging you...mistress." He hated himself for his weakness.

But she clearly couldn't see that. Or she didn't care. Clearly, all that mattered to her was winning. "Tell me you're my slave."

He let out a breath. Pleasure had never been more agonizing. "I'm...your...slave."

The light of satisfaction beamed in her eyes as she reached down to begin stroking herself, whirling her longest finger in a circle over her grandly swollen clit. As she eased her ass up and down, the movements grew slightly rougher and he pushed back, fucking her tightest opening, watching her arousal heighten, watching her finger move faster and faster over that beautiful knob of flesh at the top of her slit.

"Oh! Oh Ralen!" she cried out, and as she came, he exploded, driving up into her snug anal tunnel, finally able to release everything that had built up so painfully inside him. He growled his release with three gruff thrusts, and for those few brief seconds, heaven was his.

Unfortunately, however, when he opened his eyes afterward, he was still tied to the bed, his wife's helpless captive—and nothing was as it had been before.

He could scarcely believe it when she had the audacity to smile as she climbed off him. And when she spoke, she sounded utterly joyful. "Now you know," she said as merrily as if they'd just shared a fun, playful coupling. "Now you know a bit of what *I* feel when I submit to *you*."

No, he didn't know. Could *never* know. For her, submission was true joy. For him, it was *not*, and she just didn't understand. Didn't understand—and had ruined…everything.

He looked up into the blue, blue eyes he'd fallen in love with and said, "I hate you."

Teesia couldn't have been more stunned. "What?"

"I hate you for this," he said, his voice dry, wooden.

Oh Ares. Oh no. What had she done? She covered her mouth with her hand.

She'd only been trying to deepen their mutual pleasure, and even when he'd resisted, she'd been sure that by the time it was done he'd know the pure delights she experienced in the same position. She'd been sure—but now she knew she'd been wrong.

Perhaps the anguish in his eyes during the sex should have told her. But had she not suffered anguish at the start, too?

Still, only now did she grasp the truth—the truth that suddenly seemed so plain and clear to see. Ralen was not a man who ever wanted to submit, only to master. Shaena had told her that. As had Ralen himself. Why hadn't she listened?

217

Her heart sank in her chest. She didn't know what to do. She couldn't believe she'd just recklessly taken what had so carefully and tentatively grown between them and dashed it against the rocks like a ship at sea. "Oh Ralen," she said sadly, at a loss, kneeling next to him.

He yanked against the silk scarves again, wildly, and the look on his face told her all was truly lost. He truly hated her. And there was no fixing it.

When he got loose from the ties, he would probably rip her limb from limb.

"Untie me, you heartless whore!"

She shrank back under the ferocity of his words, truly frightened of him—in a way she'd never been before, even on their wedding night.

She knew instinctively that he'd never forgive her—that their happiness was a thing of the past.

At a loss for what to do, she leapt from the bed, grabbed up the clothes she'd discarded, and fled the room without looking back.

Chapter Ten

∞

There seemed to Teesia only one answer, and that was to run.

She loved Ralen now, loved him desperately, and was crushed by what had just happened, but it was her own fault, and irreparable. *Why, oh why, was I so stupid? Why did I think I knew him so well, better than he knew himself?* Well, that didn't matter now, all that mattered was getting away from the fortress before Ralen got free. She truly believed he might rip her to shreds in his anger—and she almost couldn't blame him.

Racing across the cool grass toward the stables, unnoticed—she hoped—by the night watchmen, she thanked Ares for the nearly full moon that lit her way. It was easy to find Vixen in the corral and lure her with a handful of clover. A moment later, Teesia had bridled the sorrel and led the horse to the mounting block, where she climbed astride her.

As her cunt stretched over the horse's back, still sensitive from sex, she was forced to remember her husband—both the horrible scene that she'd just brought about as well as all the wonder, all the passion and joy she'd experienced in his arms. "Oh Ralen," she sobbed quietly.

But this is no time for tears. You must be strong if you are to make your way home to Myrtell.

It should be simple, she thought. Follow the beach—and in a day or two she would be home. Maybe even sooner, for she planned to press Vixen into a gallop for as long as the horse was able, figuring the farther away she got from Charelton before the sun rose, the better.

And yes, Ralen would likely come for her at her father's fortress, and she wasn't sure what would happen then, but at least this was a temporary reprieve. If her father wouldn't protect her, perhaps she'd head farther north and inland to her sister's home in Rawley. Maybe Maven and Dane would hide her there until Ralen tired of searching for his "heartless whore" of a wife.

The words still burned, and the memory of the look in his eyes tormented her, but it was too late now. As Vixen neared the dunes that would give way to the sandy coastline, Teesia looked over her shoulder at the fortress in the distance from which she'd just fled. "Goodbye, my dear Ralen," she said softly. "I love you, and I'm so sorry I hurt you."

* * * * *

"Laene! Shaena! Someone get into this chamber—now!"

He couldn't believe it! First she'd emasculated him—now the little hoyden had left him trussed up like a deer brought home from the hunt.

"*Shaena! Are you out there?*" The walls were too thick, he knew—he simply had to hope someone would pass by the door and hear him bellowing.

Reduced to crying out for help like a child, he thought bitterly. And then he shook his head against the bed, still trying to fathom why Teesia had done this to him.

But perhaps it was simple—she was paying him back, reminding him how badly he'd treated her in the beginning. She was punishing someone who truly *deserved* to be punished, he supposed. As for the pleasant times they'd shared more recently, he could only presume it was all pretense on her part—her way of building his trust so that she could enact her grand scheme to humiliate him.

"Laene! Shaena! Anyone! Is anyone in this entire fortress awake?"

Just then, the door opened and Shaena burst in—horror reshaping her face when she saw him.

"Don't just stand there. Untie me!" he barked.

"Where is Teesia?" she asked, moving to the top corner of the bed to work at the silk scarf.

"Gone. But when I find her..." he began through clenched teeth.

"When you find her, what?"

He shook his head, still so deeply entrenched in his anger that he didn't care who might be right or wrong—he only knew he wanted to do her harm, wanted to make *her* pay now. "I don't know what I'll do to the evil girl, but I can promise you this—she's made a fool of me for the first and last time."

Above him, Shaena let out a heavy breath. "Made a fool of you? Is that all you can see that happened here?"

He looked up at her, met her gaze. "You knew."

As one wrist came free, he folded his hand into a fist, trying to get the feeling back into it. Shaena broke the gaze and made her way around to where his other hand was bound. "I knew you wouldn't like it, and I told her that—but yes, I knew her plan. And I hoped maybe I was wrong, that maybe you would be more charitable to the idea of permitting Teesia to have a little control in your relationship."

He swung his gaze around to look at her in her new spot. "Control in our relationship, she could have had—*did* have. Control in this bed, like *this*—" he motioned to his bindings, "—no, that just isn't in me."

Shaena nodded as she fought at the knot. "Even so, she was simply trying to...surprise you."

"It worked," he grunted.

"And ultimately to *please* you," she went on pointedly. "She thought that since she enjoyed submitting to you so deeply that you might discover you enjoyed submission, too."

"Clearly, I have given her too much freedom," he said as his other hand came loose.

"Clearly, you're taking what happened here tonight far too seriously."

It was as the two of them finally succeeded in untying the last knots and Ralen reached for his pants that Laene burst in the room—looking surprised to see Ralen naked with Shaena, given the recent developments in all their lives.

Ralen was in no mood to humor him—he only snarled. "Don't worry—your beloved hasn't betrayed you." Then he sighed. "*Mine* has betrayed *me*."

Laene's pale eyebrows knit. "Then maybe that explains…"

"What?" Ralen jerked his head up.

"One of the guards said he saw Teesia go racing up the beach on horseback. I was certain he must've been mistaken, but came to make sure."

Ralen pushed to his feet. "No, the man wasn't mistaken— my dear wife tied me up here, made a mockery of our sex, then apparently went haring off into the night." He reached for the black leather vest on the floor, then raised back up. "Let me guess. She was heading north, fleeing home to Daddy."

Laene confirmed it with a nod. "Exactly."

"Well, she won't get there. Bring Charger around. *Now.*"

"What are you going to do?" Shaena rounded the bed, her voice filled with worry. Worry for the woman who had betrayed him. He shook his head, disgusted—since when did Shaena's loyalties shift so quickly?

"I'm going to find her," he said simply.

"And then?"

"Then she'll learn that punishment is not always a game."

* * * * *

Ralen slapped the reins against Charger's neck, driving him up the beach at breakneck speed. His wanton little wife might think she had escaped, but she didn't ride *that* well and Charger would catch Vixen with ease.

His chest still burned with anger—anger and…hurt. He didn't like to admit that, even to himself. It had been a long time since he'd allowed someone to get close enough to him to hurt him. But Teesia had succeeded, and it was ripping his heart out.

Rounding a bend along a narrow stretch of sand, he caught sight of her in the moonlight, her black hair streaming behind her in the wind as she raced north. The very sight of her pummeled him inside, made him want to wound her as badly as she'd wounded him, made him want to punish her more severely than either of them could even imagine. *Why did you have to do that to me, Teesia? What did you have to do that to us?*

He drove Charger on, faster, faster, hooves beating against the sand, until he was bearing down on her. When she looked over her shoulder to find him directly behind her, her gaze filled with fear. *Well you* should *fear me, vixen*, he thought, and drew his horse alongside the sorrel as the expanse of sand widened around them.

She'd turned back ahead now, but in his mind he still saw her eyes. Love, hate, pain—it all mingled inside him, building, building, as the sea winds slashed through the night.

I love you, I hate you.

He despised the fear in her eyes, despised—suddenly— being a man who made her feel that way. And yet—was he to simply let her rule him? Hurt him? Take him back to those awful days of helplessness with his father? How could he feel anything but brutal anger toward her, the need to punish, the need to make her obey—once and for all, *forever*.

He rode near enough to grab the reins at her mount's neck, wrenching them from her grip as their legs crushed together between the horses' bodies, slowing them both, until finally he latched fiercely onto her arm and pulled them both off the horses' backs.

They tumbled roughly to the soft sand, their limbs mingling, and when she pushed to her feet, ready to run, he yanked at her leg, dragging her back down.

Their gazes met, hers a vibrant blue beneath the light of the moon and still filled with pure terror. He wanted to kill her.

Instead, he kissed her.

He didn't know why, but he bracketed her face with his hands and brought his mouth down hard and demanding on hers. He kissed her so hard he wondered if he were bruising them both, but he didn't stop, *couldn't* stop. Something deeper than even his fury drove him.

He pushed her to her back in the sand and covered her body with his, tearing at the ties on her vest, needing to get to her. She whimpered beneath him, her hands in his hair, clutching at his shoulders until he sank his mouth hungrily to her breast. He suckled her harshly and she cried out— pleasure-pain, that blessed, cursed pleasure-pain that seemed to rule them—then kissed her other breast just as vigorously, drawing his hands from the lush mounds only to work at the opening on his pants.

They both breathed hard, the sound meshing with the flow of the tide, as he pushed his palms under her skirt to her round ass and thrust deep inside her. They both yelled out at the entry, so deep, so binding—and she eagerly met each rough plunge of his cock into her hot, welcoming cunt. They cried out at each drive, at each moment when their pelvises came flush, his large shaft buried entirely within her body, and he fucked her with a rough, thorough passion that came without thought or decision. But emotion—oh yes, emotion was there, prodding him on, making him love her, love her, love her, tonight be damned.

That, he realized, was the thing driving him, the thing bigger than his anger. *Love.*

Reaching between them, he stroked her clit with his thumb, turning her cries to desperate whimpers that made him love her even more. And when she came, screaming her ecstasy, he groaned, thrusting his last inside her. He *needed* it, needed to leave part of himself behind just as she'd recently wanted, too—only this time he needed to leave it *in* her, not on her, somehow feeling it staked a claim, branded her as his in some new way because he suddenly realized how deeply he loved the girl.

A moment later, he remained inside her, but they'd both gone silent so that the shush of the sea was the only sound. The grit of sand caked his elbows and sprinkled her dark hair.

Her voice came small beneath him. "Do you truly hate me?"

His was just as muted. "No."

"I...I only wanted to pleasure you as you had pleasured me," she explained, peering up at him.

He sighed and made himself meet her gaze. "I don't like being controlled, Teesia. I don't like not being able to...well, to protect myself. I'm sorry."

It was in that moment that Teesia remembered, and fully understood. Oh Ares. She had been even more stupid than she'd realized. His father. His father had beaten him. Somehow, in the midst of her determination to pleasure him, she'd forgotten that. No wonder he'd hated being tied down so much. It must have brought back feelings of horror, total helplessness. She hugged him to her. "Oh, Ralen, I'm sorry. So sorry." She ran her hands through his thick hair and squeezed him even tighter. "I only want to make you happy."

He drew back in the embrace to look at her, their gazes melding in the moonlight. "You *do* make me happy. Happier than I ever dreamed I could be."

"I won't try to control you again," she promised, then offered him a tentative smile, adding, "master."

Slowly, he smiled back at her, and they rolled to their sides in the sand. "I apologize for the terrible things I said to you, vixen. I won't ever do that to you again."

"Then all is forgiven?" she asked hopefully.

"If you forgive me, as well."

She smiled warmly, unable to believe it was the middle of the night because it felt as if the sun had just shone into her heart.

Then, when she least expected it, her husband took on the wicked look she loved. "Will you still be my willing slave, vixen?"

"I have no choice. I'm enslaved to you for life."

"But you were running away."

She bit her lip, then admitted everything she'd been feeling before he'd caught up with her. "And even as I ran, my pussy ached for you and my ass throbbed with wanting your cock. I was just about to realize I was running in the wrong direction when you caught me."

"Promise me you'll never run from me again."

"I couldn't. You're the master of my desire."

Epilogue
3591 AD

ॐ

It was at the grand summer feast at Enrick's estate in Myrtell that he announced he had selected a husband for his youngest daughter, Laela, who had just reached bride's age. Afterward, Laela came scurrying over to the table where Teesia and Ralen sat eating. "I'm so nervous, wondering who it will be," she said to her older sister as she looked between Teesia and her husband. "And yet, perhaps I should not be. Maven and Dane are happy—dear Ares—did you know she's pregnant again? And you two are happy. Aren't you?"

Teesia couldn't resist exchanging a sensual look with her beloved before answering. "Oh yes, we are happy. Very happy indeed."

Soon after, when Laela had flitted away, Ralen leaned to whisper in his wife's ear. "I know you enjoy visiting your family, vixen, but I've discovered since we married that I no longer enjoy leaving the fortress overnight."

"Oh?"

"I'd rather be in our chamber tying you up, holding you down, finding more creative ways to fuck you."

She cast him her most coquettish look. "You think we cannot fuck here?"

He grinned. "Well, certainly. But at home, we have…certain tools."

"So you think I cannot excite you here, master, is that it?" she asked teasingly. "Well, I thought after the feast I would take you into my old bedchamber and tell you some naughty tales of the Orientation I had there."

He raised his eyebrows, clearly enticed. "Naughty tales? Give me a taste to last me through the meal."

Teesia pointed at her dear old friend Bella, who sat across the room eating, and flirting with the men on both sides of her. "Bella was my Orienter and she chose to teach by example." Reaching to press her palm between his thighs, she found Ralen's cock had gone delightfully hard, that fast. "Mmm, I see you're interested already."

"Even so, though," he complained, "it won't be the same as at home."

With a sinful smile, Teesia pulled up her finest silk dress under table and led her husband's hand to the string of overlapping disks at her hip. Then she gazed into his dark, sensual eyes to say, "And it's quite possible a filly's tail might have found its way into our trunk."

A hungry smile graced his face as his eyes glittered with heat. "You *are* the perfect sex slave."

She smiled in reply, glad to have pleased him, and glad to know she would please him even more later. Then she winked. "Perhaps we could sneak off into a dark hallway together for old time's sake, master."

Also by Lacey Alexander

ઐ

About the Author

๕

Lacey Alexander's books have been called deliciously decadent, unbelievably erotic, exceptionally arousing, blazingly sexual, and downright sinful. In each book, Lacey strives to take her readers on the ultimate erotic adventure and hopes her stories will encourage women to embrace their sexual fantasies.

Lacey resides in the Midwest with her husband, and when not penning romantic erotica, she enjoys history and traveling, often incorporating favorite travel destinations into her work.

Lacey welcomes comments from readers. You can find her website and email address on her author bio page at www.ellorascave.com.

Tell Us What You Think

We appreciate hearing reader opinions about our books. You can email us at Comments@EllorasCave.com.

Why an electronic book?

We live in the Information Age—an exciting time in the history of human civilization, in which technology rules supreme and continues to progress in leaps and bounds every minute of every day. For a multitude of reasons, more and more avid literary fans are opting to purchase e-books instead of paper books. The question from those not yet initiated into the world of electronic reading is simply: *Why?*

1. *Price.* An electronic title at Ellora's Cave Publishing and Cerridwen Press runs anywhere from 40% to 75% less than the cover price of the exact same title in paperback format. Why? Basic mathematics and cost. It is less expensive to publish an e-book (no paper and printing, no warehousing and shipping) than it is to publish a paperback, so the savings are passed along to the consumer.

2. *Space.* Running out of room in your house for your books? That is one worry you will never have with electronic books. For a low one-time cost, you can purchase a handheld device specifically designed for e-reading. Many e-readers have large, convenient screens for viewing. Better yet, hundreds of titles can be stored within your new library—on a single microchip. There are a variety of e-readers from different manufacturers. You can also read e-books on your PC or laptop computer. (Please note that Ellora's Cave does not endorse any specific brands.

You can check our websites at www.ellorascave.com or www.cerridwenpress.com for information we make available to new consumers.)

3. *Mobility.* Because your new e-library consists of only a microchip within a small, easily transportable e-reader, your entire cache of books can be taken with you wherever you go.

4. *Personal Viewing Preferences.* Are the words you are currently reading too small? Too large? Too… ANNOYING? Paperback books cannot be modified according to personal preferences, but e-books can.

5. *Instant Gratification.* Is it the middle of the night and all the bookstores near you are closed? Are you tired of waiting days, sometimes weeks, for bookstores to ship the novels you bought? Ellora's Cave Publishing sells instantaneous downloads twenty-four hours a day, seven days a week, every day of the year. Our webstore is never closed. Our e-book delivery system is 100% automated, meaning your order is filled as soon as you pay for it.

Those are a few of the top reasons why electronic books are replacing paperbacks for many avid readers.

As always, Ellora's Cave and Cerridwen Press welcome your questions and comments. We invite you to email us at Comments@ellorascave.com or write to us directly at Ellora's Cave Publishing Inc., 1056 Home Avenue, Akron, OH 44310-3502.

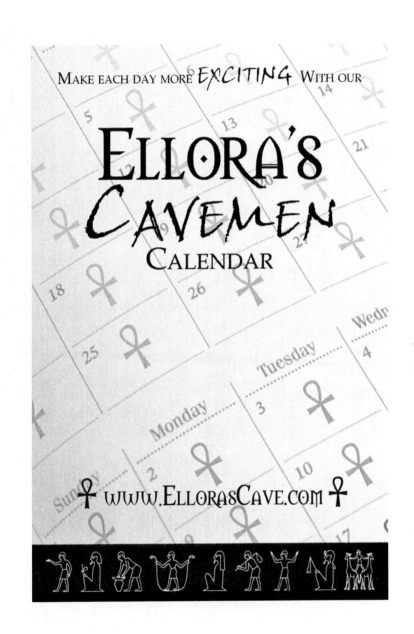

MAKE EACH DAY MORE *EXCITING* WITH OUR

ELLORA'S CAVEMEN
CALENDAR

WWW.ELLORASCAVE.COM

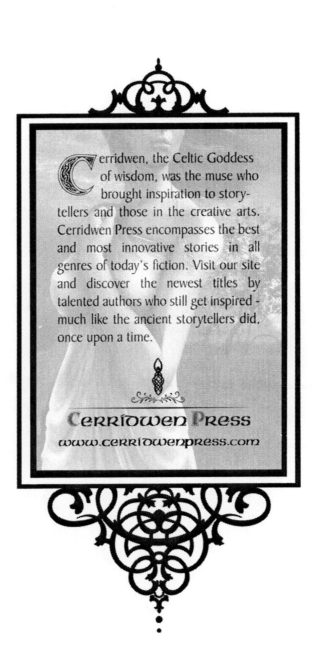

Cerridwen, the Celtic Goddess of wisdom, was the muse who brought inspiration to storytellers and those in the creative arts. Cerridwen Press encompasses the best and most innovative stories in all genres of today's fiction. Visit our site and discover the newest titles by talented authors who still get inspired - much like the ancient storytellers did, once upon a time.

CERRIDWEN PRESS

www.cerridwenpress.com

Discover for yourself why readers can't get enough
of the multiple award-winning publisher
Ellora's Cave.

Whether you prefer e-books or paperbacks,

be sure to visit EC on the web at
www.ellorascave.com

for an erotic reading experience that will leave you
breathless.